THE MARGRAVE

CATHERINE FISHER

RELIC MASTER

THE MARGRAVE

Dial Books

an imprint of Penguin Group (USA) Inc.

DIAL BOOKS

An imprint of Penguin Group (USA) Inc.

Published by The Penguin Group

Penguin Group (USA) Inc., 375 Hudson Street, New York, NY 10014, U.S.A.

Penguin Group (Canada), 90 Eglinton Avenue East, Suite 700, Toronto, Ontario, Canada M4P 2Y3 (a division of Pearson Penguin Canada Inc.) • Penguin Books Ltd, 80 Strand, London WC2R 0RL, England • Penguin Ireland, 25 St. Stephen's Green, Dublin 2, Ireland (a division of Penguin Books Ltd) • Penguin Group (Australia), 250 Camberwell Road, Camberwell, Victoria 3124, Australia (a division of Pearson Australia Group Pty Ltd) • Penguin Books India Pvt Ltd, 11 Community Centre, Panchsheel Park, New Delhi - 110 017, India • Penguin Group (NZ), 67 Apollo Drive, Auckland, North Shore 0632, New Zealand (a division of Pearson New Zealand Ltd) • Penguin Books (South Africa) (Pty) Ltd, 24 Sturdee Avenue, Rosebank, Johannesburg 2196, South Africa • Penguin Books Ltd, Registered Offices: 80 Strand, London WC2R 0RL, England

First published in the United States 2011
by Dial Books
an imprint of Penguin Group (USA), Inc.

First published in Great Britain by Red Fox 2001

Designed by Nancy R. Leo-Kelly
Text set in Sabon
Printed in the U. S. A.
1 3 5 7 9 10 8 6 4 2

Library of Congress Cataloging-in-Publication Data
Fisher, Catherine, date.
The Margrave / by Catherine Fisher.
p. cm. — (Relic Master ; 4)
Summary: Their quest to find a secret relic with great power leads
Master Galen and his sixteen-year-old apprentice, Raffi, into the Pitts
of Maar and the deep evil world at the heart of the Watch.
ISBN 978-0-8037-3676-4 (hardcover)
[1. Fantasy. 2. Apprentices—Fiction. 3. Antiquities—Fiction.] I. Title.
PZ7.F4995Mar 2011 [Fic]—dc22 2010043237

Contents

THE MARGRAVE

I think you should confide this *fear to your master,* the tree said gently.

Raffi gave a sour laugh. "No point."

He is, I admit, difficult to approach. A small sparkbird, brilliantly red, fluttered among the branches; the tree rustled thoughtfully over Raffi's head. *If he was one of my kind, he would be holly. Or dark firethorn that grows in the chasm of Zeail. Such a one is Galen.*

Raffi nodded. He lay on his back in the dappled green light, eyes closed against the sun. The tree was a birch; young, and very curious.

Tell me where it takes you, this Deep Journey.

3

"It's a vision." Raffi sat up and gazed out hopelessly into the depths of the warm spring woodland. "It happens in your mind. The Litany says there are different stages—the Cosmic Tree, the Plain of Hunger."

Hunger is a sensation?

"Emptiness. No food."

Indeed. The tree sounded fascinated. *Our roots are always storing. Rootless creatures, it seems to me, are most vulnerable. The Makers were wise, but sometimes we feel you were something of a failed experiment.*

"And then," Raffi said, half to himself, "comes something called the Barrier of Pain."

The tree was silent. Finally it whispered, *You fear that.*

He nodded. "And the last thing even more. To be a keeper every scholar must pass through utter darkness into something the books won't even describe. They call it the Crucible of Fire."

Fire! The birch shuddered down to its very roots, every leaf quivering. The sparkbird flew out with a cheep of alarm. *Fire is the worst of enemies! The Watch burned the forest of Harenak, every leaf, every sapling. Who could fail to mourn so many deaths?*

"Raffi!"

Galen had woken in a black temper. He came out of the shelter, still looking tired, and snapped, "Any news?"

"Nothing."

"As soon as there is, let me know." The keeper turned, tugging his black hair loose from the knot of string. "And stop wasting your time. Read! Flain knows you need to."

Raffi picked the book up without glancing at it. "He's a nightmare," he muttered, "since Marco died."

The tree was silent.

Galen limped between the birches to the stream. He waded in, scooping the cold water up to drink, splashing it over his face. For weeks he had been working on the sense-lines, driving himself nonstop. Already they had a chain of lines between a few known keepers and through re-awakened channels of tree-minds and earth-filaments that reached to Tasceron itself; in fact, last night, after days of effort, Galen had spoken with Shean, the keeper of the Pyramid in the Wounded City. It had been a triumph. But it had worn him out.

Looking down on him, Raffi thought of the night of Marco's death, of Galen's terrible oath, that he would seek out the Margrave. That he would kill the Margrave. "That's why he's so desperate to set the sense-grid up. And to get me through the Journey. He thinks he won't come back alive."

Now, the tree said gently, *you are really afraid.*

Raffi jumped up, brushing pollen from his clothes. Already it was back, that sickening terror he could never lose for long. He felt the tree's consciousness spiraling into him, intrigued.

Do you really believe, it whispered, curious, *that this Margrave is hunting especially for you?*

"I can't talk anymore." Raffi turned abruptly, blocking its voice out. Sickness was already surging in him, a choking stress, blurring the tree-words to a crackle of leaves. He started to stumble through to the stream, then swung around for the book, feeling the sweat on his back chill as he bent, dizziness making his vision spin. He gasped and leaned on the tree.

Raffi, it said urgently, its voice bursting through his panic. *Someone comes!*

Bewildered, he felt for the sense-lines. They were intact.

"Galen!" His voice was a whisper, a croak, but the keeper was already racing up; a firm hand grabbed him.

"The Watch?"

"Can't be. Can't feel anything." Weak, he crouched on the tree roots. Galen spun around, facing the footsteps.

It was the Sekoi.

Wiping his clammy mouth and streaming eyes, Raffi staggered up and tried to focus, but the creature was close to them before he could see it properly. Then he stared. The Sekoi was worn and ragged. Dried blood clogged its fur from a half-healed wound under one ear. Its yellow eyes were glazed with weariness.

Galen grabbed its thin shoulders. "For God's sake, did they ambush you? Have they got the Coronet?"

Exhausted, the creature collapsed onto the leafy bank. For a moment it seemed too worn out to speak. Then it whispered, "The Coronet is safe in Sarres. We were on our way back when we ran into the Watch."

"Thank God," Galen breathed, but the Sekoi seemed not to hear. Over his shoulder it glanced at Raffi. "They've got Carys," it said hopelessly.

The Broken Hills

1

When the work of the Makers stopped, Halen fell silent. He answered no one. He climbed far into the hills and built a fearsome castle. He built it in a day and a night, and no one came there but himself. Throughout its dim corridors, there were mirrors.

Book of the Seven Moons

T HE SLAP WAS HARD, and when she dragged her head up she tasted blood.

Breathing deeply, she stared at the Watch captain. Fury almost made her quiver. Fury and fear.

"I said, get in line," he snarled.

Carys stepped back, giving one glance at the old woman who lay collapsed on the verge of the road. The Watch captain turned and prodded the inert body with his boot. When it didn't move he kneeled and took out a knife.

Carys stiffened.

But all he did was slice the rope that held the woman to the rest of the prisoners.

"Are you just going to leave her there!" Carys snapped.

"She's no good to us. You there, at the front! Walk!"

The razorhounds snarled and scrabbled at the mesh of their cages, and the small line of prisoners stumbled quickly back into motion, the jerk of the rope tugging Carys on despite her anger. The road was steep, rutted with recent cart-tracks, a great gash along the flank of the mountain, plummeting on the left to a dizzy ravine. All the hot day they'd stumbled up it, with water only once at a stream, hours ago.

Carys sucked her swelling lip. Her hair and clothes were filthy with road-dust and she was almost too tired to think. Only anger kept her going. She clenched the knotted ropes around her hands as if anger was a thing she could hold on to, tight.

Around her waist the second rope slackened, sagging as the weary group closed up, stung by the irritating dart-flies that had followed all day in a buzzing cloud.

With the old woman gone, Carys was last. It was a relief not to have to hear that terrible gasping, or have the constant jerk of the rope as the woman stumbled, but the thought of the frail figure lying on the bleak road, without water, a prey to night-cats, was unbearable. Carys cursed herself for talking to the woman, for getting to know her. Her name had been Alys. At one of the pauses she had whispered to Carys that she "had a granddaughter, dear, very like you."

She looked back. The Watch captain, Quist, was far behind, striding up fast.

"Turn around!" he yelled, and she turned, grim.

They were taking no chances with her. Not now that they knew who she was. Speaking up for the woman had been useless, she'd known that. Before she met Galen she'd never have done it. But before she met Galen she'd never have been in such a mess.

It had been three days since she'd been caught. The patrol had jumped them in seconds. How the Sekoi had gotten away she had no idea, but they'd loosed the razorhounds after it instantly, thin silver beasts streaking into the wood. An hour later their handlers had dragged them back, bloodied. They'd certainly caught something.

The line stopped; she slammed into the prisoner in front. A lanky youth, older than her, pimply and stinking of sweat, one of his teeth black. "Rest," he gasped, crouching and clutching his side.

Carys didn't waste breath talking. Instead she watched Quist walk past her to the front. His number was 8472. High. No child from a Watchhouse, but a volunteer, enlisting as an adult. A dangerous, agile man.

The first thing he'd done was have her searched, and he'd found the Watch insignia. Galen had warned her often enough to get rid of them, the small silver discs with her old number, name, hard-earned promotions. But they were still part of her. She hadn't been able to let them go. Seeing them glint in the sun in Quist's fingers had been strange; as he'd read them and looked at her curiously she'd felt as if some last protection had been snatched away.

Sitting now on the edge of the road she rubbed sweat from her neck and looked around. The road edge was sheer, plunging down to a valley far below. She couldn't see over. Behind her was woodland, some squat, dark species; ahead, the road rose along the arduous slopes of the mountains. Where it led she had no idea, but it had seen heavy traffic lately, its surface cracked and worn.

The Broken Hills

The patrol was an eight-man standard. Three horses and a cart, with the razorhounds' cage and various food sacks. Ten prisoners left, all roped in line.

Water was being passed back. She stood and grabbed it from the boy's hand, clutching the dirty jug with both fists, drinking fast, then splashing the last drops on her face.

For a second, he was standing quite close to her. "Don't worry," he whispered, grinning slyly at her. "There's a plan."

She stared in astonishment. "What?"

"It's all fixed." He winked. "I'm in on it. I'll see you safe, at the castle."

He was serious.

Carys didn't know whether to laugh or feel sorry for him. But before she had time to say another word, the jug had been snatched by a Watchman, the rope jerking her to her feet.

"What's the rush?" she muttered, sullen.

"Orders. To be in before dark."

"In where?"

But he'd gone, and the line was already moving.

RELIC MASTER: THE MARGRAVE

All the hot spring afternoon and into the evening they tramped nonstop, climbing along a narrow track, so treacherous in places that loose rock slid away under their feet, rolled over the edge, and dropped for a long silent second into the distant, crashing branches. The landscape was arid; stunted lemon trees and calarna sprouting from high ravines, the road winding up under natural arches and along the very brinks of drops that made Carys dizzy to look down.

These were the Broken Hills, a shattered, convulsed highland infested with lizards and the scurrying, many-jointed purple scorpions that could kill a man with one sting. The peaks above her had slipped and shifted; it was as if some terrible bolt of the Makers' lightning had smashed the whole range to pieces centuries before. Perhaps it had. Galen would know.

The road had been repaired. Stumbling around the flank of a vertical cliff, she passed piles of cut stone, great heaps of sand. There must be quarries up some of these side-trails. Away to the west, green foothills still glimmered with late sun, but as the road wound up a riven hillside where all the trees had been hacked and felled, far

18

over the horizon she saw the smokes and vapors of the Unfinished Lands, amazingly close.

And on the last ridge, she saw the castle. It was black, half ruined or half built, some eerie Maker-structure. It was no ordinary Watchtower; the whole thing was more like a fortified hilltop, with immense walls and towering gates, and as the prisoners stumbled on she saw it was crowded with people, all working, hauling stone up scaffolds, dragging great blocks of mined rock, the racket of hammering and chiseling carrying clearly on the mountain air. As Carys gazed up, the curfew-horn sounded; a familiar distant blare from the highest part of the Keep. Abruptly all hammering stopped, the workmen climbing down wearily.

So she was part of a work-gang. If they needed them, the Watch dragged in criminals and outlaws to build their Towers; she seemed to have walked straight into that. Though this place was immense. And secure.

By the time the weary prisoners straggled through the main barbican, dusk had fallen; as they stood to be registered the faint smells of cooking from the shuttered huts and houses filled Carys with a groaning hunger. Behind her the sentinels dragged the heavy wooden gates shut with a hollow clang, then rattled enormous chains across. Under the vaulted arch it was suddenly dark, stinking of marset dung and woodsmoke.

A number was stamped on her neck; she could feel it, but not see it, and she knew it would take months to wear off. The Watch used corris-juice; she'd done it herself.

Then the line was moved on, through the twilit streets, climbing through archways and cobbled alleys between what seemed hundreds of squalid, crammed huts and shelters, up toward the Keep.

In one street a shutter slid apart; for a second Carys glimpsed a pair of eyes watching her, but a Watchman glared up and it was slammed tight. The lanky boy turned and winked at her. She looked away, and then remembered with a tingle of surprise that he had called this place the castle, as if he had known where they were going. Was he a spy? That was only too likely. It was best not to talk to any of them.

Between the great inner Keep and the rest of the castle was a chasm, too black to see into. The bridge over it was

The Broken Hills

so narrow that only one person could cross it at a time. It was lit by flaring torches, guttering at the corners.

In the very middle of it, Carys shuddered. Something had rattled and slid under her feet; breathless she took four quick strides. She knew about the trapdoors in bridges like these, opening underfoot without warning, plunging intruders to an endless, screaming fall.

On the far side was another great gate; eyes looked out of a grille and some question was barked. Quist pushed a piece of paper through and waited, whistling through his teeth, arms folded, impatient. Once he glanced back and caught her eye; she looked away immediately.

When the gate was finally opened it led to a stone tunnel; on each side were guardrooms. Above her head were murder-holes, and she saw slots for the sudden sword-racks that sprang out sideways, both doors and weapons at once. Getting out of here would tax the cleverest Watchspy.

Alert, she glanced into the chambers as she passed, but only the relentless red letters of the Rule marched down the bare walls. A hand grasped the back of her neck, twisted her head painfully.

"Don't think I've forgotten you," Quist muttered in her ear. "Keep your eyes front. I hear you've done enough damage already."

He stayed close behind her. Across a dim courtyard and down greasy steps, into a corridor where the prisoners' breath made the damp air smoke, and along a series of doorways that were obviously cells. At the door of each, a prisoner was untied and thrust inside: the two farmers, the woman with the fair hair, the lanky youth. As he went he grinned at her cheerfully. The door slammed shut behind him.

She was the last.

There were more cells, but they hurried her straight past. Quist in front now and two burly Watchmen close behind her. As they climbed some broad steps, Carys allowed herself a wry smile. She was obviously a big threat.

The steps were Maker-material, unworn. At the top was a door; Quist knocked and went in. In seconds he was back.

"Inside," he said. And then, to the Watchmen: "Stay here. No one to come in or out." Pushing Carys before him, he stepped in behind her.

The Broken Hills

⚛

THE ROOM WAS LONG. At the far end was the biggest desk she had ever seen, and sitting on a corner of it, watching her, was a woman. Carys was thrust forward. As she walked, the distance made her feel small; she passed an empty fireplace and a dead fly on the floor. There was nothing else in the room. She lifted her head, defiant. Maybe the fly was lucky.

The woman was pretty and small, with a sharp, narrow face. Her hair was scraped back; she wore a castellan's emblem on her shoulder. Her face was calm and quite unreadable. Carys walked up to the desk and stopped. There was a small stool; the woman nodded, and Quist pushed her onto it. She had forgotten the rooms of the Watch were so utterly cold.

The woman's scrutiny was thorough; her gaze traveled over Carys, taking in every scratch, every muscle of her face. Carys tried to keep the fear out of her eyes. The silence chilled her. And then she noticed the woman was fingering something. Some silver discs on a chain: the insignia. Before she thought she said, "Those are mine."

The castellan showed no surprise. Instead she put the slithering chain on the table. When she spoke her voice was oddly husky. "Welcome back to your family, Carys Arrin." Then she pushed the discs over the desk. "If they're yours," she said, "put them on."

2

*Ask questions with cold rigor. Display
one weapon on the wall, where the
subject must see it. Bring them past
closed rooms where the lash sounds. But
do not allow screams, which bring anger
and stiffen resistance. Do not threaten.
Behind you looms the shadow of the
Watch; that is threat enough.*

Directions for Interrogators, WP9/7623

FOR A LONG MOMENT Carys was still, with surprise more than anything. Then she picked up the chain
and slipped it over her neck.

The castellan gave a thin smile. She nodded at Quist,
who came and lit the two tall candles on the desk with the
spark from a tinderbox. The yellow flames lengthened,
their tiny sizzle loud in the hush.

"Good." The woman nodded. "It always helps when
the prisoner knows exactly what resources the Watch has
for dealing with her."

Carys folded her fingers together. "What is this place?"

Quist went and stood behind the castellan's chair, like

a shadow. She leaned back; he put a hand on her shoulder and to Carys's amazement the woman reached up and stroked it, without looking.

"I'm afraid I'm the one conducting the interrogation. But it will do no harm to tell you that its official designation is Watchtower 277. Broken Mountain. It once had another name, most people still use it. The Castle of Halen."

Halen. One of the Makers.

The small woman leaned forward. "Now listen to me, Carys Arrin. When my captain here sent a message on that he had captured a renegade spy I was very pleased with him. You must know that Maar has you on every wanted list?"

"I'm flattered," Carys said drily.

The castellan smiled. "You're well trained. But then, so am I. Only the flicker of your eyes is enough for me. You're afraid, Carys, and that's natural. You have everything to be afraid of."

She let the candlelight dance on her face. "Unless . . ."

Carys frowned. She knew she was supposed to ask "Unless what?" to be grasping at straws, but she wouldn't. Instead she stood up. "I'm not playing those games. If you want to interrogate me, then do it, but don't bother with the tired old tricks. I'm not some terrified farmwife."

Quist had taken a step, but the castellan waved him back. Her calm did not waver. Carys already knew she was a formidable opponent, probably a trained spy-catcher. But there was something else going on here, something she couldn't work out yet.

The castellan opened a drawer in the desk. "My name," she said unexpectedly, "is Maris Scala." She took out a thick file of paper; putting it down, she shaped the loose sheets into a tidy block with her small hands. "This is your file. It makes fascinating reading. You were seen as extremely promising from a very early age. Stubborn, intelligent, quite ruthless. A great career lay ahead of you. You would very probably have been transferred to command, even become a Watchlord in your own right. And then one day they sent you after a keeper. One Galen Harn. And how everything changed. He must be a remarkable man, Carys."

Carys sat, stonily silent. She folded her hands in her lap and looked straight ahead. But she hadn't missed that the castellan had known Galen's name without looking it up.

Scala turned the papers. "There is a new reward of forty thousand marks for you."

"Congratulations."

"Oh. I intend to do much better than that." The castellan looked at her archly. "Because, like you, I play by my own rules. I find they profit me better. Do you understand?"

She was beginning to. But somehow she had to make the situation profit herself too. "You want information. For your own ends."

"I do. And we'll begin now." The castellan nodded at Quist; he fetched paper and a quill from an alcove and went and sat on the window seat, taking one candle with him. The draft made the flame quiver wildly, and as he dipped his nib in the ink Carys glimpsed the dim outlines of the shattered hills outside. The castellan's eyes followed him fondly. Then she turned to Carys. This was it.

"What has happened," the woman asked, "to the relic called Flain's Coronet?"

The Broken Hills

"The Sekoi have it. In their Great Hoard."

"And where is this Great Hoard? Because it is no longer where you left it."

Carys blinked. "Then you know more than me."

"In this case perhaps we do. A month ago a triple patrol was sent out from Rendar, riding fast into the Sekoi country. It was known later that they found a vast arena, immensely old, with the smashed statues of ancient Sekoi blocking the road to it. The destruction had been recent, and thorough. The arena was empty. Nothing of any hoard remained, not even one gold coin."

The castellan smiled. "You look baffled. Is it that amazing?"

"Yes," Carys said, heartfelt.

"The Watch have always underrated the Sekoi." The castellan got up and wandered to the window, gazing out. "This Hoard, Carys. It was big?"

"It was beyond counting!" She remembered the hills and valleys of treasure. How could they have moved it so quickly?

"And you don't know where it is now?"

"No."

"I believe you." Scala turned abruptly. "The Sekoi keep their secrets, even under torture. I should know. How I would love, Carys, to find the place they keep their children."

Cold, suddenly weary, Carys shrugged. "Don't ask me. So the Coronet is gone, then."

Scala smiled. She looked very small in the black Watch tunic, the dark trousers, her face as delicate as a child's, her deep brown hair caught in its silver pin. "Ah. Not the Coronet. We know, as you do, that the Coronet was given by the Sekoi to the Order, after that strange mass hallucination you all suffered, when you believed you had mended the weather."

Carys shrugged. "You seem to know all about it."

"We do. The Coronet belongs to the Order now. Therefore it must be in the Order's safe house. On . . ." She came and turned a few pages, as if searching for the name, though Carys was sure she didn't need to. "On the island of Sarres."

Carys had been waiting for this. She kept her face totally closed, though a sudden memory of Felnia with her arms wide running over the grass flickered in her mind.

The Broken Hills

Scala turned. "Where is Sarres?"

Carys was silent. Then she said, "In the Unfinished Lands."

"More exactly?"

"I don't know."

Quist looked over. The castellan leaned against the table, folding her arms. "You've been there."

"I was blindfolded each time."

"The keeper still doesn't trust you, then?"

Carys shrugged. Secret delight filled her. Galen had been right. The Watch hadn't found Sarres. When she and the Sekoi had delivered the Coronet four days ago, the sacred island had been just the same, the flowers in early summer color, Felnia dragging her to see a nest of sunbirds, a new line of scrawny goslings crossing the lawn. The Coronet was safe there, with Tallis. Carys would never betray them.

A bell clanged out in the courtyard. Quist dipped his pen in the ink and turned a page. He looked up, impatient. "We're not getting far."

"Patience, lover." Scala tapped her fingers on the file. Her lips were delicately reddened. It was against the Rule.

"Look." Carys sat up and leaned forward. "You and I know that the Margrave lived in Solon the keeper for months. He saw Sarres, the Hoard, everything. What is there left for me to tell you?"

Scala lifted her head, eyes steady. "The Margrave?"

"Oh, yes." Carys stared her out. "The Kest-creature that controls the Watch. That lives down in Maar. You wonder why I gave up my glorious career, Castellan, and he's one reason. A beast and a man, mingled, bred together. A thing of evil working through you. And me, once."

She'd said too much. Shown feeling. Always a mistake. Her face was hot and they were both watching her closely; Quist had stopped taking notes. He looked at Scala. "Is this true?" He sounded appalled.

She gave a husky laugh. "Keep writing, lover. I ask the questions."

He looked back at the page quickly.

Behind Carys the door opened. An elderly man shuffled in with a flagon and three cups; no one spoke as he set them down. Carys tried to think fast. They were still only playing with her. Letting her think she was winning. She had to be very careful.

The Broken Hills

The servant shuffled out. As he closed the door a clock was chiming, far off in the castle. Ten o'clock. She felt drained, bone-weary.

The castellan poured wine into the cups. "Yes," she said. "I have heard this legend of the Margrave. I thought it a tale to terrify the people, that grew in the telling. Useful, no more. But you say it's true?"

"I've said too much."

"Carys, you and I are very alike."

That was an old line. The odd thing was, she thought Scala meant it.

"And if this creature exists, it explains a few things. Because I admit the orders concerning you have been puzzling me." Sipping from the cup, Scala reached for the first sheet of paper and swiveled it around. "Most of the things you could tell us we already know. We know Galen Harn has been calling himself the Crow . . ."

Quist went quite still; Carys noticed it.

". . . and that he claims to have spoken with the Makers. We know of Sarres, if not its location, and we know the Order is re-forming sense-lines of communication across the Western Province. We know their secret group in Tasceron is led by one Shean, from a place called the Pyramid, though I have to say when we eventually found a way into that, it was empty. All these things are important, but Maar doesn't seem to think so." She looked up. "The strange thing is there is just one demand that keeps coming, in every directive, every batch of orders. One person who has to be found, arrested, captured by any possible means. Captured alive. And I think you know him."

Carys was silent.

The castellan leaned forward. "Tell me where he is, and you can come back to us. It will be as if you never left. All your promotions back, your record wiped clean. That glorious career, Carys. If not . . ."

Carys put the tips of her fingers together. "I want time to think about this," she said carefully.

"You can have tonight. No more."

"I may not know where he is."

"You were on your way to meet him."

"He'll have moved on. Galen is unpredictable." Her mouth was dry.

The castellan nodded. "You'll have some meeting

place, I'm sure. But you misunderstand me, Carys. The urgency is not for the man Harn. These desperate orders from Maar concern only a boy."

"A boy?"

"A mere scholar. His name"—she sifted the papers—"is Raffael Morel."

Carys stared in utter shock. "Raffi?" she breathed.

The castellan smiled, and drank. "So you do know him," she said.

3

*The loyalty of the faithful is vital, though
our service to them does not depend on
that.*

Second Letter of Mardoc Archkeeper

THE TWO SMALL BOYS WERE DIGGING for shar-roots in the open field. They had a dog with them, but Galen whipped a sense-line firmly around it and said, "Go on. Remember the father's somewhere near."

Raffi wriggled through the branches and out onto the path. He walked along it making a cheerful whistling noise between his teeth, letting the boys think they saw him first. Then he stopped. "Hello."

The dog was a big one, half wolf. Sleepily it thumped its tail. The older lad glanced at it, but its stillness seemed to reassure him. "We're not to speak to tramps." He turned back to his digging.

"That's a pity." Raffi leaned on the gate. "Because I wanted you to help me. I'm looking for someone."

The boy dug, stubborn. The younger one, about six, just stared, rubbing dirty hands. Then he crouched and began to pile the roots up, arranging them in patterns.

Raffi felt Galen's impatience. "Look. You might have seen her. She's got short brown hair and she's about my height. Wearing dark green trousers and a brown coat. She's in a group of Watch prisoners, and we know they came this way. Have you seen them?"

No answer. The small spade chipped relentlessly at the hard soil. Raffi glanced behind, desperate. From the bushes the Sekoi's long hand waved him on. Then the boy said, "What are you paying?"

He shook his head, bemused. "I haven't got anything."

"Not much use asking, then."

"I could help with the digging. If you tell me."

The spade stopped. The boy looked back, then held it out. "Dig first."

Raffi cursed under his breath, then climbed over and took the dirty wooden handle. He shoved it into the clods of soil.

The Broken Hills

"Careful," the boy said crossly. "The beggars are up the top."

He dug again; briefly the sliced orange tip of a root showed. Before it could wriggle away, the boy was on it, grabbing it and tugging and scrabbling till it came out, flexed once in the damp air, and then went rigid.

"Well?" Raffi snapped.

"Two more."

The sun was overhead; it was warm. Raffi gritted his teeth and dug quickly. "All I want . . . is to know . . . if you've seen her."

"I'll tell you. When I've got my twenty."

The last root was deep, and kept wriggling deeper. Finally the boy sliced it out with his knife, cut it neatly in half, and dropped it on the pile. His brother leaned the two halves together tidily.

Raffi flung down the spade. "So?"

"Haven't seen her."

"What!"

"Haven't seen her."

"You cheeky little brat." Raffi was furious. "You said . . ."

"Didn't say anything." The boy turned toward a distant barn. "Dad! I've finished."

Instantly, before Raffi could move or the boy take another breath, Galen was out of the hedge and had both the boy's hands caught tight in a vicious grip. "Listen to me, you little wretch," he snarled, his eyes black and hard. "I know you've seen her, so you tell me where she is. Now!"

The boy went white with fear. In a sobbing whisper he gasped, "On the road. The big road. They took them all away to the Broken Mountains."

"How long ago?"

"Two days." The boy was breathless. Galen let him go and said, "Come on." In seconds he was gone, up the lane, the Sekoi racing after him.

Raffi looked at the boy. "Sorry," he said, awkward. "But you should have told me."

The boy glared at him with hatred. Then he turned and screeched, "Dad! DAD! They're killing me!"

Raffi ran.

⚛

The Broken Hills

THIS WAS HARD COUNTRY. The lanes were empty, people scarce. There were few great trees, just small gnarled orchards and the tiniest green shoots of what might be barley springing through the fallow ground. Over it, rising like the spines of a nightmare, were the Broken Mountains.

Galen and the Sekoi were waiting at the foot of the next slope, all the small white sheep huddled into the far end of the field. Raffi climbed the stone wall and dropped into the grass. "I'd have found out," he said irritably.

"We haven't got that long." Galen swung the pack off, pulled out the water flask, and drank.

Raffi shook his head. "The father might talk."

"Let him." Galen offered the water to the Sekoi, who took it and wiped the lip daintily with a square of purple silk it took from a pocket. Then it drank, the shaven patch under its ear looking sore and cold, the ragged stitches itchy. It had fidgeted too much when Galen put them in. Now it passed the flask and said, "Galen, I think the small keeper may be right in part. We shouldn't let our anxiety for Carys cause us to be careless."

Morose, Galen turned away. He stared up at the hills

and his gaze was dark and deeply uneasy; Raffi could feel the sense-lines move in an invisible unraveling all around him, into soil and stone, always searching. The keeper was worried. More than that. Curious, Raffi grasped after the feeling; it was brief and hastily hidden, but for an instant it had been clear and it astonished him. Guilt. Galen felt guilty.

As if he sensed the mind-touch, the keeper turned and looked at Raffi. "How many in that last village?"

"Only about ten. All old."

"And did you notice," the Sekoi said, fingering its shaven tribemark, "how the cattle were unmilked and the dogs hungry? The fields untended? Whatever the Watch are building, they have taken many people. It must be some vast undertaking."

Galen shouldered the pack and picked up his stick. "It must," he said grimly. "That's why we need to find out what."

The road the boy had spoken of was easy to find; every inch of it had been scarred and cracked by recent cart-wheels. In some places it had been hastily widened; in others the soft ruts churned through the mud on each side, with drifts of white dust that the Sekoi fingered and smelled and said was from freshly cut stone.

They climbed all afternoon. Twice they had to let Watchpatrols pass. The second group had prisoners, all male. Galen let them go by without a word, much to Raffi's relief. But by late afternoon they both had become aware that something terrible was waiting ahead of them; a darkness in the awen-field. Ducking under the branches of pine, suddenly, they came to it.

A great swathe of woodland had been hacked and cut to a desolation of stumps, the smell of burning still lingering, the undergrowth blackened and charred right down to the scarred soil. Galen stopped, touching the beads at his neck. He might have been praying, but he said nothing aloud, and after a fraught second walked on, fast, with Raffi close behind, white-faced at the horror of the place, the snapped energies that seemed to spark and sting them as they passed, the ghostly whispers of lost voices that cried in the empty air.

At the far side of the clearing the Sekoi paused, breathless, one hand on its side. "Galen," it pleaded. "A moment."

The keeper kept walking, never looking back. Reluctant, Raffi stopped. "He can't," he said, with difficulty. "It hurts too much."

The Sekoi took a deep breath and walked on, looking at him curiously. "You feel the pain of the dead trees?"

"No. Only their loss." It was impossible to explain the choking, the tangle in the mind. After a moment the creature nodded, its yellow eyes sharp in the light of the risen moons. It put its hand on Raffi's shoulder kindly.

Twilight deepened in the shadows of the hills, but the clearing was still too close for them to stop; for hours afterward Raffi could feel it, a sore spot in the world, falling farther and farther back, fainter and fainter, but always a nagging ache. He was tired now, and footsore, and empty with hunger, but he knew how to deal with that, just walk into it, keep walking, not let his mind jerk free from its rhythmic trance. So that the shriek, when it came, stopped him dead.

"Men?" the Sekoi whispered.

"One." Galen was moving now. "And other things. Dark things."

Before them, to the left of the road, was an area of

broken cliff, where landslips had long since crashed down, one on another. In the mixed lights of Atterix and Agramon it was sharp-edged, a mass of jagged shadows, gleams of quartz sparkling from the tilted strata. Sense-lines echoed confusingly.

They slipped silently through the rocks. Then Galen waved them still. Ahead, somewhere under the broken rock face with its springing thorns, someone was sobbing. A frail voice, high and helpless, muttering to itself incomprehensible words and prayers that rose suddenly to a shriek of "Flain, have mercy!" that cut Raffi like a knife.

Carefully, Galen moved the branches. They saw a ravine, and halfway up, on a narrow shelf that crumbled away under her, a woman. She was hard to see, crouched up tight and sobbing in the shadows, and around her in a half circle were four candles, all guttering low, with grease marks where others had been. As Raffi watched, another went out. The woman rocked herself in utter misery.

And then he saw something that filled him with terror. From the base of the cliff a dark paw reached up at her slyly. With a scream she stamped at it, beat it off.

The things were gathered in the dark; inky, silent things, hunkering low. They moved clumsily, slinking from dark place to dark place. Moonlight caught their stooped, misshapen bodies.

"What in Flain's name are those?" the Sekoi breathed.

"Jeckles," Raffi whispered.

"Too big. Too quiet." Galen glanced at the Sekoi. "You get to the woman." Then to Raffi he said quietly, "Join the lines. Use the Second Action."

"Is that all?"

The keeper turned, his profile hooked and dark. "Do as you're told. I want to see these things close up." Already the tingling energies of the Crow were gathering in him; he said, "Ready?"

Raffi nodded hastily.

The Sekoi had slipped away; now they both moved after it and apart, working their way noiselessly through the rocks, Raffi frantically making sense-lines, sending them out, frail tendrils of thought. It was hard to ignore the woman; her terror made him shiver, tangled his best efforts, but when he was almost dizzy with trying to shut her out, the powerful swoop of the Crow surged suddenly out of the dark and linked with him, snapping his eyes open. Crouched behind a tilted slab of quartz, he peered out.

The dark things were climbing. A mass of them swarmed up, over each other's heads and shoulders, snuffling and hissing, rattling small stones. He moved, over-careful, but his foot slipped. A rock fell with a crash. Every one of the creatures turned its head.

Raffi stopped breathing. In the jagged moonlight their eyes were savage and reflective, like tiny bright mirrors. For a terrible second he thought they had no faces; then one opened a crooked slit and snarled, a crackling, painful sound.

Now, Galen said silently.

The mind-net sprang between them, a swift down-drop of searing blue lines crisscrossing the night with eerie light, falling on the dark creatures, crumpling them to a tangled, screeching, infuriated heap. Raffi scrambled out, desperate to hold it in his mind, but one of the beasts flung a rock; it hit him in the chest, flinging him back.

Galen was yelling, the awen-net shriveling away from him; Raffi grabbed breathlessly after it, but for a second his mind had been blank and it was gone. Stones rained down on him. The cliff-face was a riot of noise and screeching; he staggered up and saw the net hanging ragged and Galen jumping down into a mass of escaping shadows.

A muddy paw grabbed at his throat; spinning, Raffi flung a mind-flare at it and the beast crumpled with an ugly smack into the rocks, but other paws had him now, cold, evil-smelling hands tearing him away.

"Raffi!" The Sekoi's voice was harsh, and far. A knife whistled, sliced into the neck of the beast climbing over him; warm blood spurted onto Raffi's face. Struggling up, he thumped into Galen. Back to back, they faced the things. There were hundreds of them; slinking out of the rocks, dropping from bushes, squatting in the ravine. Glancing up, Raffi saw the Sekoi with one spindly arm around the old woman; she seemed stunned, clutching at its fur.

Galen said, "When they attack . . ."

"I don't know! I don't know if I can!"

"You can," the keeper growled. "Just be ready."

From all sides the night crawled; the shadow-things

swarmed over each other, their only sound a rasping, hoarse breathing, a leathery, terrifying sound. At his back, Raffi felt the keeper tense, drag energies from the broken hills, streams, the tangled whiplash bushes. His very being altered, became remote and strange and dark. When he laughed, his voice was the crackling harshness of the Crow.

The things stopped, suddenly wary, almost at Raffi's feet. It was too late. The night exploded in their faces.

4

Long after my death, what I have begun will
continue.
Creatures I could never guess at will be bred.
Horrors I never wanted will be unleashed.
And I will be blamed.

Sorrows of Kest

"RAFFI?" THE SEKOI WAS CROUCHED, looking at him, its yellow eyes sharp in the flame light. "Come closer to the fire," it said kindly. And then, severely to Galen, "This boy is still in shock."

"He's not the only one." Galen's face was edged with firelight, the small cuts on his forehead and neck still oozing. He wrapped the blanket around the old woman and pressed the cup into her hands. "Drink all of it."

She obeyed him, silent, her eyes never leaving his face.

Raffi felt confused. As the Sekoi sat him near the crackling fire he realized he couldn't remember it being kindled, and looked around in sudden fear. There were no rocks. This was a wooded place, green and dark. Mountain ridges rose high above them on each side. Somewhere near, a cold trickle of water cooled his mind.

"You must drink some too," the creature said. "Galen, I really think there should have been more warning. His wits are totally scattered, and it was a miracle the ledge held long enough for me to leap from it." Its seven fingers pushed a cup into Raffi's; he drank thirstily. The water seemed to wake parts of him. He remembered walking now, stumbling along with the Sekoi propping him up, Galen carrying the old woman until she insisted on making her own way. For hours. Or only minutes?

His chest and ribs ached, and it hurt to breathe. Somehow he felt deaf, though he could hear perfectly well; his mind was numb, sore to use, and some great echoing crash was still going on fathoms deep inside him, over and over.

"What did you do?" he mumbled.

Galen glared at him. "What I need not have done if the net had been well made! Or held tight. Of all the scholars I could have chosen in Anara I had to choose you!"

"Not now," the Sekoi said mildly. "Let him be."

The Broken Hills

"We could have been killed!"

"But we weren't. Thanks to the Makers."

Galen gave it a sour stare.

"I'm sorry." Raffi rubbed his chest. "I think I got knocked down." He froze then, seeing the thing that lay in a heap by the fire. "Is that . . . ?"

"Don't worry. It's dead."

The beast lay on its side. Close up it looked hideous, its fur mangy and bald in patches, an odd rusty color, its distorted body crumpled in a pitiful heap.

Galen left the woman to drink and came back. With one foot he rolled the beast over, then kneeled at its side. Fascinated, the Sekoi crouched next to him. "This is no jeckle. Look, it has hands."

Galen turned one, cautiously. The paw was remarkably like the Sekoi's own but thicker and more stubby; seven jointed fingers, one a distinct thumb, the nails ridged to abnormal sharpness, bloody and split.

"It's got no nose either," Raffi whispered.

Galen turned the head. It fell back, and Raffi jumped. The beast's eye stared up. He could see himself reflected, shadowy, upside down.

"But it must breathe." Puzzled, Galen explored the fur. "There are small flaps here. Like gills."

"Gills?" The Sekoi looked disgusted.

"Similar. And here, look, these spines behind the neck." Galen snatched his hand back quickly, then crouched, bringing his face close. "They are sharp. Venomous, I should think."

"Then be careful." The Sekoi shivered. "Such Kest-poisons can harm even after death."

But Galen had turned the beast's face and opened its mouth. Its teeth were long and sharp.

There was a moment of silence, broken only by the cracking fire. Then the Sekoi said, "Certainly an eater of meat."

Galen sat back on his heels. "This is the seventh new species since the winter. Remember that antelope, the one with the striped horns? A ferocious thing."

"The jellyfish that crawled out of the stream." Raffi massaged his sore ribs.

The Sekoi made a mew of distaste. "The worst was that bloated toad."

"Crab."

The Broken Hills

"It could have been either."

Galen went back to the fire and stirred the flames. A shower of sparks lit his face. "Kest made many horrors. The Order once had a great catalog of over twenty thousand different species of creature, but even that number was nothing like the total. There may be millions. There were always things we had never seen before; the beasts interbreed or mutate." He gazed down somberly at the dead creature. "But lately there seems to have been more. And each more dangerous."

In the silence the stream sounded loud, trickling over invisible stones. Raffi's hunger came back like a sudden wave and overwhelmed him. "Can't we have something to eat?"

Galen looked at him, intensely irritated. "Is that all you can ever think about! Do what you want, for Flain's sake."

The Sekoi laughed and tipped the food bag out. There were some mushrooms, a small turnip, and the last few strips of uncooked fish, looking cold and unappetizing. Raffi didn't care. He speared one on a stick and held it hastily over the fire.

"Haven't you got any cooking things?" It was the old woman who had spoken.

Surprised, Raffi said, "Yes, but . . ."

"Then let me do it, keeper. It's the least way I can thank you." The herbal drink had done her good. Her face was tearstained and haggard, but she pushed the wisps of hair back fussily and took the pan Raffi held out.

"Not very clean." She tipped it critically.

"No."

"And you have some fat?"

He glanced at Galen, then took out the precious jar of oil. The jar was a relic—it had a strange lid that sprang open with a gentle pressure on a thumb-pad; he showed her how it worked.

She made the sign of honor furtively, then poured the oil. "At home, we have five relics."

Galen came and sat down nearby. "In your house?"

She nodded. "They are kept in secret. You may see them, if we reach that far. If you wish, keeper, and they are important, you may take them. We are always in danger of the Watch finding them."

The Broken Hills

Galen nodded. "You feel well enough to go on tomorrow?"

"My daughter and the little one will be worried sick." She looked around at them all. "Bless you again, keepers. Flain sent you to me. It was a great miracle."

The oil was hissing. Deftly she took the fish and mushrooms and set them to fry. From a bag around her waist she measured salt and a dark powder and added it; it smelled like spices, and Raffi's mouth started watering. The fish hissed and crackled.

"Will you tell us what happened?" Galen asked.

She was quiet a moment, stirring the mixture. Then she said, "My name is Alys Varro, masters. My village lies at the foot of these mountains, in the valley of the small river called Radicas, about a day's walk now from here. A quiet place, with few people. Four days ago, a Watch-patrol rode in."

Galen looked at the Sekoi. "For work slaves."

"They took twenty of us. All the men, some of the young women. And me." She managed a proud smile. "Either I was to make up the quota or I look young for my age."

"You look very young," the Sekoi said politely. It had unwrapped a parcel of small green berries and dried apple and was sitting with its back against a tree stump, long legs stretched out.

Alys nodded. "As if you would know, master. But yes, I was in the smaller group. We walked for two days, up the road."

"Where does the road lead?" Galen's voice was quiet.

She shrugged. "Some say to a castle. A great castle."

Raffi sat up. "The Castle of Halen?"

"I don't know." She flipped the sizzling, delicious-smelling fish over easily. "I was in a group of ten. No, eleven. We picked a girl up on the way."

Raffi felt the sense-lines shiver.

The Sekoi paused with a slice of apple halfway to its mouth. "A girl?"

"Yes. Quist brought her out of the wood. They let the razorhounds go, as if there had been someone else with her."

The creature scratched its stitches. It looked smug and then, barely seen, a flicker of terror went through it. Raffi dared not guess what such a chase had been like.

The Broken Hills

Galen edged forward, urgent. "This girl, Mother, is a friend of ours. Can you tell us what happened to her?"

"First, you eat. Both of you."

The Sekoi grinned. Galen almost hissed with impatience, but he had to wait while Alys divided the food, sorting the bones out, pushing the largest pieces to Raffi's corner of the pan. Ravenous, he ate quickly, tearing the dried bread from the pack to mop up every morsel.

Galen waited while the woman ate; she obviously needed it. But before she had finished, his patience had run out. "We need to know."

"You need to look after yourselves more." She licked her fingers and nodded at him. "All right. Quist was the patrol captain. He seemed to think the girl was important. When they searched her they found some discs on a chain around her neck; he sent them on ahead."

Raffi swallowed hard bread. "The insignia!"

"Was there anything else?" Galen snapped. "Did they find anything else?"

Raffi looked at him curiously, but the woman said, "No. She was a clever lass. I spoke to her once, but she never told us her name. Kept herself apart from the rest, kept her eyes open. And she wasn't scared of them, not at all. Spoke up for me when I fell."

"That's Carys." Raffi scraped up the last scraps. "But the Castle of Halen? For a start it's a ruin."

"Maybe not." Galen tossed sticks on the fire. "Not if it's being rebuilt. It would take a lot of men. And why?"

"A supply base." The Sekoi spat out a pip.

"Supplying what?"

"Is Carys all right?" Raffi turned to the old woman. "Is she hurt? And how did she get away?"

"She didn't. No. But I did." Alys smiled coyly. "Kept stumbling and coughing, making out I couldn't keep up. It was Quist, you see. I've lived a fair time; I can tell how a man is. He acted hard, but there was something about him. Last time I fell, I just didn't get up. So he cut me loose and marched them on."

"They left you for dead?" Galen laughed his harsh laugh. "So much for the mercy of the Watch!"

"Don't judge too quickly, keeper. For now I'll tell you a very strange thing. Quist yelled at them to go on, but he waited beside me. When the patrol was out of sight I felt him lift me. For a moment, yes, I thought I'd go over the

The Broken Hills

cliff, but then, masters, he laid me down soft in the wood and said, 'Keep off the road,' just as if he knew I could hear him. Then he went. When it was safe, a while after, I lifted my head. There was this bag beside me. With water. And a knife."

In the astonished silence the flames crackled comfortably. Then the Sekoi gave a low purr.

After a moment Galen said, "You do right to chide me. Even in the heart of the worst it seems the Makers still move." He looked at her sidelong. "And the girl?"

"I saw no more of them, master. I walked for two days before sleeping in that ravine. Before the beasts . . ." She stopped suddenly, her eyes flooding.

"That's enough." Galen stood and helped her up. "You must sleep. Tomorrow we take you home." He helped her over to the blankets, talking quietly.

Raffi washed the pan. The Sekoi watched him. Then it wrapped the rest of the fruit up and said suddenly, "Raffi. What is going on?"

"Going on? What do you mean?"

It was silent so long he turned and stared at it. It looked troubled. Finally it said, "For a long time, as you know, I thought Carys was not to be trusted. After our adventure with the Coronet I found to my shame that I was wrong. I would hate to go back to those suspicions."

Raffi dropped the pan. "Why should you?"

"Carys is skilled at evading pursuit," the Sekoi said quietly.

"No one better."

"Indeed." The creature leaned back against the stump, folding its arms. "No one better. At running, hiding, not being taken by surprise. So why do I feel so strongly that she *let them capture her*?"

A spark stung Raffi's hand, but he barely felt it. "What?" he whispered.

5

In his castle, Halen dreamed.
He walked the silent corridors and in the
mirrors saw only his own face.
Outside, the world descended into
Chaos. "Something evil is searching for
me," he whispered.

Book of the Seven Moons

THEY WERE TREATING HER LIKE an honored guest, Carys thought wryly.

The straw was almost clean and the drinking water had only two dead spiders in it. The plate that had been banged in through the grille of the door had bread and cheese on it, and there had even been a flea-ridden blanket in one corner of the cell to make a softer bed. Scratching the bites it had given her, her whole body stiff with the damp and the hard stones, she rolled over and sat up against the wall, pulling her jerkin on and pushing the sleep-tangled hair from her eyes. But she'd slept surprisingly well.

By the noise outside and the shaft of sunlight that slanted down the narrow embrasure of the window, it was early morning. All the work of the castle was well under way; wagons crunching by outside, the trudge of weary feet. She grinned. Maybe she wouldn't have to work after all. Pulling the plate over, she began to eat hungrily, glancing around. The cell was big. A few rusty chains hung from one wall. In the wand of light from the window she could see scratches on the damp stones; names, verses, dates laboriously crossed off. They might be worth a look later.

The cheese was strong, almost going bad, but she was glad of it. When she'd finished the last strip of bread, she fished the spiders out of the water and drank, then soaked the end of her sleeve and washed her face. Until she stopped, listening. There was a lot of noise outside; hammering, voices and yells, the clatter of wheels and marset hooves, but close by, insistent, there was something else. It was tiny, and it was inside the cell.

Tapping. An urgent, quiet tapping. After a second, she knew where it was coming from. The wall facing her was of stone, rough-edged, the ancient mortar black and

The Broken Hills

crumbling. Faint wet smudges of green algae glistened on its hacked facets. The tapping came from the other side; as she crawled closer she saw a tiny crack deep in the corner.

Picking up a piece of loose stone she tapped back. There was silence. Then a whisper, hoarse and eager. "I thought you'd never hear me."

She groaned to herself. Of course, it was the spotty boy; she'd seen them put him in the cell last night. Still, there was something she wanted to know from him.

"Have they fed you?" he whispered.

"Never mind that." She put her face close to the crack. "How did you know they were bringing us here? Out on the road, when you said the castle?" She could almost feel him grin.

"My secret. But like I said, get ready. It's all fixed, and when we break out, believe me, it'll be big!"

"Fixed? By who?"

"My uncle." His voice was breathless; his eagerness to tell her everything filled her with contempt and pity. "He's behind it. Everyone's terrified of him."

"He's going to break you out?" she asked, puzzled.

"No! The whole place is full of his people. The Watch have no idea! Lots of the workmen, the prisoners, are under his orders; we've been infiltrating this place for weeks. I was in on the plan from the start. Well"—he gave an odd, self-conscious laugh—"you could almost say it was my idea, really. He thinks the world of me. I just said, "Uncle, I've got this brilliant—'"

"I'm sure," Carys said acidly, "but what's the use of having all your men made workslaves?"

"Don't you see! It's a stroke of genius. When he attacks, we let him in. We've got weapons, brought in under the cartloads of stone. The Watch will never know what hit them!" His voice fidgeted, as if he was wriggling in delight.

Carys shook her head. "It would take an army. And what about—"

"We've got an army! My uncle's the most ferocious warlord there is!"

Bolts rattled. Instantly, Carys jerked away from the crack.

Voices rang in the stone corridor, keys clinked; it sounded as though the prisoners were being taken out to join in the work. She listened, catching the rattle of chains, waiting for them to come for her, but no one did, and the shuffle of feet and barked orders died away into an eerie silence. As if the place were empty.

After a few minutes she edged back to the crack. "Are you still there?"

No answer. So it seemed she really was spared hauling stone. That was one good thing; it gave her time to work out what to do. And for something else.

She got up, went to the door, and lifted the grille as far as it would go, a dark slot in the rusty metal of the door. Then, with all her concentration, she listened. It took at least five long minutes before she was absolutely sure there was no sentinel outside, or anywhere in the corridor. Someone was talking, but the low voices were a long way off, probably in the guardroom near the gatehouse. It seemed safe. In any case, she'd have to take the chance.

Going to the darkest corner of the cell she worked quickly. Shrugging her jerkin off, she undid the third wooden toggle. Only it wasn't wood, just carefully painted to look that way. It came apart easily, the Maker-material smoothly unscrewing, and inside it tiny lights pulsed, green and blue. There was a small button in the center; she pressed it and held it down, counting the seconds off silently. Four minutes. To make sure she made contact. She released the pressure, counted one minute, then repeated the procedure, every muscle in her body tensed, listening for the slightest rustle outside the door.

Still no one came.

While the button was held down the lights changed color, blue to red. As soon as the time was up she screwed the whole thing together hastily, pulled the jacket on, and huddled up against the wall, her heart thudding. If they had any way of knowing . . . Of course they didn't. Calm down, she told herself firmly. It was quiet now, outside. Gradually her mind relaxed.

The boy's boasting was odd. Especially if it was true. He might just be trying to impress her, but it seemed more than that. Scala worried her more. Carys had foreseen nothing like her. It was obvious the castellan and her captain were working for themselves—they wanted to know where Raffi was so they could pass the information on and pocket the rewards.

Raffi. That was the thing she couldn't grasp—why

The Broken Hills

Raffi? Was it just a way to get to the Crow? What on earth could the Margrave want with a . . . She stopped, her mind cold. Wait a minute. Just wait a minute.

She remembered now. It had been the night after they'd used the Coronet of Flain—a night stop on that hurried journey out of Sekoi lands. Just the two of them. Raffi had been huddled by the fire, oddly quiet.

She'd said so, and he'd stirred the flames. For a long time he hadn't even answered; when he did, his words were hesitant. "Carys, when we were all caught up in that vision, when the weather-net was mended, I thought . . . someone came and spoke to me."

"Someone?" she'd asked. She'd been sewing a tear in her coat. She remembered how reluctant he'd been.

"The Margrave." And then he'd reached over and caught her fingers, stopping her, blurting it all out. "He spoke to me! He told me that he was going to find me, to seek me out. Just me! He said he wanted me . . . for some sort of apprentice. That we were linked. I'm sure it was real. I'm sure of it! It's terrifying me."

She had stared at him. "Have you told Galen?"

"No."

"You should. But Raffi, we all had strange, muddled visions. I know I did. I thought I was back in the Watch-house." Had she told him that? She wasn't sure. But she thought she'd convinced him the whole thing was a nightmare, that he'd let it worry him too much. They'd ended up laughing about it, and he'd never mentioned it again. But thinking back now, he'd still been a bit quiet, right up until the time she and the Sekoi left for Sarres.

Could it be true? She shivered, dragging her knees up in the straw and wrapping her arms around them. This was serious. If Scala wasn't lying, then the Margrave really was searching for Raffi. And that complicated things.

There were two things she could do now, it seemed to her. The first was to refuse Scala's offer. If she did that she'd end up on some work-gang and the plan would be finished. The second thing was to tell them where Raffi might be found—or at least make a convincing deal with them. It was what was needed. But it was dangerous. If she did it, she might never get out of this alive.

Footsteps.

She curled instantly; the door rattled, banged open,

and Quist walked in. He looked down at her. "I know you're awake. Come on; she wants her answer."

He walked ahead down the corridor; brushing herself down, Carys followed, leaving a trail of wisps of straw. There were guards, but Quist waved them away. Opening a door to the outside, he bowed her through, mock polite.

"Have you known Scala long?" she asked, squeezing past him.

"Forget it. I've had the training too. You'll get nothing from me."

The were standing on a high gallery near the top of the keep. Watch flags flapped above them; the sudden fresh air made Carys feel giddy. It was a cool, bright day and the castle lay below her flooded with sunlight, swarming with workers. Lines of wagons were straggling out of the distant barbican; even from here she could hear the yells and whipcracks of the wagoners.

"Where are they going?"

He looked at her, as if weighing what to say. Then, as if it were no secret, he shrugged. "The Wall."

"What wall?"

"You've been away too long, Watchspy. You're out of

touch." His voice was morose, his fingers tapping restlessly on the smooth battlements. Then he turned, his dark hair lifting in the wind. "You know the Unfinished Lands are spreading."

"Everyone knows that."

He nodded. "The Watch has calculated that if the present rate of expansion continues, the Finished Lands will be halved in twenty years. We'll be surrounded by chaos and each year it will close in on us. In fifty, maybe less, it will close over our heads. Farms, towns, villages, everything gone. No one will be left alive."

Carys looked down at the bedlam of noise. "So the Watch is building a wall?"

"Not just any wall. A vast, immensely strong structure, from here to the Narrow Sea, as a start. Sixteen leagues. Eighty spans thick, of rubble and hardcore faced with the smoothest Alavian marble. Forty spans high with a parapet even higher. Towers every two leagues. Only one gate. No weak points."

"You sound very proud of it." She was silent, thinking of the immensity of the effort. "But will it work?"

"Nothing will be able to burrow under or scale it.

The Broken Hills

We'll wall in the Finished Lands. No pollution will come to them." He saw her disbelief and laughed. "Come on. She hates to be kept waiting."

The castellan's room was warm in the sunlight that slanted from its windows; in the daylight Carys saw they were thickly glazed with the unbreakable Maker glass.

Scala had her hair loose. It brushed her small shoulders as she looked up from a file of papers. "Sleep well?"

Carys didn't bother to answer. Instead she leaned on the desk with both hands and said, "I've made up my mind. These are my conditions. I want an assurance ~~from you~~ countersigned from Maar—of my reinstatement and I want copies of it sent to every Watchhouse and Tower. I want a third of all rewards and promotions. Up front, I want two thousand marks, my own armed patrol, and a permanent suite of rooms in the Tower of Song."

"I see." Scala didn't even blink. "Fairly extensive demands for a prisoner. And in return, what?"

Carys took a breath. It was a simple sentence, but it cost her a great effort to say it.

"In return I go with you to the Pits of Maar and to-

gether we inform the Margrave—face–to–face, if he exists—exactly where he can find this Raffael Morel."

There was a long silence. Then Scala smiled. "It seems fair."

"Oh, it is." Carys sat in the nearest chair. She leaned back and blew hair out of her eyes, wondering what Scala really thought.

"We'll leave as soon as possible." The castellan looked at Quist. "Get things ready."

He shrugged. "It'll take three days."

Carys thought of the spotty boy's blurted secrets. "Make it two," she said thoughtfully.

6

Are these the ladders that lead to heaven?
Who has ever climbed to their top?

Poems of Anjar Kar

THE YOUNG WOMAN ROCKED the crying child. "I suppose you've come for the babies and the lame ones now," she said savagely. "No one else is left! Who's supposed to sow and harvest? Who's supposed to milk the cows? Don't you people have any sense?"

The Watchsergeant was hot and thirsty. The hut was dank. In one corner an old woman rocked, dribbling and mumbling to herself, spitting into the fire and then giggling with an odd, manic glee. It gave him the creeps. And the place stank—the pile of marset dung outside the door was huge and fresh. His stomach heaved. He took out a rag of handkerchief and pressed it over his nose.

"I'm not taking anyone, woman. It's a search. There have been reports of bandits. A lot of them, gathering in the hills."

"Bandits!" The woman snorted and waved her free arm. "Oh, yes. Here they are, look, hundreds of them. All crammed into this luxurious palace!"

The Watchman shrugged. It was true he could see the whole of the inside of the hut and had no desire to go farther in; it was sooty and smoke-blackened, with lumps of what might be meat hanging from the rafters. One cupboard, a hearth with a dull fire, two box beds. Not much else. The floor was trodden mud. A real hovel.

The old woman cackled and looked at him suddenly with the white of one eye. Her face was filthy, her long gray hair tangled. "Beware," she said. "The owl and the kraken, the cold shadows of the moons." She spat solemnly and the fire crackled. "Death is looking for you. He has long fingers."

"Don't mind her," the young woman snapped. "Her mind's gone."

But the Watchman had had enough. He backed out,

trying not to breathe the stink. "All right, but if you see anyone . . ."

"I'll stay in and bar the door."

The giggle from the dark corner chilled him. He walked quickly back to the horse, leaving the door to slam behind him. Job for one man, they'd said. No one had told him the place was a madhouse.

After the Watchman had ridden away, the farmstead was silent for at least five minutes. Then the door burst open; the two women ran out, long spades in their hands. They cleared the great pile of dung aside quickly, then heaved up the trapdoor. Alys peered down. "Are you alive, keepers?"

Galen's hands came up; he hauled himself out. "We are. Though half choked."

Raffi was pulled out next. He had never been so glad to breathe fresh air in his life; he crouched and coughed it in till his eyes watered. The Sekoi gasped and spat and sniffed its own fur in disgust. "An ingenious idea, ladies, but I think I almost prefer capture."

"Inside," Alys said. "Quickly." The hut was almost as unbearably stuffy as the dark pit had been, but the fire cheered it. While her daughter-in-law built up the blaze, Alys smiled proudly. "Cara was superb. And you should have seen me as a madwoman."

"I'm sure it was most realistic." The Sekoi sat, stretching its long legs with a purr of relief. "But now you are safely home, we should go as soon as possible. Let the keepers see these relics."

A cheep startled Raffi. In one dim corner a cage hung, with a green markeet in it. It eyed him beadily through the smoke. Galen had seen it too; he frowned. "There should be no caged souls in a free house."

The young woman said, "Keeper, the bird is happy here."

"Set him free. If he's happy, he'll stay."

She looked down. Finally she said, "Tomorrow I'll do it."

"Tomorrow," Galen said sourly, "is never . . ." He stopped. Rigid. The red light was tiny and it burned them both like a coal. Raffi almost hissed with the sudden pain of it; with his third eye he saw it, sharp as a star, like the point of a heated sword, searing him.

The Sekoi was asking something, concerned, but all

he could feel was the Maker-light. It faded, then pulsed
again. When it was gone he felt abruptly cold. The Sekoi
watched, intent. "Can you speak?"

"Yes." Raffi turned to Galen. "It had to be a relic!
Something still alive."

Galen nodded. He stood up and went to the door and
opened it, looking out to the jagged hills.

"The relics are here." Alys went to the bird's cage and
put her hand in. "Jem pecks any strangers, so we feel it's
the safest place." The bag she pulled out was small and
covered with sawdust; hastily she brushed it clean, then
emptied the contents out onto the table and made the sign
of honor over them reverently. "These are all we have."

From the door, Galen didn't turn. "Look them over,
Raffi," he said morosely.

A little disappointed, Alys stared at his back.

Raffi fingered the objects. Already he knew there was
no energy left in them; none of these could have produced that point of power. The Sekoi, always curious,
leaned over his shoulder. There was a small bracelet and
a cube that opened and was empty inside. Beside them
lay a smooth black object with many buttons, each with

a Maker-symbol. He had seen several of these. Galen thought they had been used to control larger relics. He pressed a few buttons. Nothing happened.

The Sekoi's long fingers turned the rest; a broken silver disc, and a blue-lidded object with strange devices, which opened to show a cracked screen and more buttons.

"Anything?" Galen asked.

"No."

The keeper turned, came over, and looked down at the sorry collection. "How are the things of the Makers lost," he muttered, as if the sight chilled him. "All their power, all their greatness. Dwindled to this."

Raffi glanced up. It was unlike Galen to show doubts; his faith was always fierce and restless. Or had been, until they had lost Solon. That treachery had devastated him, perhaps even more than Galen knew. Now he said, "Put them back, Mother. Keep them safe. They're only empty shells now."

"Something made that signal." Raffi slid the relics into the bag.

The keeper turned away, his face dark. "But not from here. We must get to the castle! And before nightfall."

The Broken Hills

Raffi sighed. He'd been hoping for a good meal, a wash, maybe even some extra sleep. From its wry grin he guessed the Sekoi had too. But both of them knew Galen had made up his mind.

They left the dilapidated farm within minutes, Alys and her daughter waving them off, after cramming the packs with all the food they could spare. Galen had given them the Blessing solemnly, as if he sensed the old woman's disappointment; she kneeled in the mud to receive it, tears running down the wrinkles of her face.

"When you find the girl," she called now, "give her my thanks."

Raffi turned, walking backward. "We will. Take care of yourself."

GALEN WAS SILENT. All the way back to the road he went at a ferocious pace; Raffi scrambling after him, too breathless to complain. The Sekoi strolled behind, its long legs keeping up effortlessly. "Our friend is troubled," it said after a while.

"Guilty," Raffi gasped.

"Indeed? About what?"

"I don't know what. And he can't forget . . . about Solon."

As they climbed, the Sekoi was silent. Then it said, "Raffi. Did you believe what I told you about Carys?"

"No." And he threw himself up the slope, bending back the thorns. He didn't want to think about Carys. Not now.

For hours they climbed into the Broken Hills. The air grew colder and the road narrowed to a track winding along mountain ledges, skirting dizzy drops into the green valleys below. Finally they were so high, the mist closed in, slowing them; once Raffi only realized he was too close to the edge when his foot dislodged a stone that rattled over into silence. The wind whistled strangely, and the broken rocks confused the sense-lines; in all the ravines and arches he had the feeling of silent movements, as if the hills were busy with sly gatherings, watching eyes. His legs ached with the long effort; his lungs were raw with the damp.

Night was falling before they saw the castle. It loomed up suddenly, a blackness in the mist.

The Broken Hills

Galen stopped, then crumpled onto a stone, white-faced. He eased his stiff leg with a hiss of pain.

The Sekoi flung itself down on its back and dragged in breath, its whole body quivering. When it could speak it gasped, "Even if Carys is in this place, Galen, we cannot just walk in and ask for her. We must not rush headlong into danger. We need a plan."

"The Makers will send a way in," Galen growled.

The creature's mew of impatience was slight but audible. "Maybe. But we need—"

"We need to trust them." The keeper turned to Raffi. "Did you feel that?"

"Someone's close by."

"More than one." Galen stood wearily. "Let's get closer. Keep as quiet as you can."

The Castle of Halen was a great black wall in the dark. A deep ditch had been hacked outside it from the rock, and the Wall rose out of that, built of strange shiny black stone, glossy and volcanic, buttressed by wedges, each block as tall as Galen and smoothly fitted. Vast towers swelled out along it. Far above, linking them, a wooden palisade rose against the stars.

"Unclimbable." The Sekoi squirmed under a yewberry bush and looked up. "Unless you're a suck-foot rat."

"Perhaps we should work our way around to the gates," Raffi whispered. Familiar as his own smell, fear was churning in him, the ominous black hulk of the castle hanging over him, heavy as dread.

But then the Sekoi's fingers closed on his arm. "See there," it hissed.

A movement. Up on the parapet. Something rippling, rattling, unrolling fluidly down the Wall; two of them, no three, four, the end of the nearest flapping to and fro just in front of where they were hiding.

Ladders? *Rope ladders?*

It was the Sekoi who broke the astonished silence. "If this is luck, I don't believe it."

"I told you." Galen's voice sounded choked. "You should trust Flain."

"Galen, this has to be some trap!"

"Does it?" The keeper turned. "Look."

Suddenly the night was alive. Men were running from the rocks, scrambling down into the spiked ditch, hauling themselves hastily up the swinging, twisting ladders.

The Broken Hills

From the parapet someone yelled. Swords clashed. A trumpet blared inside the castle.

"An attack?" Raffi breathed.

"Come on!" Galen was out, running; he plunged down into the ditch, staggered, and hauled himself up. Then he grabbed the nearest ladder. And climbed.

7

*Defense is a first priority. Take any steps
necessary to keep key personnel out of
enemy hands. If important prisoners
cannot be evacuated, shoot them.*

Rule of the Watch

THE CELL DOOR BANGED OPEN. Carys jumped down from her desperate squeeze into the window embrasure. "What's going on out there!"

"The castle's under attack!" Quist grabbed her and hustled her out into the corridor, shoving her under a flickering light. "Did you know about this?"

"Me!" Her heart jumped, but she laughed coldly. "I'm hardly likely to mess up the deal of a lifetime. They can't get in, can they?"

"They're already in." The corridor was full of men, hurrying; arms were being given out, orders snapped. "The gates are open; the lower barbican's been taken.

They had help from inside." Quist looked flustered; he pushed her on.

"Who are they?"

"Outlaws. We'd had reports."

"It would take an army!"

Quist banged through a door and thrust men aside. "That's what they've got. Scala's livid. She'd hang every prisoner if she had time."

Flainsteeth! Carys thought. The spotty kid had been telling the truth. Grabbing a crossbow from a pile, she looked wildly around for bolts.

"Come on!" he yelled. "Now!"

Scala's room was empty. Quist ran to the window. "Wait here. Touch nothing." In seconds he was gone, into the noise.

Carys barely paused. She flung down the crossbow, grabbed a quill and dipped it, then scrabbled desperately for some small piece of parchment that wouldn't be missed. Anything! There was a roster for prisoners; she flipped it over and began to write hurriedly, the ink sputtering into little sprays as she rushed. It was the old code—her own. He'd worked it out once, so he could do it again. She managed barely half a dozen words; then Quist was coming back, and as he burst in with Scala running behind him, she dropped the quill and turned, blocking them from seeing it, her fingers cramming the stiff wet sheet into her pocket.

"This is unbelievable!" Scala went straight to the window. "The whole of the outer court is overrun. Most of the prisoners are armed. There are fires in three quadrants. I'll have the head of every Watchsergeant left alive after this." She was furious, but it didn't overwhelm her; even now she was planning. "Sound the retreat. I want the fourth and fifth patrols to regroup at the inner gates. We'll hold them there."

"There are ropes down every wall." Quist's voice was almost a whisper. Carys pushed in beside him and looked down.

The castle was in ferment. Fires burned everywhere; cressets and fiery torches bobbed in the dark. There were swarms of men coming over the north parapet; as she watched, a whole group came out of a turret and along the Wall-walk yelling; they cut down four astonished Watchmen and sliced the ropes of the great artillery machines with precision. Then they were gone, swinging down into the fight. The courtyard was an inferno of noise. Arrows thwacked against the stones; the clang of swords was deafening.

"Whoever they are, they're experts," she muttered.

Directly below them there was a roar and a great yell of triumph. The inner gates crashed in; horses and men rampaged through them, the last Watchmen hacked down as they fled.

Carys turned. "This place is finished."

"Not so," the castellan said icily. "We can defend the keep for as long as it takes."

"You won't get all your men in here."

"Then we won't. Those left outside will die."

"But we'll be trapped! Maybe for months! Have you got that sort of time to waste?"

"She's right," Quist muttered.

"You think I should leave my command? Desert all our men?" It was impossible to tell whether she was angry now, or teasing them.

"Listen to me." Quist caught her elbows. "Horses are ready at the secret gate. We can ride straight to Maar.

The Broken Hills

Whatever report you put in, I'll back it. We can't afford to be trapped here, not now we've got this chance. Someone else might find the boy, and we'll have lost everything!"

Scala stared at him. She seemed amused; her lips curled in suppressed laughter. "You've changed, lover. You're getting as ruthless as the best of us."

"I've had a good teacher."

They were silent, till Carys snapped, "Well? Or we'll never get out."

For answer Scala swung to the desk; she grabbed a packet of papers from one drawer and a strongbox from another. Quist caught a dark cloak from a hook and swung it around her. Then they were running.

The corridors were deserted now, and shadowy. Flame light reflected through arrow-slits and the acrid, choking stench of smoke was everywhere. They raced down the stairs, past the prisoners' cells, then turned a corner and stopped. All the doors were unlocked.

And barring their way, with a sword far too big for him and a bunch of keys, was the spotty boy.

GALEN DUCKED as a fire-arrow slashed over his head. "Hurry!" he said, reaching down. Raffi felt the strong grip on his sleeve, hauling him rapidly over the battlements. Breathless, he crawled to the inner edge and looked down.

It was a battle. The gates were wide, and as he stared another set of inner gates crashed down. The invaders were hard to see in the dark confusion of flame and shadow, but they were well-armed and seemed to know exactly what they were doing. Fire-arrows fell like rain; the noise of yelling and the clatter of metal almost deafened him.

The Sekoi flung itself down behind him. "Now what! She could be anywhere!"

"She's important." Galen pointed up through the smoke. "She'll be in there." The keep stood like a solid rectangular outcrop of rock. From all its battlements and galleries, parapets and arrow-slits, a hail of bolts was flying, and every few seconds a whistling wave of arrows slashed down into the turmoil below. Beacon fires blazed from its top. Huge wooden artillery fired with fierce discipline.

Raffi's mouth was dry. "We can't get in there."

The Broken Hills

"We've gotten this far." Galen scrambled up. "There's one entrance—that narrow bridge." He ran along the walkway; two Watchmen turned, but he shoved one aside ruthlessly and the Sekoi caught the other and had cracked the man's head hard against the wall before Raffi could move. After that they were lucky. The fight in the courtyard was fierce; all the defense was concentrated there. Racing down a spiral staircase they forced open a door at the bottom and came into some dark kitchen entry, slippery with fat. All the torches had burned away except one; the Sekoi grabbed it as they passed, then flung it down with a snarl as it went out. At the end was an archway; they took a breath, then ran across the trampled mud, to the bridge.

Raffi was terrified. The battle was raging all around; just behind him a Watchman fell with a screech and instantly had his throat cut by a tall man with a sword who swiveled on the Sekoi. The creature leaped back. "I'm no Watchman, friend!" The man spat, and swore, and vanished into the throng.

Galen hauled Raffi away from the corpse. The bridge was only wide enough for one at a time; one torch burned on it. At the far end the portcullis was raised.

"Something's wrong. Why isn't it watched?" The keeper sent a swift sense-line across. Then he said, "Wait." Grabbing both rails, he crossed quickly, then turned. "It's safe. Come on."

The Sekoi shoved Raffi on. He took three paces and then stopped.

"Hurry!" Galen yelled.

Raffi couldn't move. A point of danger churned in him; he couldn't tell what it was, but he was sweating and gray.

He put his foot down, on the central slab.

"LEAVE THIS TO ME," Carys muttered. Without hesitation she ran down and flung her arms around the boy before he could move, pinning him so tight, he dropped the keys with a squawk. "It's . . . it's all right," he spluttered. "I said I'd save you. I'm here."

In his ear she whispered, "Shut up. Give this to the keeper." Paper was shoved into his pocket.

He stared over her shoulder, appalled. "Isn't that the castellan?"

The Broken Hills

Carys jumped back. "Where?"

"There!" He turned.

Instantly she hit him hard, in the stomach, and again, in the back of the neck. He collapsed like a sack, splayed in the straw.

"Sorry," she whispered.

Quist leaped over him. "Who was that?"

"Just a prisoner. Lead on."

Scala had her own keys. They unlocked a tiny postern door near the guard room and beyond it was an icy stone tunnel with a wooden gate at the end. Bursting through that, they found the horses, three already saddled.

Scala gave Quist a haughty look. "That sure I'd come!"

"Always."

Carys had climbed onto the best horse. She realized now they were down in the dry moat; high overhead, the keep's defenses roared and smoked; the fiery moon Pyra burned above. Behind her, Quist wheeled his mount. Then a shout made her look up. On the bridge, directly above her, she saw Raffi.

HIS FOOT CAME DOWN, the slab seemed solid . . .

"For Flain's sake!" Galen raged.

Raffi barely heard him. All his instincts were crawling with horror; as his weight pressed harder, second by second, he seemed to himself to be already falling, plummeting into some great pit in his mind. Then, with a click that jarred his very heart, the trapdoor crashed open.

Raffi! The word leaped into Carys's throat; she choked it to silence.

He seemed to hang a moment; then as he fell, she gasped, the Sekoi lunging vainly after him, Galen grabbing at air.

For Raffi, the black square of darkness rose up like a great mouth; with a scream, he reached out, grabbed, slid, grabbed again, and Galen's hands had his sleeves, but the whole of his body was swinging in the dark, a sick giddiness.

"I can't hold him!" Galen was yelling. His hands slipped. Something dark leaped right over Raffi's head; then the Sekoi's seven fingers hauled powerfully on his arms, the cloth tearing. He looked down. Under his feet, far below, Raffi saw Carys.

Her face was white, tiny. And then she had turned away and was galloping, the horse clattering right under him, and as Galen hauled him up he lost sight of her in the smoke, and collapsed on the bridge, weak with shock, shivering. The Sekoi pulled him upright and held him. "We have to get inside!"

Arrows were bouncing from the rails. One fell through the trapdoor; Raffi saw how it plummeted into the dark. Then they were dragging him into the keep. He wanted to shout that it didn't matter, that she'd gone, but somehow the despair of that knowledge kept him dumb; he didn't want to say it, because that would make it real.

They raced down the corridor of cells; from above, wooden boards were being slammed down on the bridge; the invaders hurrying across. The cells were all empty. Galen paused in the last, glancing around. "She was here."

"Not anymore." The Sekoi looked up nervously. "This castle has been captured."

"And so have you!" The words were fierce; the sword

that came out of the shadows so sharp against the creature's neck that it breathed in alarm. Out from behind the door stepped a bruised lanky youth, his face pocked with spots.

"You're my prisoners." He grinned, his teeth black.

"We're looking for a girl," Galen snapped. "A prisoner. Carys Arrin."

"Her!" The boy scowled. "She's gone."

"Gone?"

"With the castellan."

Galen said nothing. Men were trampling down the corridor, a bodyguard of at least ten, hefty and threatening. "Uncle!" The boy turned, almost swelling with pride. "Uncle, it's me! It's Milo!"

"Milo." The voice was dry and resigned. "You had to still be alive."

"Yes I am!" The boy waved the sword, flushed. "And I've captured these prisoners, look. They're not Watch, either."

The bodyguards were shoved aside. Out from among them came a tiny man, his face narrow and sly, wide-lipped, his clothes masterpieces of gaudy show. Behind him, a girl in silver armor and a broad-chested bearded man stood, stock-still with amazement.

The dwarf saw the Sekoi, and he paled. When he saw Raffi his face went ashen. Taking a deep breath, he closed his eyes. Then he turned around, and opened them.

"Hello, Alberic," Galen said quietly. The silence was terrible. Until Alberic snatched the sword from his nephew's hand and began to beat him with it, mercilessly, viciously.

"You useless, weak-kneed lump of clinker!" he howled. "You brainless, addle-headed flea off a rat's back!"

"What have I done!" the boy squeaked.

"What have you done! You've brought me the one man I never, ever want to set eyes on as long as I live!"

The Sekoi folded its arms. "You can see the family resemblance," it said thoughtfully.

The Mirrors of Halen

8

"What do you want?" the Emperor said.
   The great keeper, Imalan, bowed.
"Mercy on your captives, lord. Let the
Sekoi prisoners go free."
   The Emperor stroked the small blue
lapdog. "I am not in the mood for
mercy," he said quietly.
   Imalan answered, "It is the Makers
who will persuade you, not I."

                    The Deeds of Imalan

THE SLIVER OF SUNLIGHT was like a wand—
Soren's wand, when she struck the flame trees and made
them burn.

Raffi lay with his eyes open, watching it. He was supposed to be making a dawn meditation, but the light
distracted him; it had slid between the shutters and was
glowing, a beautiful red, on the stones. Outside he could
hear voices, the clatter of a bucket. After its exhausted
night, the castle was waking.

Galen had found this room. When Alberic had stormed
off last night in a black fury, the keeper had only laughed
and turned away. When the Sekoi had wondered inno-

cently what they should do, he had said, "Sleep. Since we seem to be old friends of the new owner." Now the creature still lay curled in its nest of stolen blankets, snoring softly.

Raffi envied it. He had slept badly, tossing and turning, worrying over Carys, about himself. Since he had seen the Margrave clearly, since that moment of icy terror when it had whispered that it was searching for him, fear had kept coming back, in waves. Fear of the dark. Of silence. Even of dreaming. And how could he make the Deep Journey like this? For weeks he had only pretended to meditate, sitting with the beads clasped tight in his hands, repeating the Litany desperately to fill the silence, because if he stopped and let the third eye of the Makers open, that dreadful profile would creep back into his memory, the turning, misshapen face, the dry rustle of its reptilian skin.

HIS BACK WAS WET WITH SWEAT, his heart thudding under his ribs. He flung the blankets off, tugged his jerkin on, and crossed to the window, lifting the bar and pushing the wooden shutters wide. Cold air swooped in. Behind him, the Sekoi groaned. Raffi leaned his elbows on the sill and looked down. The castle was eerily quiet. The stench of smoke was everywhere; far below him the inner gates were a mass of twisted metals and smoking, blackened stumps. Walls were scorched, battered into holes, but already, high above the keep, the Watch standard was down and a gaudy pennant of red and gold rippled in the mountain breeze. He rubbed sweat from his hair.

"What's it like out there?" the Sekoi murmured sleepily.

"Quiet. Everyone's under cover."

"Indeed. I wonder where we might get something to eat."

Raffi turned desperately. "Listen. Carys saw us. She saw me fall, but she didn't stop, didn't make any sign. She just galloped away. I could have fallen and she . . ." He shook his head. He couldn't finish.

The creature stretched and scratched through the long fur at the back of its neck. "Small keeper," it said carefully, "something is going on that we know nothing of."

The door slammed open. Galen grabbed some sheets

and pulled the blankets off the Sekoi. "Come on! I need you both." He was gone almost at once. Raffi raced out after him, the Sekoi hopping far behind, hastily pulling its boots on.

"What's wrong?"

"Wounded."

"But Alberic's got a whole squadron of surgeons and—"

"Not Alberic's men. The Watch. Their wretched leaders have abandoned them and left them to die. They're worth nothing to Alberic."

"Galen!" Raffi caught up to him and grabbed his arm. The keeper glared at him.

"Don't say it, Raffi."

"I have to! We need to be careful! If we help these men and they live, they'll remember us. They'll file reports. Our names. What we look like." A shiver of terror crossed his mind.

Galen may have felt it. He pulled away and looked darkly at Raffi, a look of contempt. "So we should leave them to rot?"

"No! I just think . . ."

The Mirrors of Halen

"You don't think, boy." He glanced at the Sekoi. "I suppose you feel the same?"

The creature shrugged. "To the Watch one striped Sekoi looks very like another. But for you . . ."

"I . . . *We* . . . have a duty to anyone who needs help." Galen turned and strode down some steps to a locked door. One of Alberic's men was posted outside. He scrambled up, then scowled when he saw who it was.

"Listen, keeper. You've looked in here once."

"Open it."

"The chief won't like this."

Galen's eyes were black with anger. "I said, open it!"

The man spat. Then he turned and unbolted the door. The smell was the first thing that struck them. A stench of sickness, of blood, that sent Raffi's stomach heaving. For once he was glad to have eaten nothing.

The cellar was dark, but as their eyes adjusted, they saw it was crammed with men, dozens of them, sprawled or lying huddled, the remnants of the defeated Watch garrison. They were in a terrible state, exhausted and in pain. Most had been wounded. Some slept, others were so miserable, they could only rock themselves from side to side moaning softly, barely glancing at the opened door. One man, lying crooked at Raffi's feet, was obviously dead.

The Sekoi snarled something bitter in the Tongue. Galen pushed past, down the steps; after a moment, hot with shame and anger, Raffi followed. They had brought water, and Galen tore up the sheets for bandages, sending Raffi racing back for more, and any food he could find. The Watchmen seemed too deep in shock to care, though one or two crawled up to help, and the Sekoi bent to comfort an older man, sobbing helplessly over his ruined leg.

When Raffi brought water they snatched it and drank thirstily, barely looking at him, and he tried not to look too closely at their wounds, black with dried blood, wrapped in rags and hasty field-dressings, already filthy. Galen and the Sekoi picked their way among them, rebinding an arm or a leg, making a few men comfortable, yelling at the guard to carry out the bodies of the dead.

"You'll have to see the chief about that," he said, sullen.

The Mirrors of Halen

Galen straightened. He was hot with rage; Raffi could feel it, simmering out from him.

"Some of these men," the Sekoi said quietly, "need urgent help. Some must lose limbs, before infection sets in."

"We can't do that!" Raffi was aghast.

"Not without killing them." Galen bent and wrapped the last blanket around a Watchman's shoulder; the man stared up with dull eyes. Then the keeper turned. "I think," he said sourly, "that it's time we spoiled Alberic's little victory."

IT WAS A LONG ROOM, high up in the keep, and had probably been the castellan's, Raffi thought. But Alberic had made a few changes. The desk had been spread with a white cloth and was covered with dishes of hot food: steamy tureens, chicken legs, fresh soft bread. A small hog was roasting on a spit over the fire. All around the room plunder was stacked; sacks of metal objects, with candlesticks and goblets spilling out, piles of clothing, a scatter of silver ingots and whole arsenals of weapons. Alberic sat with a chicken bone in one hand and a great cup of wine in the other, in a high jeweled chair that had obviously been made to fit him. His feet were propped up on the desk. Behind, near the window, a luxurious bed with one glass ball on each bedpost spilled its silken sheets onto the floor.

When they saw Galen, the three bodyguards on the bench by the door stood up as one. The keeper eyed them. "You never used to be so timid, warlord."

Alberic dropped the picked bone and licked his fingers. "Flain's bloody thumb," he said acidly. "It really is you. Not a bad dream after all."

"No dream." Galen came forward, picked up a chicken leg, and tossed it to Raffi, who caught it deftly. "Only too real."

Alberic scowled and jerked his head ungraciously at the men, who sat. He was wearing a very fine dressing gown of ivory brocade—Raffi had never seen anything so sumptuous. Sikka was sitting with him, and on the other side of the table, his big, bearded henchman Godric, who waved Raffi over. "Come on, boy! God, how I remember what your master calls breakfast. There's plenty here."

The Mirrors of Halen

Raffi edged nearer, but Galen stopped him with a glance.

"Well, keeper." Alberic sipped the wine. "I can't say I'm thrilled you're here, but I'm not a man to bear hard feelings." Godric almost choked; the dwarf eyed him coldly. "You're free to go. As far as you like."

"That's very kind." Galen pulled up a chair and sat on it sideways. "However, I think you'll be seeing a little more of us, thief-lord."

"More? I don't think you get my meaning."

"Or you mine. We're staying."

"I knew it!" Alberic flung down the wine cup. "And now you're going to spin me some yarn that the Makers arranged all this! That my strategy—my brilliant strategy—and months of planning were just some ploy to get you and your worthless rabble in here!"

"I couldn't have put it better myself."

Raffi's chicken bone was picked clean. He went and dropped it on a plate. Godric winked, and passed him a peppered chop and a hunk of bread.

Alberic jumped down from his chair. He prowled wrathfully around the room, kicking a goblet that rolled across the floor. "You're a fanatic, Galen, and dangerous to know. I've never got over that curse you put on me. I don't think I've had a good night's sleep since. Whatever you're up to, you can count me out! I want nothing to do with you, your Order, your crazy tales or your talking trees." He stopped, slapping himself on the forehead. "Flainsteeth! Listen to me! Who's in charge here anyway!" He spun and clicked his fingers at the bodyguards, who stood menacingly. "What's to stop me selling you all to the Watch! What a price the Crow would make."

Galen looked around, totally unconcerned. The Sekoi came up behind him and surveyed the breakfast table. "We're your friends, Alberic, remember. Don't you eat any fruit?"

"Friends!" The dwarf stared up in disbelief. "God, you people have got a nerve."

"Why the Castle of Halen?" Galen asked quietly.

It was Godric who answered. "Had to move out from the old place. A plague of flies came out of the Unfinished Lands. Bloodflies. Or something like. As big as your hand with a sting to match. They got into the food, the clothes, demolished crops, even had a go at livestock. Everyone fled; there was no one left to rob. So the chief said he fancied a castle, and we found this one." He poured out more wine, and some for the Sekoi. "Took a bit of planning. Infiltrated the place for weeks."

Galen looked up. "What about your prisoners?"

"Prisoners?" Alberic spat. "The Watch riff-raff? Who cares?"

"I care." The Relic Master stood. Suddenly he looked angry and dangerous. "There are about sixty men herded in a filthy cellar below here. They need surgeons and food and by God, Alberic, you'll provide them."

Alberic stared. Then he jumped onto the chair and up onto the table, kicking plates out of the way. He brought his face close to Galen's. "You owe the Watch no favors. Let them rot. And don't threaten me, Relic Master."

"I haven't. Yet." Galen ignored Sikka's sword quietly unsheathing. "I'm asking you to do it for your own sake." His voice was hard with sarcasm. "People will be only too glad to surrender to you if they think they'll be treated well. Word will get around. When you release them . . ."

"*Release them!* You addle-headed . . ."

"Uncle!" Milo was fidgeting nervously in the doorway.

Without taking a breath or his eyes from Galen, Alberic roared, "What?"

"It's all ready. For the hangings."

Galen's face darkened. "What hangings?"

Alberic moved back and smiled sweetly at him. "A few deserters from my war band. Discipline has to be kept up, keeper. You'd know nothing about it. If you want, you can come and watch." He shoved plates aside and leaped down, marching out to the balcony, his whole entourage hurrying after him.

Galen stood up. The Sekoi muttered, "Be careful. We could all end up with a knife in the back."

On the balcony, horn players were blowing an elaborate fanfare. A box had been carefully hidden behind the low parapet; Alberic leaped up onto it lightly. Then he looked down. It was a mistake. The keep was enormous, the courtyard far below crowded with his ragtag army and all the Watch's released workers. They cheered when they saw him, an eruption of noise.

Alberic went white. He turned hastily and tottered off

the box; his face was ashen. "You blundering fool!" he snarled at Milo. "It's too high!"

"But, Uncle. You said—"

"I don't like heights!" For a second he looked so sick, Raffi almost felt sorry for him. Then Galen had pushed forward. "Stop him," the dwarf croaked.

It was too late. Galen was already addressing the crowd. "Friends! Some of you may remember me." There was a murmur below. "I'm very grateful to our chief for allowing me to be the one to break the good news. As part of his deeply felt and powerful conversion to the beliefs and truths of the Makers, Alberic has ordered that every hanging is to be called off, and every deserter is to be given mercy. And his life." A puzzled silence answered him. Then disappointed, muted applause.

"For Flain's sake, get him down!" Alberic raged. "Can't you see what he's doing!" None of his people moved. Turning in utter fury, he found out why. No one had seen the Sekoi pick up the crossbow. Now it was pointed straight between his eyes.

"Let's hear what the keeper has to say, shall we?" the creature whispered pleasantly.

"Every one of you," Galen yelled, "will be given a fair share of the plunder." The crowd whooped. They liked that. Alberic swore ferociously. "Also," Galen went on recklessly, "the chief intends to treat the Watch prisoners with the utmost courtesy and set them free! No one will say Alberic is mean-spirited." A roar of laughter.

"Get on the box." The Sekoi jerked the bow. "Wave. And smile."

"Drop dead," Alberic snarled.

The creature's finger tightened on the taut trigger. "I'm a teeny bit tense," it whispered. With a glare of hatred, Alberic obeyed. But he didn't look down.

"Every man, woman, and child brought here by the Watch is to go free." Galen's voice rang out, echoing in archways and battlements. "And they must take this message with them, to everyone they meet. Spread it wide, my friends! The Crow has returned to Anara! The Crow is here, and he has gathered his army, and Alberic is with him! No more running and hiding in the dark! From this day, together, we will begin the destruction of the Watch!"

He spread his arms wide. Awen-power crackled and spat at his fingertips; it made Alberic jump back in sudden alarm. Long blue tendrils of Maker energies soared into the air above the courtyard, coiling and intertwining in the form of an immense black bird, darkening the upturned faces, swelling until it hung like an ominous cloud over the whole Castle of Halen, wingtip to wingtip. Then it faded, slowly, without a sound. There was a vast silence. Until the crowd roared, a great outcry of delight and amazement and joy.

Alberic's face was white. He stalked back into the room, and above the uproar outside, he turned and rounded on Galen. "You've finished me!" he hissed. "Once the Watch hear of this, they'll hunt us down like rats! They'll never stop!"

"They'll think you and I planned it all together," Galen said, folding his arms. "It seems you've finally been converted, Alberic. I always told you it would come to this. And one day you'll thank me for it."

At the back of the crowd Raffi felt a sudden anxious pull at his sleeve. It was Milo. He looked scared. "Does your master have a bad temper?" he hissed.

"Terrible." Raffi was fascinated by Alberic's screeching rage.

"Then is this a good time to give him the letter?"

"What letter?"

"The girl's."

For a second Raffi was utterly still. Then he turned.

"*What girl?*" he breathed.

9

Swear no oaths.
Oaths are chains on the soul.

Poems of Anjar Kar

RAFFI GRABBED THE BOY and hustled him out into the corridor. "Show me!"

Milo searched his pockets and found a grimy piece of paper. "She knocked me out," he said sullenly. "After all I did for her!"

Raffi stared down at the dirty sheet, then turned to find some light. The boy trailed after him, complaining bitterly. "I helped her out on the road. They treated her roughly, and I stood up for her. Got water for her. Even warned her about Uncle's plan. How was I to know she was a spy?"

"Shut up," Raffi said fiercely. He tried a door and

it opened. The room seemed full of light. A movement ahead made him jump, until he saw it was his own reflection, grimy and cobwebbed in a vast mirror that leaned in front of a stack of others.

Behind him, the spotty boy peered in. "Don't like this room," he muttered.

But Raffi was too interested in the paper. It was a list, a roster of some sort. On the back a few words had been scrawled in a hurried line that blotted and smudged and broke off abruptly. And it was in code. It looked like Carys's writing.

"Did she say it was for Galen? What did she say!"

The boy wandered in. He rubbed the dust from a mirror with his finger. "Yes. For the keeper. Then she knocked me out."

"Was anyone else there?"

"The castellan. And Captain Quist."

Raffi turned. "He brought you in."

Milo nodded. "She didn't want them to know, because she whispered it and shoved the paper in my pocket." He examined a bruise on his face in the dusty glass, jutting his jaw this way and that. "Then she knocked me out."

The Mirrors of Halen

"I'll knock you out," Raffi snapped, "if you say that again." He tried to think. Why had she gone with them? What was going on? And if the Sekoi was right, why had she gotten herself deliberately captured? He looked up. Thirty other Raffis looked up too.

The chamber was a labyrinth of mirrors. They were stacked in great piles, higher than his head. Milo was climbing one heap like a ladder, up into the dim vaults. Glass slabs gleamed; they were slanted, forming archways and tunnels, and in the thousands of reproductions of the room, only light was reflected and Raffi himself repeated endlessly, from the front, sides, and back, looking unfamiliar in the depths of the myriad looking glasses.

"I need a pen." He turned, ducked under a tent of glass; looking up, he saw his own face, grotesquely foreshortened, staring down. "What is this place?"

"The Watch brought them all in here." Milo's voice, muffled with distance, came from somewhere near the ceiling. "They didn't like them. They were all over the castle. One of the prisoners told me there's supposed to be a ghost in one, but no one knows which. Of someone crazy who used to look in them."

"Halen's mirrors!" Raffi stared. They were all sizes and shapes, oval, tiny, enormous, elaborately gilded. In them he looked dirty and harassed and for a second thought he saw, far back, the shadow of a man, reflected from one to another. He turned, unsure. The sense-lines were reflected too. They tangled and confused him. Just as he felt dizzy, a small object dropped from above, landing with a rattle.

"Pencil. That's all I've got."

Raffi took a deep breath. Halen had lost his mind here. That was what Galen thought. Tormented by the Makers' failure, by the thought of Kest's treachery.

He bent down and groped after the pencil; when he found it, it was small and the end had been chewed away. He looked at it in disgust. "Thanks."

He sat in the dust with his back against one of the mirrors and worked on the code. Carys had taught him how codes were broken; he was sure she would be using one of those she had invented herself, and hurriedly he listed alphabets, slotting in the different code words they had agreed on. At the fourth attempt the words started to make sense. "Got it," he whispered. The room was oddly silent. He raised his head. "Milo?"

The Mirrors of Halen

The mirrors were empty. Only a spider ran across the floor, or the reflection of one. He worked quickly. The message formed, letter by letter, along the edge of the grimy paper. GONE TO MAAR AS PLAN. IMPORTANT. MARGRAVE LOOKING FOR

He stared at it, cold. Looking for what? There was another word, completely smudged. Was it *Raffi*? Without knowing it, he crumpled the paper, staring at himself in the dim recesses of glass. The Margrave is looking for Raffi. His vision had been right. It was true. She had found out.

He forced himself not to panic, smoothing out the paper, rubbing his tired eyes. It might not be. It might not. Staring at it didn't help. It had five letters. Or four. It could be Crow. But they knew the Margrave must be looking for the Crow. Why would she bother telling him that?

"Got you!"

With a yell that made him jump, a shadow fell from the stack of mirrors and crashed against him; Raffi cried out and rolled in shock, whipping out a mind-flare that made Milo huddle up with a screech.

He banged his head against a mirror and stared. "What was that?"

Raffi was shaking, sweating. "Brainless idiot!" He rubbed one hand down his face. For a moment he had thought . . . but that was stupid.

"And what does she mean by 'plan'?" he whispered.

GALEN WAS DOWN in the ground-floor hall, a vast assembly chamber with a tiny fire blazing at each end. He and the Sekoi were organizing care for the wounded; as Raffi came in, a crowd of Alberic's men streamed out past him. Raffi was almost too angry to speak.

Galen turned, but before he could say anything, Raffi flung the crumpled letter down on the floor.

"Why didn't you tell me?"

The keeper looked at him steadily, then down at the letter. "What is that?"

"A message. From Carys."

The Sekoi made a small mew of surprise. Neither of them looked around. Galen took a step toward the paper, but instantly Raffi stamped his foot on it. He felt as though his whole body was trembling with wrath.

Galen sensed it. He looked at Raffi, sidelong, a dark look. "Say what you want to say, boy."

"You should have told me! You let us think that she'd been captured, that they could be torturing her! Or worse, that she'd gone back! And you knew all along!"

"Explain," the Sekoi said tightly, sitting on a table.

Raffi swung to it. "It was all a plan! Their plan—the two of them. You were right—she let herself be taken—and she's using relics to mark her route for him, to pinpoint where she is. But I don't understand why!"

He rounded on Galen, who was watching him, ominously calm. "Don't you realize what danger you've put her in! If they find out, if they find the relics, they'll burn her alive. After all she's done to them, how could you put her through that!"

Galen looked grim. "You know I can't make Carys do anything she doesn't want. It was her idea as much as mine."

"She wouldn't say no! She's as hotheaded as you. But you should have had more sense!"

Galen's temper snapped. "By God, Raffi, don't lecture

me. We've got our backs to the wall here! We need every bit of information we can get—"

"About the Margrave!" The truth leaped into Raffi's mind like a flame; he crouched and grabbed the paper and thrust it out. "That's what you want her to do. To lead you to the Margrave!"

Sparks of energy snapped and coiled between them. The Sekoi watched, fascinated.

"What better way is there?" Galen snarled. "We need to find the creature."

"You do! You need to find him because of that stupid, stupid oath you took! You swore to kill him and now you've put Carys into Maar! Because that's where she's gone—just like you told her to!"

Galen's mind-flare struck him hard between the eyes; he hissed with pain, staggering back.

"Galen!" The Sekoi leaped up instantly.

"Stay out of it!" The keeper snatched the letter, his eyes black with fury. All the great hall seemed crammed with an inky, crackling darkness; they were both lost in it, swamped by months of pent-up wrath.

Raffi hit the wall and crumpled. He felt so sick and

furious, he could hardly see, but Galen came after him, crouching, grabbing his coat and dragging him up so that his head jerked back.

"Yes, I swore that oath! What else was I to do? He destroyed Solon. He mined right into the heart of us, infected us, Sarres, everything, and we never even knew it! All the planet is tainted with his crimes, all of it!"

"You didn't know," Raffi croaked. "That's what makes you so angry. That you didn't know."

Galen flung him down. Then he turned and shoved the anxious Sekoi aside with one hand, stalking down to the other end of the hall. They stared appalled as he flung a table over, picked up a jug, and smashed it viciously against the wall.

When he turned, he was someone else. The glossy darkness of the Crow had overwhelmed him. Even the fires died down before it; his face was shadowed, long hair fallen loose, the black and green awen-crystals tangled around one hand. "Think about me for once, Raffi," he breathed, his voice painfully harsh, unrecognizable. "How it is for me. I have this presence inside me and it burns me, consumes me, and I have to use it, allow it to work, and I daren't. Yes, I should have known about Solon, and the torment of that is bitter. All the things I've done may be wrong. I let Solon go through the Door of Air, but I don't know where he is or why the Makers haven't kept their promise. Where are they? Why don't they come?" He dragged both hands over his face and through his hair. "Haven't I done enough? God knows, I've tried. For years we've struggled, living like animals, hunted, burned out, always running, always trying to keep the relics, to keep the people close to what should be true. Have *we* become relics now? Where is Flain, and Soren, and Tamar? Are they dead, have they forgotten us, don't they care about our agony? *Why don't they come?*"

The sweat on Raffi's back was cold. For a moment he thought a stranger was there; then Galen turned, his dark, hooked face eyeing them sidelong. "If faith dies, Raffi," he whispered, "what's left?"

Into the terrible silence the Sekoi said, "They will come. My people know that."

"It will be too late. Unless the Margrave is destroyed."

Raffi shivered; he felt confused and chilled, but he

pulled himself up onto his knees. "Not me. I can't be part of this."

Galen came back. He said sourly, "You go where I go."

"No. Not Maar." He was shaking, and his teeth were almost chattering with sudden cold, with the reaction, but he stammered it out anyway. "The Margrave is looking for me. Carys says so. He wants me . . . He . . . he doesn't want you."

For a moment the hall was utterly silent. A door banged, far off in the castle. The fires flared up. And softly, Galen laughed. His laugh was cold, and rare, and it never failed to chill Raffi to the soul.

"It's true," Raffi whispered hopelessly. "I know it's true!"

"You! What in God's name does he want with you!"

"I don't know!" Raffi hugged himself. "I just—"

"So this is what you've been terrifying yourself with since the Coronet. You saw him in that vision and it was just too much for you." Galen stood over him, then crouched and faced him. "You've let it prey on your mind, Raffi, and if I keep secrets from you, you do the same, and yours are just as destructive. The Margrave doesn't want you, he doesn't even know who you are! This is a vision-echo and it has to be overcome before it grows and smothers you!"

It was useless. He had always known Galen would never believe him. Now the keeper dragged him up and dumped him on a chair, then limped to the fire, leaning on the high mantel. He looked drained, as if some vast energy had washed out of him.

"There's only one way of dealing with it. As for Carys," he muttered, staring into the fire, "do you think I haven't blamed myself over and over for that? I prayed we'd find her here . . ."

"We could get her back. Give up the Margrave."

"No. I swore an oath and I meant every word of it. But first we both need to pray and fast for forgiveness. For our weakness. And then—"

"You'll leave. How lovely." Alberic was leaning in the doorway, Godric behind him. Raffi wondered dully how much they had overheard. Galen looked over. There was something in his spent anguish that wiped the sly smile off the dwarf's face.

"We stay. At least until Soren's Day. We hold the feast

here—reopen the shrine and do it properly, as it should be done. Because on that day"—he glanced at Raffi, his eyes black and hurt—"my scholar, my loyal, exemplary scholar, will finally attempt the Deep Journey."

Alberic glanced at Raffi's white face. "Him?" he muttered drily. "He looks scared stiff to me."

10

Starmen are curious about our friend-
ship with the owls. It is more than
friendship. The Silent Ones and the Sekoi
speak one tongue and have one concern.
There is little else I can say without
betraying secrets, but this much is true—
that when Anara is cleansed, they and we
shall rule together.

Words of a Sekoi Karamax,
recorded by Kallebran

SCALA SLEPT CURLED UP, her hair loose on the pillow. There was something childlike about her like that, Carys thought, taking another step back, feeling for the door handle. And it was the strangest of the moons, Atterix, that was shining on her, through the bare window of the cottage, the pale light falling over the small collection of cracked cups and plates on the dresser.

Her fingers touched the bolt. She drew it back, wincing at the faint squeak. The inner curtain to the storeroom stayed closed. Quist was in there on a mattress, squeezed between sacks of grain and hanging, overripe cheeses.

Scala slept without moving.

Gently Carys pushed the door open and slipped through. The night was brilliant with moonlight. Atterix and Agramon, Pyra and Lar were all full, and far to the west beyond the jagged hills, another of the sisters must be rising, her ghostly glow lighting the dim clouds.

The sisters. Carys grinned, moving into the shadow of the house. She'd been around keepers too long. Raffi had filled her head with all those old folktales; things old Jellie had never taught, or only mentioned with scorn.

The cottage had been deserted when they'd ridden in, but the ashes of the fire were barely cold and some milk in a jug on the windowsill still fresh. Whoever lived here had abandoned the place in a hurry; they might well be hiding up there in the hills, thinking Scala had been leading a patrol, or maybe they'd already been taken for the castle or the Wall. Or they might be closer than that, watching.

There were some outbuildings. An empty stable that would do. Rats rustled in the straw. Carys stepped inside without a sound, into a shadowy, dung-smelling corner, and listened. Then she unscrewed the relic. The small lights seemed brighter than before; maybe it was the moonlight that affected them. They were tiny points of blue; as she held down the button they instantly went red. It never ceased to fascinate her.

She had to keep it operating for the right amount of time. Galen had said that the relic still had power, that if he was close enough he would feel it, and even if he was too far it would leave a trace of its presence here, a faint glimmer of energy he could detect when he came.

Thumb tight on the button, Carys counted anxious seconds. The Sekoi was alive—one good thing. She'd seen it jump on the bridge. And Raffi—they would have hauled Raffi up through the trapdoor. Of course they would. The whiteness of his face came back to her, the sudden terror of that plunging fall.

Her thumb slipped. The lights went blue. "Blast," she hissed. She pressed again—it was tiny and awkward, and then a movement up in the rafters brought the sweat out on her back. Hastily she screwed the relic tight, whipped a knife out of her belt, and turned.

"All right," she said firmly. "I know you're there. Come out and you won't get hurt." The darkness of the barn was utterly silent. Even the rats seemed to have gone. Through a rectangular opening in the roof she could see stars, and moonlight falling onto the hay loft, the last tumbled bales, their long stalks spilling, gnawed, dragged out by birds. Then something answered her.

It was a low, churring noise, high up, so eerie, it made the hairs on her neck prickle.

She stared through the dark. "We're the Watch," she hissed, breathless. "Give yourself up."

A narrow gray object drifted past her shoulder, down through the moonlight. Her heart gave a great leap; she grabbed at the thing and caught it left-handed. It was a feather. She turned instantly, her whole body alert.

The owl was enormous. It had perched on the crossbar above her, a species she had never seen before, its face smooth and pale, the small beak hooked. Maybe it was a ghost-owl, or one of the Great Blacks that had gathered and mourned over the fields of the dead after the Sekoi battles.

Its eyes unnerved her. They were perfectly round pools

of faceted darkness; she imagined how she must look to it—an upturned white face, shifting planes of light, unprotected. She stepped back.

The owl's stare was unblinking. She saw, with a thrill of surprise, that it wore around its neck a thin, jeweled collar. Carys swallowed. "Can you understand me?" she whispered.

The owl made no movement, no sound. Its huge stillness made her feel foolish and threatened, but she went on quickly. "I know you can understand the Sekoi. One of them is coming, a gray striped one, with two Starmen. In a few days, maybe. Tell them I was here. Tell them we're heading for the Wall at a place called Flor's Tower, west of here. Remember that. The Wall."

The owl made a small churr. It stared at her and blinked once, swiveled its head and watched a spider run speedily into a crack, then swiveled back.

Carys frowned. "I must be crazy," she breathed.

The door creaked. The owl opened vast wings. Without the slightest sound it flew, brushing so close to her face she felt its draft, up out of the roof-hole and away, blotting out the stars.

She turned. Quist was in the doorway. He glanced quickly at the knife. "What are you doing out here? Not trying to run off, I hope."

Carys smiled sourly. "I heard something. Thought maybe the owners had come back."

He glanced around. "Have they?"

"It was an owl. Ugly great thing."

He stared at her for a moment as the owl had stared, so she put the knife away and said, "What about you?"

"Call of nature."

"Then I'll get out."

He stood aside, and she went out into the moonlight and slammed the door. Then she breathed deep, folded her arms, and looked out at the stars. She believed him just as much as he believed her.

THEY RODE WEST. It was a damp morning; the faintest of drizzles that they could hardly see, but it clouded the tops of the trees and clung like mist in hollows, turning the path into a muddy slough. They were three days out of the castle. Last night had been the first chance

The Mirrors of Halen

Carys had had to get a signal out, but she was sure it had been too brief. Her horse plunged into a puddle, and she swore, clutching tight. Still. At least Raffi would have had his warning.

"So why the Tower of Song?" Scala asked suddenly.

"What?"

"The Tower of Song. You asked for rooms there."

Carys tried to remember her demands. "I stayed there last year. An amazing place."

Scala shrugged gracefully. "I've never been. Quist used to work there." She glanced at him, over the horse's ears. "Didn't you, lover."

He had been quiet all morning. Now he pushed back his hood and let the branches drip on his hair. "Once."

"In what department?" Carys asked casually.

"Records. In the Overpalace."

"I thought that was classified."

"It is."

She looked at him thoughtfully. She had nothing to lose, so she said, "When I was there I tried to find out about myself. Where I came from. Against the Rule, I know, but the Rule isn't everything, is it?"

Scala's red lips smiled. "No indeed. And what did you find out?"

"Nothing."

Quist's horse brushed through a bush of spring-mallow that released clouds of white seed. "What year were you?" he asked.

She shrugged. "One forty-six WE."

"What house?"

"Marn Mountain."

Maybe his horse stumbled. He twisted, for a second seemed off balance, caught by surprise. More than that. Shock. Carys looked away. In that instant she sensed, without doubt, that he knew something. So being around keepers had some use. "Ring any bells?" She kept the anxiety out of her voice.

It took him a moment to answer, and when he did, his face was set. "Only that that was the house where they took the children of Mathravale."

The name echoed vaguely. "Where?"

But Scala had stopped her horse across the path. She gave Quist a swift, angry look. "That's classified," she snapped. "And we don't discuss it with renegades.

Now speed up. And stop talking." She turned.

Quist looked after her, a strange, half-resentful stare. Then he caught Carys's eye and laughed sourly. "You heard the castellan. If the castellan commands, we must obey."

"Even you?"

He looked away, into the misty trees. "Especially me."

ALL DAY SHE HELD THE NAME steady in her mind. *Mathravale.* She had heard it before—or no, not heard it. Seen it. On some written page. Maybe in one of Galen's books, or in the library on Sarres. But it took her all that day, the long ride down from the misty hills, the drizzling rain, the sparse supper in the tiny Watch outpost at Depra, the two women there flustered and Scala being gracious and sardonic, a whole day of mental struggle till she lay in a cold bed just about to fall asleep, for the memory, suddenly and completely, to come back.

She sat up in the dark. Watch history. Second lesson. Wednesday mornings. The thick yellow pages of clumsy print, four pages a week, to be learned by heart. Tactics, battles, the Sekoi revolt, the piecemeal destruction of the filthy and sorcerous Order. And on page 654 the word. *Mathravale.* The sentence came back to her; with all her training, she made herself remember it.

The supreme tactical triumph of the Watch, it had said, *came at Mathravale, where . . .* and they had turned over, bored and cold and weary, and every book in the class had had the next four pages torn out. Every book. No one had dared to ask why. Old Jeltok had mumbled and sworn in the dim classroom, then had creaked down between the rows of desks and muttered, "Get on. Get on!" and the boy reading had done just that, and the history had jumped a year, as if whatever happened at Mathravale had been blotted out.

It had just been one mystery among many. She remembered how she had rubbed the torn edges with her finger. And as far as she knew she'd never come across the word again. Until today. She lay back on the hard pillow. It made sense. If the children at Marn had been from this place, it made sense that whatever happened there wouldn't be mentioned. It must have been important.

Galen would know. But Galen was far away. It was

Quist she'd have to work on. Turning over, she closed her eyes. Was she one of the children of Mathravale? Was that home?

THEY LEFT EARLY IN THE MORNING, much to the Watchwomen's relief, climbing again, high into woods. It was warm, and Carys took her damp jacket off, tying it to the saddle. These were sheshorn trees; they murmured and susurrated in the high winds, a gentle sound. Carys wondered what they were saying.

Near the top of the ridge Scala turned. "We'll have to do something about you, Carys."

"Do something?" For a moment she was chilled, but Scala only smiled coyly and held out a bronze insignia chain. "Wear this. I'm afraid it demotes you, but it's the only substitute we have."

Carys took it. The number was 2778. The name, Greta Rothesy. "Who was she?"

"An adjutant. She died." The castellan turned and gathered up the horse's reins in her small, gloved grip. "We'll need to keep your identity secret from now on.

The camp commander at Flor's Tower is a very astute man; if he found out who you were, Quist and I would instantly be imprisoned for abetting a spy." She smiled. "And you'd be hard put to make deals with him. Believe me. He always goes by the book."

"Not like you. Or Braylwin." Carys changed the insignia quickly.

"Arno Braylwin?" Scala laughed, amused. "Oh, you won't come across him. He had to be ransomed from some petty warlord. Last time I heard, he'd been demoted to a supply clerk in some whaling station on the Ice Coast."

Ducking under a branch, Carys grinned. "He'll be back. He had a whole network of bribery and blackmail."

The trees were thick now, the path dwindling to a thread of fallen leaves.

"How far are we from this place, anyway?"

Ahead, Scala came to the top of the ridge, and a stiff wind blew out her hair. "Not far at all," she said.

Carys's horse stopped; she swung herself off, pushed past Quist, who was standing on a rock, and stared down into the valley. It was like something out of one of the Sekoi stories.

The Mirrors of Halen

Black, immense, unbelievable, crawling with men, littered with cranes and gantries and scaffolding, engines of wood hauling huge blocks, mountains of mortar and sand and viaducts of water, the noise and stink and squalor and splendor of it rising, even to here. It stretched into the distance, complete, towered, bristling with weapons. It had no end, as far as she could see.

It was the Wall.

11

Some never wake but die on the Journey.
Others come back but their minds are
broken, and ever after are vacant and
foolish, and scream at night. Some
lose their speech, some their eyesight.
The Journey is a peril that must be
undertaken, but its dangers are great.
Those that live through it never forget it.

Second Letter of Mardoc Archkeeper

THE SINGING WAS DRIVING HIM CRAZY. Raffi threw the Book down and put his hands over his head; then he got up and flung open the window. He was not supposed to speak to anyone, but he couldn't stand this. "Shut up!" he yelled savagely. "I'm trying to study!"

The scrawny man below stopped twanging the hand-harp and looked around, astonished. It took him a minute to find Raffi's face at the window. "Nobody studies in Alberic's army."

"Well, I do!"

"Listen, lad, I've got a job to do. I'm Alberic's poet and he'll want a song about his battle."

"I don't care!" Raffi yelled. "Shut up or I'll get Alberic to hang you from the keep by your harp strings!" He slammed the casement and turned away, leaning against the wall. Then he slid down it, and sat, knees up, hands over his head, in despair.

The Ordeals should have taken a week, but they didn't have that much time. Galen had said two days would have to do, and that until sunset on Soren's Day, neither of them would touch food, and would drink only water. He had been more morose than ever; Raffi knew he was bitterly regretting his lapse into despair, punishing them both for it.

Raffi was beyond hunger. He was empty and worn out. The first day he'd spent outside the castle, at first with Galen, then alone, moving his mind along the sense-lines, deep into the trees and into the soil of Anara until he had almost forgotten his own name or who he was; his self a broken, shattered thing, like the mountains, all fragmented. He'd wandered back late, and Galen had ordered him to bed, letting no one talk to him. All night he had dreamed strange dreams, tossing and waking and unable to remember what they were.

The Mirrors of Halen

Yesterday, for hours, Galen had questioned him, on every chapter of the Book, the Litany, every prophecy, story, testing the details over and over, angry at every mistake. He'd had to recite the tale of Flain in the Underworld, of Kest's fight with the Dragon, of the Makers' war against the creatures of the Poisoned Sea, every one word-perfect. It had been exhausting, and when Galen had finally been satisfied, Raffi had wandered the corridors of the castle like a shadow, avoiding people and the smells of food, seeming always to end up at the room crowded with mirrors, sitting there, staring at his own pale reflection. Remorse was tormenting him. He should be meditating; he should be so filled with joy, with desire to make the Journey. But he wasn't. He was terrified. And the hours seemed endless and yet went too quickly, and there was no one to talk to but Flain and Soren and Theriss and Kest, and though he longed to beg them to call it off, to make something happen, he couldn't. "Give me the strength to get through it," he muttered desperately. "Don't let me let Galen down." And silently, not even in words. *Don't let me lose my mind.* But today was Soren's Day. In an hour it would all begin.

Outside, the harp started again, a defiant twanging. Raffi gripped fistfuls of his hair. Then someone tapped on the door, and the Sekoi's striped face peered around. "I know you're in isolation, small keeper, but I wanted to say good luck." It slid back.

Raffi jumped up. "Wait! Don't go!"

The yellow eyes came back, surprised. "I thought . . ."

"I'm sick of being on my own. Please."

The creature slipped quietly inside. "Galen will be angry."

"Galen's always angry."

The Sekoi looked at him attentively. Then it went and sat on the bed, leaning against the straw bolster. There was a moment of quiet. Only the voice of the poet rose throatily from below. Finally the Sekoi said, "I'm sure everyone who attempts this ordeal must be apprehensive."

"Galen wasn't. He told me how he longed for the Journey."

"In retrospect, maybe. But I'm sure at the time he was afraid." The creature interlaced its long fingers. "Raffi, you must not think yourself unworthy. This is what you have worked toward for many years."

"But I'm not ready! It's too soon." He paced anxiously.

The Mirrors of Halen

"I don't remember half the responses, or the Prophecies. I don't really know the Wisdom of the Calarna or how to open and close Flain's Gate, how to make the awen-power come fully into the Blessing. Galen keeps drumming it into me, but I keep forgetting, and there's so much else going on, with Carys missing, and all of it! I get everything wrong! Look at that business with those jeckle-things."

The Sekoi was silent a moment. Then it said, "Maybe you should not just blame yourself. Has it never struck you that Galen might not be the best of teachers?"

Raffi stopped and stared. "He's always making me learn."

"Yes, but it takes more than that. It seems to me you were happier working with Tallis. Galen is not the most patient of men. And I think he finds it . . . difficult, to enter into what another might feel."

Raffi shook his head sourly. "Someone with less faith, you mean."

"Even Galen's faith is not perfect." The Sekoi bit a nail. "And, as we know, the Crow is in him. That alone makes him no ordinary master."

Raffi poured some water into a bowl and soaked his

face and hair. It made him feel better, but the chill of his nerves made his stomach ache and his breath come short. "There are stories," he whispered. "Scholars whose minds have broken, who've never been the same after . . ."

"Raffi."

"I'm sorry." He turned abruptly. "Talk about something else. I feel as though I've been locked in here for weeks. What's Alberic up to?"

The Sekoi laughed, an uneasy bark. "Ah, yes. Our gracious host. Well, it will surprise you—it astonished me— but the dreaded warlord has had a change of heart. Last night he summoned Galen to his upper room, so I went too, out of curiosity. Such nightclothes, Raffi! Palest blue silk . . ."

"Yes, but what did he want?"

"He was sly, as ever. He said that as Galen had proclaimed war and announced to the world they were allies, and as the news would be raging through every village and Watchhouse for miles by now, it may as well be true. He agreed to become the Crow's ally for the price of one million gold pieces and the overlordship of Tasceron, if and when the city was captured."

The Mirrors of Halen

Raffi stared. "What did Galen say?"

"You know the keeper. He laughed. *That* laugh. He said the Order has no money and that this was a war of souls, not weapons. But that after Soren's Day Alberic must lead a march on this Wall. The dwarf did not find that amusing. They argued hotly."

"He wants to run things." Raffi sat on the bed. "I don't trust him."

"Nor I, small keeper. He will always be a slippery friend. I hope Galen knows what he's doing."

A bell began to ring, far off in the castle. The Sekoi stood hastily. "I must go. Good luck, Raffi. Remember, you will emerge from this ordeal. You have grown much in the past years." At the door it paused and looked back. "My people have a saying. 'Even in darkness, the river runs.'"

WHEN GALEN CAME, he carried new clothes. A white shirt and dark green trousers. Raffi had to strip and wash himself from head to toe. The water was icy; he had to grit his teeth to bear it, and afterward he couldn't stop shivering. Galen anointed his hands and neck and fore-head with some pungent, sharp-scented oil.

The clothes felt fresh, smelling slightly of bergamot. He wondered where Galen had gotten them. Silently he dressed. His feet were bare.

Galen looked at him. "The beads," he said.

Clumsily Raffi took them off. The seven strands of blue and purple crystals that marked the scholar; he had worn them now for so long his neck felt bare without them. As he handed them over, they were warm and heavy and slipped easily out of his hand.

"You are between the Branches now," Galen said softly. "Between ignorance and knowledge. Between Darkness and Light. Let the visions Flain sends you be good ones."

"And may I emerge from the darkness transformed like the satinfly from its sheath." Raffi whispered the Response. He wanted to say something else, something of his own, but Galen turned away. Raffi felt numb and cold. So cold.

Only at the door did Galen turn. He looked dark and troubled, his hooked face sharp. "I know how you feel. But believe me, Raffi, tomorrow the whole world will be different for you. You'll be a Relic Master and all Anara will be yours. The joy will be like nothing you've ever known. Keep the vision moving. Follow the Makers. Don't let yourself be distracted. Remember all I've taught you."

Raffi nodded. He couldn't speak. His tongue felt swollen, his face white, drained of life.

AS THEY WALKED DOWN the corridors, Alberic's people stood back to let them pass. Most didn't know what was happening, but the keeper's dark presence made talk falter and laughter fade. The place was busy. Rich cooking smells of meats and spices rose from the vast kitchens, making Raffi's mouth water and his empty stomach rumble. Alberic was obviously going to celebrate Soren's Day in some style.

The shrine was a large one, and had been cleared of the debris and stacked supplies of the Watch. As he came in, his feet cold on the stones, Raffi's breath tightened in his throat. Miraculously, the frescoes had survived. High on the rounded wall they looked down at him; Flain the

Tall, strong Tamar, dark Halen, and in the middle of them all Soren, Lady of Leaves, with seeds scattering from the hems of her green dress. She smiled at him, a kind, pitying smile. "Help me through this," he breathed.

All around, on every shelf and in racks and rows on the floor, hundreds of candles burned and dripped, their spilled wax forming grotesque stalagmites; the warmth and flicker of them cheered the bare room. The floor was scattered with petals. They felt soft under his feet, petals of fireweed and primroses and early tormentil, blue and red and purple, and the smell of them was sweet, almost cloying.

On the low table in the center of the room the relics were waiting. They were all familiar, the objects he had known for years, the seeing-tube, the blue box, a crystal coil, the broken remnants of the Makers' treasures. Galen must have found a few more around the castle, but the Watch had left little, and the collection looked suddenly small and sorry. Some power lingered in them. Raffi could feel it.

Beyond the candles, in shadow, people were standing. Raffi didn't look around, but he sensed them, and

The Mirrors of Halen

as Galen began formally to chant the Litany, their voices joined in, hesitant, stumbling, and he was surprised at how many there were. Glancing sidelong, he saw women and small children, some of Alberic's war band, a scatter of girls. The Sekoi was there, tall and elegant, and Godric next to it. The big man winked. Raffi turned quickly.

The words rose around him, the breath of them agitating the flames. He realized that for some of these people, these words had not been spoken aloud for decades, or not ever, not since the Watch had forbidden them.

The Litany ended. Galen turned to face Raffi. In the candlelight his eyes were black, pinpointed with tiny flames. "What is your name?" he asked, his voice low.

"Raffael Morel."

"Why are you here?"

"To enter the Deep Journey."

"Where does the Journey lead?"

"Through darkness, to light."

"With whom does the Journey end?"

"With Flain and the Makers."

Galen nodded, very slightly. A rustle came from behind him, a small commotion near the door. Alberic had come in, his bodyguard carrying a chair and a small scarlet cushion. He climbed up and sat, waving the proceedings on.

Galen turned back. He faced the relics, his face a mask of shadows. "Soren, Lady of the Leaves. On this, your day, this scholar takes the road that leads down into the dark, through the veins and hollows, through the mind-threads of your world. Come to meet him, lady. Lead him over the Plain of Hunger, through the Barrier of Pain. In the Crucible give him your courage, that he may return safely as one of your sons. Speak your word to him, that he might be transformed."

He spread his hands. From each palm a blue thread of energy flickered briefly; it moved among the relics, sparking and cracking with a loudness that made the watchers uneasy, causing the small dials in the octagonal slab to whirl their needles wildly, and the buttons on the cubes to flicker on and off.

Out of the power, Galen made the seven moons. They hung in the air, huge, over the table, each seeming solid and real, glowing with their individual brilliant lights. Then he turned. "Raffi."

The Mirrors of Halen

There was a wooden couch before the relic table.

A small cushion lay at its head. For a moment Raffi knew that his limbs were too frozen to move; his bare feet frosted to the floor. But somehow he walked and kneeled down.

Galen laid both hands on his head. "Take the awen-power," he said, his voice too quiet for anyone but Raffi to hear. "Make the Journey. Be free. Enter the world."

The pain came suddenly. It surged into him, into his head so that he gasped and cried out. It was an agony of power, it burned his veins like inner fire, and as he plummeted into it, it was a darkness that swallowed him, hands that caught him as he fell.

Gently Galen laid him down on the wooden couch, crossed his arms, placed the cushion under his head. Raffi's face was white, his eyes closed.

"How long will it be?" the Sekoi whispered anxiously.

Galen stood. "A day. Maybe two. He must wake before the third."

"And if he doesn't?"

The keeper turned and began snuffing out the candles, his hand shaking slightly. "Then we'll have lost him."

12

"I have lost all direction," Halen murmured.
"I am in darkness. I do not know who I am."
   His hair was long, his nails overgrown.
   Tamar held up the lantern. "I've come to
find you, brother."

Book of the Seven Moons

THIS WAS WRONG. Something was wrong. He had controlled the Ride, the first mad, headlong flight of his tumbling soul. He had seen, in the misty distance, the Great Tree, rising over the barren plain. For hours, it seemed, he had been stumbling toward it, over this endless scorching desert, where nothing grew, where tiny red lizards ran into holes and the unbearable sands blistered his bare feet. But the Tree was no nearer. If anything, it seemed farther than when he had started, and the sting of flies was tormenting him, and the pain in his chest hurt so much he had had to stop, crouching, reckless with thirst.

And now, someone was behind him. Standing. A

shadow on the sand, long and dark, a cool shade. He wanted to crawl into its darkness. But he kept still, and didn't look around.

"Are you hot?" a voice asked gently.

He nodded.

"Thirsty?" It was a voice of hisses and crackles; sounds that were dry and scratchy, as if the desert spoke. A croak was all he could make in reply.

"You could go back. Going back would be the wise thing to do."

"No." His tongue was swollen. It was hard to swallow. "I have to go on."

"Then you need this." A hand reached over his shoulder, a gloved hand, holding a small gilt cup like the one he had drunk from once on Sarres. He grasped after it desperately, but as he took the cup, the glove came too, and he saw the hand. It had seven fingers. Each was long and clawed, with tiny iridescent scales. He turned instantly. No one was there.

All around him the desert burned, an emptiness of rock, shimmering. It took him a long time, a bitter struggle, before he poured the cup of clear water away into the sand.

The Mirrors of Halen

IT WAS RAINING. The rain came from nowhere; he had barely noticed, as he trudged, how the skies had grown dark with cloud, but now it thundered, and he looked up suddenly, and great drops of water began to fall, plopping into tiny craters in the sand. He laughed, and stumbled into a run, head up, and the rain crashed on him; in an instant it had soaked him and he was drinking it, scooping it up from the flooding streambeds where it ran and gathered in gullies, splashed down rock-falls. Animals came from caves and cracks and holes, all around him; warthogs and night-cats and candorils and zabrays, they crowded the edges of the flooding streams, drinking thirstily, and tiny snakes burrowed out of the mud and launched themselves into the gushing brown water.

Raffi kneeled and drank. This was better. He had passed some test, done something right. Maybe that had been the Plain of Hunger, and he had crossed it. He felt so elated, he wanted to shout.

And in that moment, he saw Flain.

The Maker was far off, on the opposite side of the

stream, standing under the trees at the edge of a great forest. He was tiny in the distance, but Raffi knew him at once, his coat of stars, the darkness of his hair.

"*Flain,*" he breathed. "*Wait for me.*"

For a second, Flain looked at him. Then he turned and strode in among the trees.

"Wait!" Raffi struggled after him, but the animals were a herd now, mad for water, a gathering host. More and more of every species slithered and galloped down to the flood, and he had to push and shove through the snuffling, yelping, barking, hissing crowd. Great leathery creatures put their heads down and threatened him; he dodged unicorns and pale striped antelopes with twisted horns; snapping avancs menaced him at knee-height. "Flain!" he yelled, and his cry startled birds, flocks of white cranes, into the sky.

The stink and noise were unbearable; he pushed his way out and took one step into the swift, plunging river.

AND EVERYTHING CHANGED.

He was back in the castle. Still wet, breathless, he stared around. How could he be here! This wasn't supposed to happen, was it? Bewildered, he rubbed his face with his hands. The room was dark, and it took him a few giddy seconds to recognize it, but when he did his hands went chill and his heart beat loud in his chest.

It was the Room of Mirrors. But someone had rearranged them. Now they made a pathway, a maze that led between images of himself, a labyrinth of twists and turns, dead ends, and always, everywhere, endlessly repeated, his own tired, grubby reflection. He looked at himself with sudden loathing. "Look at you," he thought. "How can you be a Relic Master?"

"Raffi!"

He jumped. In the mirror to his left Carys was looking out at him. She was sitting, knees up. She jumped to her feet. "Thank God! I'm here to warn you. I haven't got much time."

She was wearing a Watch uniform. He had never seen her in one before and it made her look like a stranger, an enemy, because the uniform meant gallows and checkpoints, burning houses. Her hair was hacked short. She wore a bronze insignia. "Raffi, listen. He's here. You've brought him with you."

"What's happened to you?" he breathed.

"Never mind me! I'm telling you! He's here; he's . . ." Her eyes moved, looking behind him.

He turned. The door was closing; as he watched, it slammed loudly and when he ran to it and shook the handle furiously, it was locked. There was no key. He spun back. The mirror was empty.

WAS IT THE SAME ROOM? It seemed bigger. Very quietly, he began to edge among the mirrors, making no sound, his bare feet muffled among the layers of thick dust. A glimmer of light came from somewhere high up. Shapes moved around him, reflections, looming shadows. His foot touched something icy; he picked it up and found it was a gold coin, a shining Sekoi coin. And there was another, lying just out of the light. He padded over and crouched for it. It was a trail, leading around a corner, deeper into the maze. Was it to help him? Or a trap? He didn't know. The gold clinked together in his hand.

Far off in the maze, something slithered. Hands hot

on the sticky coins, Raffi kept absolutely still. His very breathing seemed enormous, ragged and jerky.

Something else was in here with him. Frozen, he traced its footsteps, the odd crackle and rustle of its progress. It moved among the mirrors, down corridors of glass. Any minute and he might see it, a thousand images of it at once, flashing into the dim panes.

It was looking for him.

He tried a single step, to his left. The slithering stopped. He imagined the creature's head turned to one side, alert, listening. His heart hammered; he moved deeper into darkness and saw another coin, but as he bent for it he banged against glass and knew it was only a reflection, and he turned quickly, and smelled the creature. He had smelled it before, this mustiness, heard this crackle of scaly skin.

The Margrave.

Soren, he whispered. *Please.* He backed desperately into the maze, banging into glass, against himself, into dead ends. Every turn he took brought him to face himself, or in the shadowier places, someone who looked like him, because Halen had walked here before him, endlessly tormented by whispers and small noises and shadows seen out of the corners of his eyes. Until Tamar had come.

As if the name triggered it, every mirror became a doorway. He stopped dead, staring. Sarres was through one; he could see Felnia lying on her stomach under a tree, turning the pages of a book. She didn't look up. In others, as he circled, he saw unaccountable visions: a drowned palace, deep forests, a great herd of martlets migrating over a plain, a Sekoi tent, all cushioned. And a cottage, where a woman was washing clothes. A woman he knew.

His mother.

Amazed, he stepped forward, his hands gripping the mirror's ornate frame. She looked older. Threads of gray streaked her hair. The familiar house seemed grimy and small; steamy from the hot water. Sudden, bitter longing took hold of him. "Can you hear me?" he whispered.

It was a mistake. In all the corners of the maze the question echoed, softly distorted. Something fell and rattled, disturbed by vibrations. A spider ran over his bare foot. There was a tiny crackle of movement just behind him.

He couldn't turn. In front of him the cottage steamed.

The Mirrors of Halen

His mother dunked the clothes and pushed a wisp of hair wearily from her face.

"You might go there," the voice said over his shoulder. "Step through and speak to her."

"She won't hear me."

"How do you know? This is a vision. Anything can happen."

Raffi's fingers were tight on the dusty frame. "My vision. My Journey. But it's all going wrong. Because of you."

A dry, rasping chuckle. "I'm only here, Raffi, because you brought me in with you. You would not let me stay outside. I came in here hidden in your heart, and you know it."

He felt giddy. His palms were sweating and there was a pain throbbing in his head. The thump of his heart made him breathless.

"Won't you look?" the voice pleaded. "You know who I am, Raffi. Are you so afraid to see me again?"

He lifted his head; it was like a weight. Gripping the mirror to stay upright, he turned. The Margrave was so close he could have touched it. Its eyes were very bright;

its lipless, distorted profile dim against the mirrors. It raised its hand. "You're still afraid of me. There's no need. I would not hurt you; you know that. I think you have known it a long time now, and that's what you fear. Take my hand."

"No." He couldn't step back; the mirror glass was hard at his back.

"Please. Because no human has touched me since Kest. No one has spoken to me. Your Order teaches you that the lonely are to be pitied, I think. And I am the loneliest being in the world, Raffi."

Its hand was close to his.

Slowly, disbelieving, he reached out and took it. Their fingers clasped. And behind him, the mirror glass melted, and he fell through.

BREATH. ANOTHER BREATH. Convulsions of pain in his chest.

"Hold him!" A voice yelled. "Tighter! Don't let him hurt himself."

He rolled, was sick, violently, and then again, shuddering over and over, his whole body a fever of sweat. Pain burned behind his eyes; someone held him up and forced him to drink some sweet water and he was sick again, and all the time he knew, hopelessly, bitterly, that it was over, that he had failed, that he would never be a Relic Master.

It took an age to come out of the coma, for Galen and the Sekoi to get liquid into him, to stop the terrible trembling, to give him something for the pain. He couldn't remember much of it; perhaps he slept. Because when he finally opened his eyes he was up in his room, in bed, and Galen was sitting with his back to the window, his face grim and set. And weary.

Through wet eyes, Raffi watched him. The keeper said coldly, "How do you feel?"

He could barely answer. "Better."

Galen stood quickly. "Raffi, what happened? How could it fail? You were only on the Journey for two hours. Two hours! Why did you come out? I don't understand what went wrong!"

"Galen!" The Sekoi came in. "For Flain's sake, not now. You told me he can try again."

"We haven't got time! We leave for Maar tomorrow."

"NO!" Raffi struggled up. "I can't—I won't go there!"

"I've told you we're going!" Galen's eyes were black with anger; he turned away and then swung back savagely. "This is my fault. I've been too soft with you, and now there's no time, because all that matters is destroying the Margrave. We have to, Raffi, even if both of us die in the attempt. Even if you're the only poor excuse for a keeper left to take my place!"

He crouched. "What happened—tell me!"

Raffi couldn't. He dared not. "I . . . It's all confused. I don't know."

Galen's look cut him to the heart.

"I'm sorry." He shook his head helplessly. "I know I've failed you. I'm all mixed up . . ." He was mumbling hopelessly; the Sekoi came over and its long, cool palms pushed him back onto the pillow.

"Go to sleep. It doesn't matter."

"Doesn't matter! It's a disaster!" Galen was rigid with contempt. "Are you a coward, Raffi, is that it? What sort of scholar have I wasted all these years on? Dear God, what am I going to do with you! What good are you to the Order, to me, to any of us! What good are you!" His voice was icy. It was more appalling than his anger. Raffi closed his eyes in despair. When he opened them, Galen had gone and the Sekoi was scratching its tribemark.

"Take no notice, small keeper," it said, into the terrible silence. "He's disappointed. He'll get over it."

Raffi couldn't answer. He turned over and buried his face. Pain and misery swept over him, in every vein, every sense-line. As soon as the creature crept out, he sobbed it all into the stiff pillow bitterly, his tears hot and heavy, biting his hand to make no sound. There was no one he could tell, not the horror of the Journey, not the pain, not his terror of Maar. Carys was gone, Galen despised him. Even the Sekoi would not understand. He was alone. He had never been so alone.

ALL NIGHT LONG he could not sleep. Before dawn he crept out of bed, pulled on clothes and boots, took an empty pack, and wandered half dazed down through the sleeping dimness of the castle. In the kitchens the remnants of Alberic's feast were piled on tables. He took water and some food, and fumbled his way out to a small, secret gate he had found the day before. It led into the dry moat. He let himself out silently.

The sky was purple. Atterix and Lar hung among the frosty stars; to the east the faintest pink flushed the clouds. A sparkbird whistled, flitting over the battlements.

Raffi closed the door. For some reason it was important to lock it, so he did, and then threw the key into the mud because he found himself staring at it stupidly. After a second he took the awen-beads out of his pocket and looked at them a long time, their purple and blue crystals deep and secret in the predawn chill. Finally, he threw them after the key. Then, numbly and without feeling, he stumbled out of the ditch and turned west. Away from the castle. Away from Maar.

The Barrier of Pain

13

Investigation of personal history is forbidden. Relationships between serving officers are forbidden. Love is forbidden.

Rule of the Watch

CARYS POURED OUT ANOTHER CUP of the sweet yellow ale and slid it across the tabletop. "So tell me," she said, chin on hand, "how long have you been stuck here?"

"In this stinking hole?" The Watchsergeant scowled, raised the glass and downed half its contents, leaving a yellow scum over his ragged mustache. "Ten stinking months."

"A long time."

He licked his lips. "A long stinking time and I've never tasted this cask in all of it. Where did you get it?"

"Officers' cellar." She sipped from her glass, watching

him. He was suspicious. And it was important not to get him so drunk that he wouldn't talk. Just enough that he wouldn't remember what he'd said.

The room was crowded and smoky. Behind her a raucous dice game was going on, with a lot of argument and complicated calculation. The Sekoi would have loved it.

"I hear you've seen a bit of action." She tried to sound admiring.

He wagged his head. "Some."

"At Tasceron?"

"Oh, aye. There." He drank again.

She sipped the foul ale. He wasn't the boasting kind. Just her luck. She decided to be direct. "And Mathravale?"

He looked at her over the leather tankard. When he put it down he seemed slightly less drunk. "I was there."

His voice had hardened. It didn't encourage questions, but she had to hurry, because at eight bells she had to report to Scala.

"You saw it?" she ventured. "All of it?"

"All." He tapped the tankard; she refilled it, wishing

she knew anything about what had happened, so that she could lead him on. At random she tried the obvious. "Did you lose any of your patrol?"

"Us!" He laughed, mirthless. "None of us died. They died, though. Thousands."

"They?"

"You know. The Order. Villagers. We cut them down. Women, children." His voice was slurred, reluctant. "Bloody mess," he whispered.

Carys was icy cold. She ran her finger around the lip of her cup, unable to drink. Behind her, the dice players roared. "It was a massacre?" she said quietly.

"Of course it was a stinking massacre." He glared at her angrily. "Didn't you read about it at school?"

"Yes, but . . ."

"Cut to pieces." He slumped, morose now. "Blood to the elbow. I remember a girl . . . young girl she was, holding my arm. Screaming. Couldn't stop, though. Orders." He shook his head, his voice fading. "Hanging; we hanged all of them . . ."

"Not the children." She wanted to shake him, but it would have been too dangerous. As it was she kept her voice low and a sickly smile on her face, because there were at least two men in the room watching them both.

"Sure. Most. Some they took . . ."

"Carys!" Quist was standing behind her, a dark shadow. "What's this?" he snapped.

"Drinking." She sipped the ale grimly.

"This place is off limits to Watch personnel and you know it." He looked the sergeant over in disgust. "What's your number?"

"Seven . . . six . . ." The man stammered.

"Get yourself out of here!"

They watched him stagger out, falling against the tables, shoved aside by workers. Carys stood up. "Not really afraid I'll run off, Captain?"

He took her arm and pushed her toward the door. "I'm not sure of anything you might do. Scala's got the permits. We're leaving right away."

"Thank God," Carys muttered. They had been two days at Flor's Tower, but to move along the Wall they needed permits, a new set for each section, which would mean at least five until they finally came to Maar, where the only gate went through into the Unfinished Lands.

The Barrier of Pain

Security was tight. Scala, she knew, would have had to use all her charm on the local commander.

"She had supper with him last night," Quist said abruptly.

For a moment she almost felt he had heard her thoughts; amazed, she waited till they'd gotten outside and were crossing the muddy street before she said, "Why should it worry you?"

He didn't look at her, ducking under scaffolding. "You know why."

She did, but to her astonishment he said, "Because I love her."

Carys didn't know what to say. Luckily, a convoy of wagons was rattling past, the heavy martlets with their heads down, the clatter of their hooves drowning everything. Yes, she'd known; she'd guessed a while ago. But the way he had come straight out with it astounded her. It was so unlike the Watch. And the whole thing was against the Rule. When it was quieter she said, "Does Scala feel the same?"

His voice was sour. "Scala's a mystery. Even to me."

Ahead of them, the castellan was waiting by the horses

impatiently. Her hair was pinned neatly and she held a packet of papers up at Carys with a quiet smile. "We can go. Get your things."

"It didn't take you long," Carys muttered, with grudging respect.

Scala looked coy. "It never does." She flicked Quist's shoulder with the papers. "Cheer up, lover. Soon, very soon, we'll be rich."

THE ROAD BEHIND THE WALL led out of Flor's Tower eastward; at first it was an easy ride, flat and well-paved, the immense black masonry slabs rising high on their right. Apart from the wagons of quarried stone there was little traffic, and beyond the first league-stone they could even gallop for a while.

But Carys was worried. How could Galen and Raffi follow her through this? It would take an army to get them through. And she had to leave a longer message behind; the spotty boy might well have been too stupid to give them the letter, and as for the owl . . . She frowned. Maybe, maybe not. The Sekoi's relationship with the owls puzzled her. Were they servants, or allies, or what? She had learned nothing about it in the Cage of Stories. If she asked the Sekoi, it would just shrug gracefully. As her horse ran, blowing through its nostrils, she wondered for a sudden, lonely moment where the creature was, where Raffi was. How close behind her were they?

By late afternoon the road was a track, blocked by landslides. It trailed through wooded country, split and mined for its dark stone. The horses stumbled in deep ruts, and when the clouds closed in, they brought an early darkness and then rain, a steady, relentless downpour. Scala looked snug in her long traveling cloak; Carys had to make do with the borrowed Watch-coat, and it was too small for her. Water trickled in through a tear at the back, soaking her neck and, slowly, her clothes. She was stiff now, and tired, and lost; the high, tangled thickets of the forest surrounded them with darkness. They had detoured far to the south and the Wall was out of sight.

Abruptly, rounding a high rock, Quist stopped.

"What?" Scala pulled up beside him. The red paint

dripped from her horse's neck into lurid puddles. "What is it?"

"Someone's there." He was sitting still, head slightly to one side. "Ahead. Down the track."

"How many?" Scala's crossbow was out; she loaded it expertly, her small fingers winding back the bolt.

"I'm not sure. The plants are confusing me."

Carys listened. She could only hear the rain, its torrents hissing on leaves, dripping and splashing; the branches roaring in the gusty wind. "Plants? Those monsters?" There had been a few along the track; great fleshy-leaved things, house high. Now in the darkness all around she saw thickets of them, sprouting out of the ruins of fallen leaves and matting the forest floor; immense growths of tough, barb-edged green spears, suppurating with a yellow glistening oil that gathered in a noisome pool at the heart of each. Rain plopped in all around.

"Deathwort. Man-eaters, every one." Quist slid down and took one step. The nearest plant stirred; Carys felt her skin crawl as she saw how the long fronds rippled and creaked along the ground toward him.

The Barrier of Pain

"Keep well away from them," he said.

Carys stared. "How can they eat you?"

He glanced up at her. "Easily." Picking up a stone, he threw it at the nearest; it landed in the central pool. Instantly the plant threshed and flailed; the liquid bubbled, a foul acid stink rising from it. The fleshy leaves slithered greedily up tight, folding over and over each other with amazing speed as if it huddled over its meal.

"The oil breaks up the prey and the plant sucks the life out of it." Quist remounted. "Kest's work, all of it. Whoever's picked this place for an ambush knows what they're doing."

Scala balanced the bow. "So do we. I'll go first." She smiled at him sweetly through the rain. "You last. Weapons ready. Are you sure you don't know numbers?"

"Not until we're closer."

For a moment Carys thought he sounded just like a keeper. "How could you know?" she asked.

He ignored her. Scala's horse moved off, into the squall.

It would be a vicious place to be trapped. The track led into a dark, overgrown plantation, clusters of ivied trunks rising on each side and the deathwort sprouting in vast thickets, their leathery, barbed spears groping into the path. The horses were uneasy, whickering and sidestepping. Far off, thunder rolled, an ominous threat.

Scala rode ahead, hood back, alert.

Carys's fingers gripped the wet bow. As her horse paced on, all her senses tingled; every part of her was tensed and ready. This was where she missed Galen. If only she had sense-lines, what a gift that would be. Sense-lines. For half a second her concentration flickered. She turned to Quist.

In that instant a tree crashed behind them. Quist shouted, and out of the ground under Scala's horse a figure jumped up, scuttling, yelling. The horse reared; Scala fought for control and out of the trees a hail of missiles slashed down around them; stones, arrows, thudding wildly.

Carys slid off her horse. As she dived for cover every deathwort swiveled toward her; a fleshy leaf groped at her and she jerked away, cursing, rolling into shadow. It was a confusion of darkness. Quist was yelling something; a horse screamed in pain.

Scala was down, her bow lost; as Carys scrambled over

she saw a figure jerk from the dark, the brief cold glint of a knife. She struck sideways with the bow. He crashed down, struggled up, the knife still in his hand; ignoring her, he scuttled oddly toward the castellan. Scala froze. Between the knife and the slithering plants she yelled at Carys. "Kill him! Kill him!"

It was a small man, fair-haired. He was filthy, bloody.

"Do it!" Scala was furious. "NOW!"

Carys raised the bow. Her finger touched the trigger. The man whirled, soaked, screaming out at her. "Watch scum!" he yelled. "Filthy Watch murderers!" She aimed instantly.

"No!" Quist's hand grabbed the bow and yanked it down; out of the dark he walked up to the man, ignoring his hysteria, the wicked waving gleam of the knife. He said nothing, did nothing. But the man was silenced between one sobbed curse and the next. Chest heaving, he crumpled.

Quist kicked the knife aside carelessly and turned to Carys. "There's just him, and he's blind. Leave him."

As he crossed to Scala, Carys stared at him in amazement. "There were shots."

"Rigged up before. He's alone."

The castellan was furious, blood smudged down her cheek. "I want him dead!" she snarled.

Quist rubbed the blood off gently, with his gloved hand. "No you don't," he muttered.

14

The Emperor was furious. "Crops destroyed, cattle sick! Now our houses shaken. But I will never be forced into mercy."

"Indeed," Imalan murmured, "it cannot be forced. But the Makers have told me that if you will not relent neither will they have mercy on you. On the fourth day the spores of their wrath will fall."

"Then I will wait and see them," the Emperor said.

Deeds of Imalan

THE SEKOI TOOK A LONG DRINK of the wine and sighed. "That, my friend, was most welcome."

"Help yourself, Graycat." Godric nudged the flagon with his foot. "There's plenty. What's the news on the laddie?"

"Not good." The creature was dusty from its long ride; its yellow eyes narrowed. "But the first to hear it should be the keeper. Where is he?"

"Under that calarna. Never speaks. Never eats. Even the chief's getting worried."

The Sekoi hesitated, then emptied the cup and put it down. It turned and walked through the hectic camp, around Alberic's lavish tent, past the hastily built ovens steaming with the war band's evening meal. In the faint twilight above the trees, Pyra burned red.

Galen was sitting in shadow, knees drawn up. His hair was a long tangle; his face edged with that brooding darkness that the creature had come to recognize as the Crow, a darkness that seldom left him now.

The Sekoi bit a nail absently, and crouched.

"Galen."

The keeper stirred. He looked up, eyes black. Then he said, "You don't need to tell me. You haven't found him."

There was no way of softening it. "No." The creature sat by the dying fire and piled dry sticks on it, glad of having something to do.

"I knew you wouldn't."

"Did you?" The Sekoi sounded sour. "Well, you were right. I have ridden for two days through every village and settlement for miles. Sikka's group went as far as Elerna. Nothing. As if he had disappeared from the world."

"He has." Galen lifted his palm up; the purple and blue crystals swung from his fingers. "Do you think I haven't been looking too? There's no trace of him, not in the soil, not among the trees."

"Then we must search harder." The creature stood, began pacing. Its whole body was agitated. "I will ask Alberic to send more men out. Raffi is ill, you know that. This Journey he made—he is not whole after it, and we have to find him before the Watch do! Galen, I say again, you must give up this oath and forget the Margrave. Raffi is more important!"

The keeper was silent, the flame light making sharp angles of his face. Even before he answered, the Sekoi crouched slowly in despair.

"I know you blame me." Galen's voice was raw with pain. "I blame myself. I pushed him too hard. It was too soon, and I should have seen that. I've always pushed him hard, because I've never known from day to day whether I would still be alive at nightfall, and someone has to carry on, to keep the secrets of the Order. He was afraid, and I ignored it. When he failed I said things I will never forgive myself for." He turned the beads, running them gently through his fingers. "I must pay for that. And if I could, God knows I'd look for him over the whole planet if I had to. But I made the oath by everything I hold most sacred, and it binds me." He looked up. "My friend, I know you find our ways strange . . ."

"Mad," the Sekoi muttered.

". . . but like us, you know about faith. I have to leave Raffi in the hands of the Makers, hard though that is. They will take care of him. He's in less danger away from us—I have to believe that."

"It will tear you in two," the creature said softly.

Galen looked away. "If that's what the Makers want."

"And will he have sense-lines? Will he be recovered enough to guard himself?"

"I don't know."

"And if the Watch should find him! If he is tortured . . ."

"*I don't know!*" Tormented, the keeper stood and limped out of the light. He caught at a low bough of the tree and held it as if it gave him strange support. He didn't look around, but his voice was harsh, oddly distorted. "It might take months to find him. And I cannot turn away from the Margrave. Not now. This is why the Crow came. This is what he has been sent to do."

The Sekoi looked gloomily into the fire. "For us," it

whispered, "our children matter more than all the world."

A shriek startled them, a thin, high scream. Galen turned. "What's that?"

"It sounds like Alberic."

Instantly Galen ran, the Sekoi close behind, racing through the camp, the gaudy haphazard tents, bursting into Alberic's silken, private pavilion. The dwarf was in his high bed, both hands clutching the coverlet. His bodyguards had clustered around him, and they were all staring in disbelief at the growing tear in the ceiling.

"What is it?" the dwarf hissed.

"It's coming in, Chief." Godric hefted his ax. "Sit tight."

The cloth tore. A huge head peered in, its eyes perfectly round, unblinking. Then with a speed that amazed them all, an enormous black owl squeezed its body through and sank like a silent cloud. It perched on the rail at the foot of the bed. Alberic was out and behind Godric in seconds. "Kill it! For Flain's sake get rid of it!"

Godric lifted the ax. He looked very reluctant to move. "How, exactly?"

The Sekoi pushed forward impatiently. Shoving the ax aside, it stepped out in front of the owl and spoke, a long fluent sentence in the Tongue.

The owl answered in a fluty voice.

"Flainsteeth!" Alberic grabbed Galen. "What's going on?"

"Be quiet!" The keeper watched, intent.

The Sekoi nodded, and folded its long arms. It was listening courteously, asking rapid questions. When it turned, its face was lit with relief. "Good news. The Silent One has seen Carys."

"When!" Galen took a step forward.

"Two days ago. At a smallholding a league from here."

"Alone?"

"When they spoke. But there was a woman asleep in the house and another, a man in Watch uniform."

"Is she safe?"

"She seems her own, highly confident self." The Sekoi turned back and spoke; the owl answered, its head swiveling, its round eyes fixed on Alberic.

"What's it looking at me for?" the dwarf muttered uneasily.

The Barrier of Pain

"You are the leader of this flock, so it pays you respect."

"Fascinating." Alberic's greedy eyes glinted. "I never knew those things could talk. What a spy network they'd be. Can you teach me that lingo?"

"That would not be allowed."

"Not even for twenty gold pieces?"

The Sekoi's eyes flickered sideways. "Fifty, and I might consider it."

"Thirty."

"For Flain's sake!" Galen raged. "What did she say!"

The owl churred.

"She told it we were coming, and that she was heading for Flor's Tower, traveling west, along the Wall. The Watch have built this folly to try to stop the spread of chaos. Apparently there is no way through the Wall for twenty leagues, until you reach the great Watchtower of Maar. That is the only gate." It asked another question; the owl answered and preened a feather carefully out from under its wing.

"Beyond the gate," the Sekoi said quietly, "the Unfinished Lands burn and erupt. The Pits of Maar are a day's flight out beyond the Wall. The Silent Ones do not go there. Nothing can live there."

Alberic had sidled forward. His eyes were sharp; his small finger jabbed out. "Look at that. It's wearing jewels."

The owl swiveled its head and looked down at him as if he were a particularly juicy mouse.

"It says," the Sekoi muttered, "that it would peck your eyes out before a bow could be fired. I recommend you to believe it."

"What happened to respect?" Alberic folded his arms. "Anyway, owls don't wear collars. Why's this one different?"

The Sekoi shrugged gracefully.

"Don't give me that, tale-spinner. You know. Your fur's all fluffed up."

It was true. The fur at the creature's neck was stiff, a sure sign of tension.

Galen said, "Has it seen Raffi?"

"No." The Sekoi glared at Alberic. "And these things are not for you, thief-lord. They are Sekoi matters."

"Touchy!" Alberic grinned, sly. "I hear you've had to

move that Hoard of yours. Now there would be a nice little find."

The Sekoi made a small mew of disgust; turning back, it spoke again, urgently. The owl churred and spread vast wings. Alberic ducked as it flew straight at him, circled low, and was gone through the tent flap before he could yell an order.

"Blast you, keeper, your spies and your messages." He turned and scrambled back into bed, fussily arranging the pillows. "That girl was always trouble. We're better off without her. Now go on, tell me we're heading for Flor's Tower."

Galen stared down at him morosely.

"We're heading for Maar."

"WHAT!" The dwarf sat bolt upright. "Now wait a minute!"

"You heard me." Galen bent and grabbed a handful of the gold silk nightshirt. His eyes were black with despair; the Sekoi took an uneasy step forward. "You're going to attack the gate just long enough for me to get through it. After that I don't care what you do. You can rot in your own greed."

Alberic looked at him shrewdly. "As long as you don't expect me to wait around."

"I expect nothing from you."

"Just as well. If you go in there it would be a waste of time; you won't be coming back. Stop creasing my outfit, keeper. If you hadn't expected too much from your boy, he'd still be with you."

For a split second they stared at each other, eye to eye. Then Galen dropped him like a sack and swung around. He shoved past the Sekoi and limped out into the dark. Alberic straightened his clothes and snapped small fingers; Milo came running up with a goblet of wine. The dwarf took it in both hands and leaned back on the pillow. Looking at the Sekoi he said, "He's on the edge."

"He's always been difficult."

"He's a godforsaken lunatic, and if he thinks I'm as suicidal as he is, he's wrong. I joined up with the Crow to win, not to be martyred. You tell him." He sipped thoughtfully. "I'll keep men out looking for Raffi. Though the poor kid's not had much of a life. He's better off out of it. Now, I'll go to forty gold pieces to learn a few words of that owl chat."

The Barrier of Pain

The creature sighed. "Perhaps another time."

Alberic nodded, and drank. "You just keep an eye on that fanatic."

The Sekoi ducked under the tent flap and went out, looking up at the Arch of the Seven Moons.

"Hey. Excuse me." A boy stood in the tree-shadow. For a second the creature's fur tingled; then its keen night-sight adjusted, and it saw the spotted boy, Alberic's kin, standing awkwardly by.

"It's just . . ." Milo came forward, wringing his hands. "Now Raffi's gone, the keeper needs a new scholar, right? I was just wondering . . . I mean, Uncle depends on me, of course . . . Well, he couldn't do without me but I'd really like . . . that magic and stuff. Maybe if you could just ask Galen . . ."

The Sekoi shuddered delicately. "That would not be a good idea."

"I'm bright. I could learn."

"I'm sure. But the keeper is very upset. This is not the time."

The boy looked downcast. "Later, then?"

The Sekoi shrugged, and said kindly, "Perhaps." It

watched the boy wander off. The camp was quiet now. The Sekoi walked to the trees and stood, listening. Around it the whole planet of Anara slept, trunk and root, tunnel and vein, a billion leaves and beasts and birds, and in every one the same thread of life, that inexplicable tingle of energy. And somewhere, lost in all of it, alone, was Raffi.

"Small keeper," it breathed sadly. "Where are you?"

15

*I am in darkness, and abandoned,
my eyes without sight, my mind without
memory.
I am forgotten by my friends.
Even God has turned his back on me.*

Litany of the Makers

HE LAY STILL. His eyes were gummy and his mouth dry; as he dragged a hand up to his face, he felt the ache of bruises, the stiffness of his legs lying crookedly under him. The touch of his own skin was rough, unfamiliar.

He didn't know where he was. His fingers went to his neck and felt absently for something that should have been there, but he couldn't remember what. His mind had deep black holes in it and they were joining up. Blotting him out. With a struggle he managed to sit up. There was a pack beside him; he recognized it vaguely and rummaged inside. A few crumbs of dried bread. The water was all gone.

He only knew he was thirsty. The agony of it was a dull pain between his eyes, crowding out everything else; he staggered up, through the neat stacks of baled hay. It was some sort of barn. When he found the door he pushed it open weakly, blinking in the brilliant sunlight.

"God, son," someone said. "You look rough."

He stumbled out. The men were sitting in a row. They wore dark clothes and their horses cropped the abandoned fields. They had a table with maps spread on it. And they had water.

Raffi moved toward it quickly. Someone tripped him and he fell; everyone roared with laughter. Then they tossed a small leather flask to him, and he drank, desperately, endlessly.

"Hey!" one of them shouted, but he ignored that, drinking and drinking until the cold water was all gone. Then he looked at them.

They were Watch.

The knowledge jolted him. Why hadn't he seen that! What was the matter with him?

"Is he worth taking?" A Watchman got up, casually unwinding rope from his waist.

The Barrier of Pain

"Makes up the quota." The one who had thrown the water came over. "Not much muscle, though. What's your name, boy?"

Raffi rubbed his face. Someone was telling him not to speak, but he ignored it, groping after the name and saying it carefully. "Raffael."

"What?"

"More . . . More."

"Papers?"

He stared up at the man, blank. "What papers?"

"God! What sort of a bender have you been on!" Roughly, expertly, the man hauled him up and searched him. "Nothing! Where are they?"

"I don't know."

The Watchman slapped him, hard. "Don't mess with me. Everyone has papers!"

Stunned, Raffi shook his head. He tried to hang on to his balance, but he was too dizzy. He crumpled into the mud on his knees, and shook his head hopelessly. "Not me," he whispered.

⊗

HE WAS IN A CART. Being jolted. Other bodies were packed in around him; someone elbowed him in the ribs. "Move over. And stop mumbling!"

It was dark. Through a slot there were stars, and six of the moons. He counted them over and over, trying to pin their names on in bright letters, Atterix, Cyrax, Lar, but the letters kept falling off and one name was always missing. He groped after it, back in darkness.

"FLAINSTEETH! Are these the best you could get! An idiot and a cripple!" The bald overseer behind the table made a gloomy note on his paper. "With this sort of rubbish, no wonder we're behind schedule. When I said get anyone, I didn't mean *anyone*."

"The boy's wiry, though his brain's gone. This one can work too, despite the arm. Sign for them and finish it."

Fascinated, Raffi watched the overseer's pen scratch over the grimy paper. Someone grabbed his arm; something cold was pressed onto his neck. "Number twenty-seven," a voice snapped. "Remember that." All around

him gangs of workers hauled stone, chipped stone, chis-
eled stone. The noise was deafening, the air thick with
flying dust.

"Get them started. Fourth section. Cato's Cleft."

A great hairy rope was put in his hands and he heaved
on it. All day he dragged the rope, and others dragged,
and the one nearest him was a scrawny one-armed man
who whispered, "Put your back into it, son. Slack off
when they're not looking. That's it. You've got it," until
it was hours later and he was slumped in exhaustion and
his hands were raw and the one-armed man was eating
both their rations of food.

Out of nowhere, clarity swung into Raffi's mind. He
struggled up. "That's mine. You're eating mine."

The man stared. "You can speak?"

"Of course I can speak."

"God help us, boy, you've gone all day without a word!
Two days, come to that. I thought you were weak in the
head." He glanced ruefully at the hard bread and onions
and then laughed. "Well, you'd better eat too."

Raffi tore the bread and sucked it; it was too dry to
bite. The onions made his eyes water.

"So why the dumb act?" The one-armed man considered him.

"It's not an act."

"No. You look sick, lad. Feverish." He backed off hastily. "Not catching, is it?"

Raffi drank some water clumsily. His hands were so sore; the pain had come out of nowhere, into his back and shoulders, and to hide from it he said, "Where are we? Are we prisoners?"

The man roared with laughter, showing broken yellow teeth. "Flainsthumb, son! You *are* an idiot." But then he stopped abruptly and said, "This is the Wall we're building. This is Cato's Cleft, in the Sarno hills, three leagues from Maar, and they've had fourteen men crushed here in the last week in rock-falls. Our chances don't look good."

"Maar?" Raffi whispered. "Did you say Maar?"

"Sure. Just up the road."

It was a syllable of horror. He didn't know why. Like a touch on a raw wound, his mind flinched away from it.

The man was watching him carefully. "You've had some bang on the head, haven't you? What do they call you?"

The Barrier of Pain

"Raffi." He looked up suddenly. "Do the Watch know my name? Did I tell them?"

"You told them some name. Is it important?"

"I don't know." Raffi looked around, utterly confused. They were in a small wooden hut, the door chained and bolted. It was crammed with prisoners, men and women. Most were asleep, others huddled together open-eyed. They were all filthy. So, he realized, was he. His hair was matted with mud; as he scratched, things crawled in it.

"Look . . ."

"Silas."

"Look, Silas, something's happened to me. I've been ill. For days . . . I think . . . perhaps days . . ."

"Take it easy." The man edged closer. "Keep your voice down and tell me quietly. Anyone in here could be a spy."

Knees up, Raffi struggled to think. It was getting harder again. "Including you," he said slowly.

"Sure, son." The man rubbed his stump; it ended in a filthy dressing at the elbow. "Sure I could. And so could you. But if you want to talk, I'll listen. If not, get some sleep. You need it. Tomorrow's a long day."

"It's just . . . I get lost . . . my mind drifts. I was on some sort of journey." He shivered, putting his forehead on his knees. "Galen would know, but . . ."

"Galen?" the man asked quickly.

Raffi shook his head.

"Who's Galen?" Silas leaned nearer. He stank of onions and sweat.

"I can't remember. It's just, if I start saying things . . . the Watch . . ."

"Then keep shut. Like you did today. Say nothing."

"But if I do, will you warn me? If I tell them?" He was so giddy, he couldn't sit up anymore, and had to lie on the damp floor, struggling through weariness for the words. "If I tell them things. Do you understand?"

"Things?"

"Secrets." His voice trailed off; his eyes closed.

Silas bent and whispered in his ear, "Whose secrets, Raffi?"

Raffi turned sleepily. When he answered, his voice was barely there. "The Order's."

Silas stared down at him a long time, and then nodded. "Sure," he muttered. "Sure. I understand."

The Barrier of Pain

THEY WORKED FROM DAYBREAK until dark. Cato's Cleft was a fearsome place. The Wall had to cross it, a sheer ravine of loose scree where the streambed had been hastily diverted and the rock-falls made the task of raising the highest levels dangerous. It was hard labor: hauling rock or carrying it in great baskets, up the hills of rubble, tipping it into the infill of the Wall, the dust choking them, filling their eyes. There was little water, less food. For three days Raffi worked almost without thinking, the rare moments of clarity flecking his bruised mind like shafts of sunlight in a dark wood. He kept silent as much as possible. Slowly, he forced himself to remember that he was a prisoner of the Watch, that this was the Wall, that there was someone called Galen and someone else called Carys who didn't know where he was. There was some great unhappiness just behind him; he became convinced it was following him like a shadow, a nightmare that would devour him if he even let himself think of it. Only at night would the knowledge wake him out of terrified dreams; a distorted creature watching him from a maze of mirrors, but when he woke and sat shivering and rocking himself among the sleeping slaves, he could never remember what the terror had been or whose long, strange hand had gripped his.

Silas stayed close. The scrawny man worked stripped to the waist, a makeshift scarf wound around head and mouth and nose. He made one for Raffi too, and though it was hot and smelled of horses, Raffi was glad to wear it, because it made him feel disguised, hidden, and his tangled hair and ragged shirt were unrecognizable too. Silas was a survivor; he quipped with the guards, stole water, kept them off the dangerous jobs.

"I'm looking out for you, boy," he would mutter, hauling a basket of broken stone one-handed onto the barrow. "Your head's getting better. You even remembered my name this morning."

Once, when the terrible blankness had gone for a moment, Raffi asked him about his hand.

Silas spat. "You've guessed, or you should have. Cut off for theft. I was lucky not to lose both."

"You!" A Watchman came up; Raffi ducked his head instantly, his heart thudding. "Silas! You and your idiot friend up on the top, now. They need a few extra hands."

"Sure," Silas said drily. "So do I." He pushed Raffi toward the ladders. "Go on, lad. It's a chance to get out of the dust, at least."

Scaling the ladder, Raffi felt the dizziness creep back, had the feeling he was climbing and climbing into some great castle, but as he hauled himself wearily over the edge, a roaring wind struck him and he staggered up, balanced on the half-built top of the mighty Wall. Out there, like a nightmare, stretched the Unfinished Lands.

Here, they were stark and empty. A great desert of hot sand, in places vitrified by some intense heat, with oily black pools that bubbled and spat and stank. Not far off was a structure that might once have been a house. Now it was a ruin in the sand, half lost, its cracked roof glinting with tiny rainbows.

"God!" Silas gripped Raffi's shoulder, staring out into the raging wind. "So that's what we're keeping out," he yelled. "No wonder the Makers left!"

Small flies buzzed up here, clouds of them. Raffi beat them off feverishly. "Makers?" he whispered. And instantly, the light went on in his brain. He gasped, clutching his head in agony. It was a small red light, and it pulsed right through him. For a second, all around him, a net of sense-lines woke and crackled.

"Raffi. Get up!" Silas was hauling at him.

"I can feel it," he gasped. "It's the signal!"

"Signal?"

"It must be Carys! The relic!" It was all flooding back. The relic power lit his mind like a Maker-lamp in a dark room; it energized him. He remembered everything. He grabbed the man's arm. "She must be close. Somewhere near!"

Silas looked around. Two Watchmen were closing in. "For God's sake, Raffi . . ."

It was too late. A crossbow jabbed Raffi's ribs. "All right, what's going on? Get on your feet."

He was hauled up; a whip flicked. Stinging pain slashed down one arm. "Leave me alone." Raffi snarled it; the Watchman's eyes widened.

"Since when could you talk!"

"He's not been well," Silas said hastily. "Had a bit of a knock."

"Has he! Then I'll give him another one." The

The Barrier of Pain

Watchman caught hold of Raffi, dragging him around.

"*Don't touch me!*" Anger charged him; it surged from the awen-field. The air cracked with a vivid explosion, a blue spark that struck the Watchman full in the chest and flung him back, senseless, hard against the heaped stone.

There was a stunned silence. All work had stopped. Raffi glanced around. A ring of crossbows pointed at him.

Silas stepped back quickly, raising his hand.

"He's nothing to do with me," he said rapidly. "Don't bring me into this."

"He was with you," a Watchman hissed.

"I don't know him. But I can tell you what he mutters in his sleep."

Something shifted behind; before Raffi could turn, a rope was around him, pinning his arms tight. He was grabbed and hauled down, struggling, kicking.

Silas gazed down at him. "It's about the Order," he said, his voice very quiet. "A lot of stuff about the Order."

16

History can be rewritten. A story depends on who tells it.

Rule of the Watch

THE BLIND MAN HAD BEEN TIED between two deathwort plants. Any movement would have been lethal; it had to have been Scala's idea. Carys crouched at his feet and said, "For Flain's sake, won't you shut up!"

"Why should I?" he hissed. "You murderers killed my wife. If I could see, I'd slice every one of you up slowly. God, so slowly."

"You listen, and listen hard." Carys took the letter out of her secret pocket. "I'm not in the Watch. Got that? I'm working undercover. I'm a spy for the Order."

"Are you? And I'm the Emperor's lapdog." His hatred was like a wall, a solid barrier between them.

"I haven't got time to argue. These two are the enemy here, not me. Now take this. If anyone finds it on you, destroy it." She shoved the letter inside his shirt; he squirmed and kicked out blindly as if it were poisoned. Carys jumped back. "It's true," she snarled fiercely. "The letter is for a keeper. His name's Galen Harn. He'll be here in hours. Or should be."

"You must think I'm totally stupid!" The blind man had stopped struggling. Now he gazed toward her, head tilted, his features distorted with loathing. "And that bitch of a castellan wants me dead."

"You knocked her down. She's not the sort to forget." Carys looked around anxiously. "But Quist's talked her out of it. They're just going to leave you here. Listen! Get the letter to Galen. It's important! Tell him the Margrave wants Raffi! He's got to leave Raffi behind. Have you got that?"

For a second he looked doubtful. "A keeper."

"Yes."

"They're all dead."

"Not this one." She scrambled up. "I've got to go. We're riding on." She walked away, then stopped and turned and stood for a second looking down on him. "Have you ever heard of a place called Mathravale?"

There was silence. Then, deliberately, he spat at her. "You lying, murderous scum," he whispered.

"AND I SUPPOSE YOU WANT ME to attack this as well?" Alberic gazed sourly at Flor's Tower through the relic-tube; Galen took it from him impatiently and snapped it up.

"No. Carys came through here, so we have to follow. What do your people say?"

The dwarf leaned back against the birch trunk. "They say the road's all broken up with mudslides. We'll have to go through the Hungry Wood."

"May I ask," the Sekoi asked apprehensively from up in the tree, "just why it's called that?"

"Deathwort. Clusters of it."

"Ah."

The dwarf scrambled up, Milo hastily brushing leaves from his clothes. Alberic gave him an absent clip around the ear. "Stop fussing me, boy."

"Sorry, Uncle."

"And stop Uncle-ing me! It's Chief to you. Go and find Taran; tell him he's to take over the rearguard."

As the boy ran off, Alberic stared after him in exasperation. "Never promise your sister you'll make a warlord of her son."

"You have a sister?" the Sekoi asked politely, dropping through the branches.

Alberic scowled. "Ugly as sin. Looks nothing like me."

They made their way down the track. Below, in a hollow, the war band rested and drank, their gaudy greens and scarlets lighting the wood. Galen stalked ahead, dark and morose, bending under the low branches with their delicate spring leaves. Last night, the Sekoi knew, he had been deep in the newly made sense-grid, sending messages to Tallis and to the keepers at Tasceron. Shean and his group had left the Pyramid; things were so bad in the city they were searching for the House of Trees, and three new keepers in the forest of Alkadis had been traced. But none of them had any news of Raffi. When the Sekoi had asked what Tallis had said, Galen had shaken his head sourly.

The Barrier of Pain

"She wasn't surprised."

"She said that?"

"She didn't need to."

Now, watching the keeper climb into the saddle of one of Alberic's horses, the creature felt Godric at its elbow. "Well, Graycat," the big man said. "What's at Maar for him?"

The Sekoi scratched gloomily. "Death."

"His?"

"Or the Margrave's. It will come to that."

Godric picked his teeth. "Do you really think that thing exists? Half man, half animal? That they could have made something like that?"

"Oh, I think so," the Sekoi said softly. "I think they were capable of that."

"And could he kill it? I mean, the Order, they think all life is holy, right? Even plants! Could he bring himself to kill anything in cold blood?"

"That's what I wonder, friend." The Sekoi was watching Galen.

Godric shrugged. "Mind you," he said. "With his temper . . ."

"SHE'S TAKING HER TIME just to fetch a glove." Quist looked back through the trees anxiously.

Carys sat among the roots of a barnut and chewed a piece of sweetgrass. "Relax," she muttered. "Scala doesn't need you to look after her."

Quist glared. "You talk too much."

They were silent a moment; an awkward silence filled with the varied birdsong of the copse, and the distant yelping of a pack of jeckles invisible in an abandoned clearing of green corn. Then Carys threw the grass stalk down. "I want you to tell me about Mathravale," she said quietly. "You were there, weren't you?"

She had caught him off guard. His glance was quick and wary; then he wouldn't look at her at all. Instead he pulled tiny mosses off the tree with his fingers. Finally he said, "Yes. I was."

"You said some of the children were taken to Marn Mountain. That might have been me."

"Maybe, but—"

"But nothing." Suddenly she was angry. "I want to

know what happened. I have a right to! Everyone else does." She stood up and came close behind him. "Do you have any idea of what it's like not to know who you are? Where you came from? Who your parents were? I don't know any of that. All I can remember is that pit of a Workhouse. I want more than that."

He stared steadily back along the track. "What if the truth is worse?"

"I still want to hear it."

"It's against the Rule."

She snorted; he smiled sourly. "No. That's never counted for much. But Scala . . ."

"Scala needn't know. Just tell me!" For a second she thought he wouldn't and felt a surge of despair that surprised her. But then he crouched, leaning against the tree, and began to pick fern leaves, shredding them rapidly.

"I was in the tenth patrol. We gathered at Carmelan, over three hundred of us, from all the towers around. It was just before dawn. I was young and scared and excited. The story was that there were keepers in Mathravale, a whole nest of them, with all their sorcery. The people there were hiding them. So we lined up and at dawn we rode down, like a great wave, whooping and yelling, and it was fine, Carys, it was fine. I hated it, and yet I felt so alive. The orders were clear: Find the keepers. Use any methods that were necessary."

He didn't look up. "Mathravale is a long, wide valley with a river that runs slowly. It was filled with ripe corn-fields, and there were sheep and geese outside the cottages. I remember thinking, as we roared down, how peaceful it was. Then the dogs in the nearest farm started barking, and all hell broke loose." His fingers never stopped moving, the pieces of fern torn smaller and smaller.

"They—we—dragged the families out. The commander—Darmon, his name was, he'd lost an eye in some Sekoi battle, and he was half mad. He roared out that all he wanted was the keepers, only them, and if they gave themselves up, no one else would be hurt. But no one came. No one moved. He screamed at the people to tell us where they were."

"And did they?" She knew the answer already.

"No. The silence was terrible. There was only a baby crying; I remember its mother was desperate to hush it, pushing the corner of her shawl into its mouth in terror."

"What did they do?" She was close behind him, her heart thudding, a slight sweat dampening her back.

"Darmon killed a young boy. Dragged him out and held a sword to his neck and when still no one spoke, cut it. Then the men went wild and attacked us. God knows why they did it. They had no weapons, just pitchforks and spades, they must have known it was hopeless. Why didn't they just tell us what we wanted to know?" He was arguing with himself bitterly, lost in memory. "It was a massacre. They stood no chance. The women ran into the houses, but we burned everything, buildings and crops. Cut down anyone who crawled out, even the dogs and cats. The screaming is what you never forget. Nothing was left. Nothing but ashes and smoke. And silence."

He stood abruptly, brushing the leaves off. "All down the valley it was the same. We came down like a black storm. Darmon lost control. We all lost control. It was a madness. At some stage a woman came running from the hills, an old woman on a stick, with two boys screaming at us to stop, that they were the keepers, the only keepers. They were trampled, their bodies cut to pieces, whether they were telling the truth or not. Darmon had to have some trophies." He looked down the track at Scala coming through the trees. "An old woman," he whispered, appalled. "And two boys."

Carys's throat was dry, but she forced herself to ask, "About the children. You said . . ."

"A few survivors were found. About thirty children were sent off to Marn Mountain." For the first time, he looked at her. "That doesn't mean . . ."

"Sixteen years ago. Right?"

"Yes."

"Then it was us. There were that many in our year. They worked hardest on us . . . we always knew that, but we never knew why." She met his eyes, cold.

He took a step forward. "Carys, the Order was to blame! To hide behind the people like that, to fill them so full of their faith that they would even die for it! They should have come out of hiding."

"If they were even there."

"They were! We knew. Our spies . . ."

"Spies!" It was like a knife wound; she drew in her breath hard. "And you killed everyone!"

The Barrier of Pain

"It was our orders. You know."

"Oh, I know." She stared at him, cold as ice. "I know."

"Sorry to keep you." Scala was smiling sweetly, pulling on her left glove. She looked smug and slightly heated, her fine skin smooth. "Shall we go?"

Carys turned without a word and climbed on the horse. She couldn't speak. She was so angry and bewildered, she was frozen by it, and that was good because when it melted, she didn't know what sort of pain would come. Her parents must have been there, brothers, sisters, who knows what. Killed because they wouldn't betray the Order.

"You're both very quiet." Scala took the crossbow off her back and slung it at the saddle. "We haven't had an argument, I hope?"

"No." Quist rode ahead grimly. "You were a time."

"Just something I had to finish, lover." She rode after him, Carys trailing last. The horse walked slowly and she let it, staring into the dense trees. What would her family think of her now? How would they feel if they knew their daughter had done the betraying for them?

✖

"IT'S DESERTED, but they've been here very recently."
Galen crouched beside Godric.

"The chief said to wait for him," the big man said. "It's
the way we do things."

Galen snorted. "I don't need your help." He pushed
out onto the track and began to walk down it, tall and
reckless. The Sekoi slid after him; with a brief oath, Godric yelled an order and the advance guard moved on
wearily.

Soon they all had to dismount. The deathwort terrified
the horses. They edged carefully around a great clump of
it, and saw Galen standing in a small clearing, looking
down.

The Sekoi clapped a hand over its nose. "Dear God,"
it muttered.

It had once been a fair-haired man. He had been tightly
tied between two deathworts, so that almost any movement would have brought him in range of their slithering
leaves. But it hadn't been the plants that had killed him.
It had been the crossbow bolt through his heart. He had

fallen sideways. The plant on the left had already found him, dragging part of the body into its acid pool. The stench was unbearable, the flies gathering.

Galen kneeled. He said some words from the Litany quietly, and closed the man's eyes. Then he reached out and examined the jutting end of the bolt. "Watch."

"I'd never have guessed." Godric came up. "Poor devil. Why tie him up first?"

"I don't know." Galen slid a hand under the jacket, beating flies away. He glanced at the Sekoi, a sudden tense look. Then he pulled out the paper. In seconds he had it open. "It's coded. It's from Carys!"

The Sekoi stared. "She did this?

"Of course not!"

"But if the Watch knew of the message, then why not take the letter. It does not make sense."

Godric nodded to his men. "Maybe she's traveling with someone more dangerous than she thinks. We'll get what's left of him buried before the chief comes. He's a bit squeamish." He turned. "If that's all right with you."

Galen was staring at the letter. He didn't speak.

The Sekoi edged nearer, biting a nail. "Bad news?"

When the keeper looked up, it seemed to the creature that it had never seen such intense, controlled despair. "He was right," Galen breathed, his voice barely audible. "And God help me, I didn't believe him."

"Right? Who?"

Convulsively, Galen tore the letter in half, as if his hands worked without his knowing. Then he whispered, "Carys says the Margrave is searching for Raffi. Searching everywhere."

17

With Flain gone, all Anara mourned.
Plants would not grow; the beasts lay
down and died. Even the skies wept a
gray snow, and the Makers sat cold and
silent around an empty throne.

Book of the Seven Moons

THEY HAD TIED HIM and put him on a horse, though he was so stiff, he could hardly sit. For about three hours, as far as he could tell, they had ridden west; one Watchman leading, two others behind.

No one spoke. It was dark, a warm mothy twilight, and to suppress the threads of terror that squirmed through him, Raffi let his mind surge out into the sense-lines, into the relief of finding them again after the blank shock of the Journey. Above him the moons rose slowly, swinging over the stark line of the Wall, but the only sounds were the rippling brooks the road crossed on narrow arches, and the hoot of an owl far off in some woodland.

The night was peaceful, and he let it soothe him. He knew they were taking him to Maar, but his mind veered off that darkness and he was happy to let it. He had always thought it would be some stark, forbidding place, but this was a quiet cultivated countryside, the fields freshly sown, smelling of rain, the small farmsteads with candle-flickers inside their unshuttered windows. He sent lines into the houses as he passed, rocking for a second in the cradle of a baby, tucked in under warm sheets, kissed on his forehead.

The horse stumbled. "Keep awake," a Watchman snarled.

With both hands, Raffi grabbed the rough mane. They were taking him to Maar. After all his efforts, his foolish running, he was going there, where the Makers must want him to go. "We can never fall out of the hands of the Makers." He almost heard Galen's scorn. Oddly enough, it was some comfort. Carys might be at Maar, Galen close behind. It would be all right, he told himself carefully, intently. "Flain," he whispered, "keep me in your hand."

Down the lanes the horses clattered, weary now. And ahead, rising out of the Wall, he saw a shape. It was black against the stars, so black at first, his eyes could not understand what it was, its darkness astounding him; a low cube without windows, without any decoration or surface features, completely and utterly smooth. A Maker-building. Intact.

Its blackness was so matte, it was hard to focus on, as if it were a vacuum, an absence, a cube of nothing. Only the lack of stars showed where it was. As he rode nearer, the harness creaking in the silence, he saw how the glow of the moons did not reflect from it. It swallowed light, a place of non-being that even the sense-lines could not penetrate. All around it, stirring in the warm breeze, tiny black flowers covered the ground. In the dark Raffi could hardly see them, but he felt them, and they were like nothing else on Anara. Their smell was sweet, almost cloying.

Before the building the Watchmen halted. The one in front rode a few steps forward, and waited. He made no signal as far as Raffi could see, but after a moment, abruptly, a small door slid open and a man came out, in Watch uniform. He and the guard spoke quietly, glancing back.

Raffi looked around. He was so tense, he felt sick. He had to do something, but what? He could startle the horses, maybe even the men, but he was tied and at the first gallop would fall, and what use would that be?

The horse whickered, sidestepped, and a cold blade was pressed into the back of his neck. "Any sorcery," the guard said briefly, "and you're dead. Understand?"

He nodded. It was too late anyway. The Watchman turned and waved. The others dragged Raffi down and shoved him forward, standing well back. "Not coming?" he said, shivering with fear.

"Not us." The guard grinned. "Nobody goes in there. Go on. Walk. It's the last walk you'll ever get."

He stepped between the black flowers. They drew aside from his feet; he felt the surface beneath them, and it wasn't rock. It was solid and wouldn't admit his mind. And from the low building ahead, he felt a constant hum, never varying.

The Watchman by the door wore a different uniform; his insignia was gold, and a small gold stripe crossed his sleeve. He had no weapons, and didn't speak, gesturing with his head for Raffi to go first. At the last second he wanted to struggle, run, but there was nowhere to run to. He stepped inside, and the door snicked shut behind them.

This was Maar.

IT WAS DARK. Corridors ran in all directions, lit only by a glimmer of blue Maker-power at ankle level along the walls. Raffi walked beside the guard, amazed. There was no sound, no scurry, no one. Even their footsteps were muffled. He had expected something like Carys's description of the Tower of Song—a vast swarming anthill, a hub of Watch organization, but this sleek, faintly warm darkness terrified him more. And what were the Watch doing with all this Maker-power?

The guard stopped. On the wall was a relic, a red light. He touched it, and it turned green. Raffi breathed a prayer silently; the Watchman gave him a glance of contempt, but said nothing.

A door slid open. Beyond it was a tiny cell, completely enclosed. Instantly Raffi took a step back. "No!" he gasped, but the Watchman pushed him in firmly, so that he fell against the smooth Maker-wall, his tied hands flat. To his surprise the guard stepped in after him. The door snicked shut.

Back against the wall, Raffi faced the man. "I won't tell you anything," he said.

"Shut up." The Watchman touched a dial. Without warning, the room dropped. It plummeted, and Raffi almost cried out with the terror of it, his stomach tingling in shock. The guard stood calmly watching. Raffi grabbed at the smooth walls. "Will it stop?" he whispered.

The man smiled, mirthless. "Let's hope so."

Down and down they fell, all the sense-lines dragged after them until he couldn't hold them anymore and they snapped and snagged, tiny points of pain behind his eyes: down and down into the depths of the planet, leaving behind roots and veined rocks and the sky, until with a smooth whoosh the fall had ended and he staggered against the guard, who caught his arm.

The door opened. Complete darkness was waiting for him.

The Barrier of Pain

"CATO'S CLEFT." Quist stood back to let a wagon of stones roll by. "We'd better eat here. Permission for Maar could take hours."

They crossed to a few makeshift tables of piled stone outside a shack with steam coming from its roof. A slatternly woman came out.

Scala flicked dirt off the bench. "Hardly what I'm used to." She gave the woman a warm smile. "What have you to offer us, then?"

"Stew, Castellan."

"Is that all?"

"Today's Agramonsday, so it's stew. Watch ration."

Scala sighed, and nodded. When the woman was gone she reached out and began to play with the fingers of Quist's hand on the table. He watched lazily.

Carys frowned. "So now what? They're not just going to let me walk into Maar."

"Even as our prisoner?"

"What!"

"Don't worry! It's just a little plan." Scala bent Quist's thumb back, trying to make him wince. "We say we have to deliver you in person. Tie you loosely."

"No chance!" Carys fixed her with a cold stare. "We're partners in this. I'm not giving up my weapons. You agreed."

"Oh come now, Carys." Scala's bright eyes were watching her, ignoring the dishes of stew being plonked down. "Don't you trust us? We get you to Maar—you give us the information about the boy, we all share the reward. You're reinstated, I'm promoted. We're all happy." Delicately she picked up the wooden spoon.

Carys knew something was wrong. Old Jellie's warnings came back and crawled down her spine—*when they're trying to distract you, be careful. Extra careful.* Picking up her own spoon she tasted the greasy liquid. Scala had some plan, all right, and if they suspected her now, she was finished. She had to lead Galen to the Margrave. Then she realized Quist wasn't eating. Instead he was staring at Scala with a curious fixity, his meal getting cold, the work racket and dust around them forgotten.

Scala paused, the spoon to her red lips. "What? What's the matter?"

"My God," he breathed slowly, in disbelief. "You did it. You really did it!"

The Barrier of Pain

"Did what?" She blew on the stew and sipped at it, making a face, but he leaned over and caught her arm, spilling it on the table.

"*You killed him.*" His voice was hoarse; his hand shook.

She tugged briskly away.

Carys was chilled. "Killed who?"

"The blind man." He was staring at Scala as if he had never seen her before, the very skin on his face white and drawn.

Scala sipped calmly. Then she said, "Yes."

"How do you know?" Carys asked.

Scala smiled. "Yes, tell her how you know, lover."

He looked sick. "How could you do that! You promised me . . ."

"He struck me." There was nothing to show her anger, but it was there, deep and venomous, and she tore the hard bread carefully with her small nails. "No one does that. I owed it to myself to—"

"He was blind, for Flain's sake!" Quist stood up, his chair falling back with a smack. A few Watchmen looked around.

Scala's smile was icy. "Don't make a scene. Sit down. Do you want us all taken in for questioning?"

For a moment, Carys thought he wouldn't; then slowly, stiffly, he picked up the chair and sat on it.

"You should put all that behind you, Captain. I thought you'd have learned by now." She glanced at Carys. "Carys understands."

Carys put the spoon down. Not answering was dangerous, but she could barely manage to say "Of course I do," and she couldn't look at Quist.

"Good. Now. When I was signing us in I had news of our lost castle. The warlord who took Halen is one Alberic . . ."

Carys swallowed a piece of bread whole.

". . . and he's obviously ambitious. He's moving west along the Wall. The Crow is with him."

"The Crow!" Quist said.

"Yes." Scala was watching Carys. "Your old friend, my dear. They have an army and a divine mission: the total destruction of the Watch. Word is that the disaffected are flocking to join them: outlaws, thieves, keepers. The host is growing every day." She smiled sweetly at them both. "It appears to be war. Everyone will be busy. Too busy to notice us."

"Meaning?" Carys said quietly.

"Meaning that we go to Maar now, without permits. And bluff our way in."

GALEN HAD TAKEN THE BEADS APART and spread them in a hasty spiral, the purple and blue interspaced with his own black and green. In the center he put the candles Godric had found and the bowl of water carefully between them. "It is clean? No one's drunk from it?"

"No one."

"And the vessel? Not tainted with anything?"

"Keeper, that's my best fingerbowl. It's Palmyrian silver and was looted from a very wealthy merchant in my days on the Tasceron road." Alberic leaned forward, his sly wide-lipped reflection rocking on the water.

Galen shoved him back. His anxiety crackled out of him, small blue snaps that made some of the crystals glow. He kneeled and began to speak Maker-words; the Sekoi recognized some of them. It was the prayer known as the Opening—one of the seven great powers of the Order. Tamar had sung it first, over the Lake Imakel, when the Makers had tried all methods to find the soul of Flain, lost in the Underworld. It was one of the creature's favorite stories, and for a second it allowed itself the honeyed pleasure of slipping into the tale, spreading its seven fingers, speaking the words through Tamar, becoming the strong Starman on the snowy shore. Then, with a sigh, it slid back to itself.

Galen had finished; the silence was intense. All around him Alberic's war band crowded, curious and quiet. Milo peered under the Sekoi's arm. "What will happen?"

"Hush. The keeper will travel to Maar through the water."

"Why there?"

"He fears that Raffi will be there."

As it spoke, they saw the water ripple. A shape came into it, a low darkness. Curious, the Sekoi strained forward. All the crystals were charged, small energies leaping from one to the next. The creature thought for a moment that it saw a building, a strange blank cube with a group of riders outside it, and then there was nothing, except on the surface of the water a few floating petals that seemed black.

Galen reached out and picked them up. He looked at them carefully, then rolled them in his fingers and turned. "Saddle up. It's time to go."

"Is that it?" Alberic was peeved. "No bangs, no flashes? Nothing to excite the troops? You're slipping, keeper."

Galen's eyes were black as the petals. "I know where he is."

"Why didn't you find out sooner?"

"I didn't know where to look. I was too deep in doubt." He laughed, in a way that made the dwarf eye him warily. "All the time I was telling him to have faith, I had none in him."

"Clear off. All of you." Suddenly imperious, Alberic waved his people away; disappointed, they drifted into the wood, leaving only the Sekoi leaning against a birch trunk. Alberic crouched. "He's at Maar then."

Galen nodded.

"Long?"

"No."

"Have they hurt him?"

Galen looked away. "I don't know."

"They will. You know it as well as I."

There was a moment of silence. Instead of answering, Galen said, "Do you know how I first came across him?"

"Tell me." Alberic glanced at the Sekoi and sat on the dry ground, on his green silk coat-ends.

"I came to his mother's farm. Flain had told me this was the place. There were a lot of children—seven, maybe eight. From the doorway, as I was talking to her, I saw him. He was in the middle of the row, all of them on a bench by the fire, swinging their feet, eating—but he wasn't eating, he was staring at me. And later, when I had said the Litany, I came and laid out on the table seven small images a wood-painter in some village had given me. They were of the Makers, and I had decided that whoever chose the image of Theriss—it was her day— would be my scholar. When it was Raffi's turn to choose, I felt the power in him, the curiosity. The longing. It was strong, for a boy so young. I knew he was the one." He picked up the beads quickly. "She asked me to take care of him."

The Barrier of Pain

Alberic shrugged. "Mothers fuss. You did, in your way."

"Not well enough. And now we have to find him. To go even into Maar."

"You'll go, friend. Not me."

Galen stood and looked down, his dark hair loose. Then he put out a hand and took the dwarf's and pulled him up. He turned, but Alberic said, "Did he choose Theriss?"

The Relic Master stopped and looked back. "No," he said softly. "He chose Kest."

18

*Many ask "What are these spores?"
They are doubt and despair. They eat
into mind and flesh. None can withstand
them. And the Emperor stood on a high
balcony and saw their work, and in great
bitterness called Imalan to him and said,
"Ask Flain to stop this. I will do as he
asks. But tell him, this is through fear,
and not mercy."*

Deeds of Imalan

HE WAS WORN OUT, but they wouldn't let him sleep. At intervals a buzzer would sound, ringing through the cell. The first time he had heard it, he'd jumped up in total terror, but now he lay in the dark hopelessly, waiting for it.

The room was completely empty, pitch-black. He had groped his way around it three times and couldn't find the door, or any other flaw in its perfect walls. He had tried sense-lines, but the material was impervious. The very things of the Makers seemed like enemies here. With no light, there was no time. He could have been here hours or days. Terror was eating him; he couldn't stop shivering. He had said the whole Litany, worked through the Book, even tried the endless Prophecies of Askelon. And every time he drifted off to blessed sleep, the cold authority of the buzzer stunned him back into the nightmare. When the door finally slid open, it was almost a relief.

Lights flickered on, dazzling him. He sat up, heart thudding. Two Watchmen marched in; one dumped a chair and shoved him into it, the other carried a wide table, made of dark materials. An empty chair was placed behind it. Then they left.

Blinded by the light, Raffi had to put a hand over his eyes. He watched the dark, open doorway in agony, knowing the waiting was deliberate. Finally a tall man came in. He had cropped, yellow hair and he carried nothing in his hands but a small metal box, which he placed carefully in the very center of the table. Then he sat down behind it.

Raffi felt so tired, he could barely focus; the last time he had slept had been between shifts on the Wall. His lips were cracked; he licked them nervously, wanting to scratch the lice in his hair.

The interrogator leaned back. "I am here to ask you

questions. You may call me *sir*. What is your name?"

He didn't know what to say. Presumably they knew. "Raffael Morel."

The man nodded mildly. "Good. You're sensible. You are the scholar of Galen Harn, called the Crow."

"Ex-scholar." He said it quietly.

The man raised a cool eyebrow. "How unfortunate. But it makes no difference. You will have heard that Harn has an army now. It seems the Order's desire for peace is as false as their other beliefs."

Raffi looked down.

The interrogator said, "I want to know the motives of this man Alberic. I want to know their plan of attack. I want to know every detail of the source of the Crow's power, how extensive it is and how he intends to use it. I want to know the whereabouts of the relic called the Coronet, and finally, I want your . . . assistance in leading a patrol to the island called Sarres."

It was what he'd expected. He'd rehearsed the answer for hours, but it seemed weak, a terrified whisper even to him. "I won't give you any information, even if you kill me."

The man nodded pleasantly. Between them on the

table the box jerked, just a fraction. Raffi stared at it.

"Ah, yes. If only it were that simple." The man leaned back. "We won't kill you, keeper, as you well know. At least, not at first. We've developed expert techniques in torture and they have never failed on anyone. Terrible devices that you could barely imagine, that twist the body, inflicting unbelievable pain."

The box shifted again. Raffi's eyes slid back to it. Sweat trickled down his back.

"We won't need all that with you." The interrogator linked his fingers. He sounded almost bored. "You're young, and you're weak. You will be easy. You'll be screaming, very soon now, to tell me what you know. That is the truth."

"No." Raffi's voice was a whisper.

"No, *sir*." The interrogator waited.

Raffi was silent.

The man considered him, then said, "If you answer, everything will be different. Time is short, keeper."

Raffi shook his head, speechless.

Unsmiling, the man leaned forward. He took the lid off the box.

The Barrier of Pain

⚛

"HOW THE HELL AM I SUPPOSED TO storm a building with no windows, no door, no gates, and that you can only see if you squint at it sideways!" Alberic waved a small, perfectly gloved hand in disgust.

They had all been silenced by the sight of the Watchhouse of Maar; the Sekoi chilled to its heart, the war band rebellious, Godric silent, even Galen saying nothing. Only the dwarf seemed unaffected. His sarcasm was a relief to them. "Of course," he said acidly, "you'll tell me it has its good points. Give me the joy of hearing them, boys and girls."

"No ditch, Chief." Sikka crouched, leaning on her upright sword.

"No openings for defenders," Godric said.

"No defenders?" Taran muttered.

"Ah, but are there?" Alberic glared at Galen. "What's in there, keeper? What's the plan?"

"I brought you here for that," Galen said darkly. "Strategy is your business."

"*You* brought *me*!" Alberic scoffed. "That's a joke."

"They say"—Galen flashed a look at the Sekoi—"there's no fortress on the planet you can't take."

The creature scratched its short fur. "So my people have heard. Such a reputation . . ."

"Cut the flannel." The dwarf stood, hands on hips, in the cold dawn light. "I don't fall for that. Still, I admit, I enjoy a challenge." He folded his arms and stared at the ominous outline of the cube, his crafty mind working. "It's Maker-work. Will it collapse or explode when we attack? Will it sprout crazy weapons? What sort of beings will pour out of it? I need information, Galen."

Galen came and stood beside him and looked down. "It is Maker-work, but these are the Watch. They may not know how to use it. I'll find the door, and I'll open the door. After that, it will be up to you. But I don't want slaughter, thief-lord, if we can avoid it."

The dwarf looked sour. "You want a miracle."

"Yes." Galen fingered the crystals at his neck. "I do."

"Uncle!" The voice came from the back of the hedge, through the field where the war band had gathered; horses moved aside, snuffling in the long grass. "Uncle!"

The Barrier of Pain

"Flainsteeth!" Alberic growled. "If that addle-brained kid comes near me now . . ."

Milo pushed past Godric and ran up, breathless. Thistledown was all over his clothes; he brushed it off hastily and a cloud settled on the dwarf's goldwork tunic. "Uncle, I'm sorry! Let me . . ."

"Look at me! I'll kill him!" Alberic roared, but Galen caught the boy's arm quickly and pulled him close.

"What is it? What's disturbing you?"

Milo seemed paralyzed by the keeper's black gaze. "She's here," he whispered. "She's riding up the lane."

"Who?"

"The girl who gave me the letter. Carys."

THE SENSE-LINE SLID into her mind so gently, she barely felt it, but maybe the horse did, because it stopped and backed, and that gave her the idea. "Wait. My horse is lame." Before they could turn and see it was a lie, she had jumped off and lifted the beast's front hoof and was poking at it. Her heart thudded; she glanced into the scrubby woodland to her left. It seemed empty in the early mist.

Scala unslung her crossbow. "Well, this seems as good a place as any."

Quist looked uneasy. The castellan raised the bow and pointed it at Carys.

Carys froze. "What are you doing!"

"Covering our backs. We know all about you, Carys, and the little trail you've been leaving."

She glanced at Quist. He dismounted and came over. Carys dropped the horse's hoof. *Galen,* she thought. *Where are you?*

"Arms out."

She did it, glaring at him. He took her bow and then looked at the buttons on her coat, tugging the second one off and unscrewing it rapidly. "This is it."

Scala said. "You see, Carys, we decided from the beginning to let you bring your friend Galen and his boy along. It's the boy we want, after all. Now we've got the relic, we'll arrange a little welcome for him, away from his army. I'm sure it won't be difficult."

Carys turned on Quist. He was the one who had to be kept busy, so she threw herself at him, punching, and he reeled back, grabbing at her. "You traitor!" she yelled.

The Barrier of Pain

"All the time you've known things, about me, about the land, about what she did back there. And you don't like the killing, do you? You don't like what the Watch does to people."

He had her wrists, tight.

"There's only one way you could know," she gasped. "Sense-lines. You've got sense-lines! You were a keeper!"

"No!" He pushed her off. "I was never . . ."

"Don't be coy, lover." Scala's horse sidestepped. "Tell her the truth." When he wouldn't speak, she said, "He nearly was. Didn't make the final test. But he's good enough for me."

Carys was furious, and it wasn't all pretense. "You used what they taught you against them!"

"It's just what you do against the Watch."

"The Watch is evil! I know it. And you know it too!"

She grabbed at him and swung him toward her. "Think about Mathravale. Go on, face it! Think about what she is!"

Something rustled in the trees. Scala jerked around, but neither of them was looking at her now. "I do think about her." Quist's voice was a whisper. "That's why I stay. To keep her from—"

"You can't change her."

"I can. She despises the Watch too."

Scala swung back, amused. "Only when it suits me."

"She does." Quist was pacing now, deep in his own anxiety. "When we get the reward, we'll leave, go somewhere far off. Away from the Watch."

"It's a dream! She won't change. I should know: I used to be just like her."

Quist stopped. "But you're not now," he said.

The words silenced her. And instantly, before she could move or prevent it, his eyes widened and he gasped, "They're here!"

An arrow slashed from the trees; it missed Scala by a hairsbreadth. With a squeal, she fired back. The horses reared and whinnied. Then at least fifty men stepped out and aimed bows at them. After a grim second Scala climbed down from her horse. "If you knew about this and didn't tell me, lover," she snarled, "I'll never forgive you."

"Carys." Galen was behind her. The relief of seeing him after all this time was so great, she almost ran to him; then she controlled it, smiled, and walked over.

The Barrier of Pain

"This wasn't in the plan. Not that I'm complaining."

"Plans change."

It was then that she saw how grim he looked, how haunted. She glanced behind him; the Sekoi raised an elegant hand. "Where's Raffi?" she asked quickly.

THE TWO WATCHMEN WERE BACK. They came in and held him down in the chair, one on each side. He barely noticed, staring at the box, so cold with fear that it hurt him to breathe. It was full of a swarming mass of worms. Tiny, blind things they were, obscenely pale. They spilled and wriggled like bubbling milk, a loathsome heap of unending hunger. "We keep them in metal," the interrogator said quietly. "They eat through everything else."

Raffi was shaking, he knew it. Ashamed, he knew too that this was what he had feared for years, in nightmares, hiding under hedges, ever since he had understood what happened to keepers.

"You know what they do, of course." The interrogator had taken out a pair of finest chain-mail gloves; now he slipped them on, without haste. "We use just one, at first, on your chest, or your back. In seconds it will have burrowed its way deep into your flesh. It will eat its way through you with remarkable speed, an agony of searing pain. And then we will add another. And another. They tell me it is all but unbearable." He stood. "I've seen what they leave of a man, keeper, and it isn't pleasant."

The Watchmen grabbed Raffi. He squirmed and fought desperately. The interrogator put his hands on the table and leaned over. His voice changed suddenly, became quick and low. "For your own sake, Raffi, you must tell us. What are the Crow's plans? Where does his power come from?"

"I don't know," he gasped.

"What's the point of needless pain? You'll tell us anyway, you know that. You know your own weaknesses. I could help you."

"No."

Struggling, he prayed for a mind-flare. Nothing came.

"Galen wouldn't want you to suffer. He'd tell you to . . ."

"NO." He shook his head, screaming it out. "No! *NO!*"

The Barrier of Pain

The man straightened. The coldness slid back over his face like a lid. "I see," he said distantly. He took a pair of fine tweezers from his pocket and reached into the box with them, delicately lifting one tiny worm and bringing it around the table.

Raffi fought and screamed. "No!" he yelled. "Flain! *Flain!*"

AN EXPLOSION ROCKED THE ROOM; the lights flickered. The interrogator was so surprised, he almost dropped the tweezers. He stood over Raffi, listening. Another crash, immensely loud. At once he swiveled. "What's going on! Find out!" A Watchman ran out hurriedly. The interrogator's eyes looked down at Raffi in fury. "It's a pity they're too late," he whispered.

Raffi moved with the strength of raw panic. He flung the guard forward so that both men crashed into the table. The box tipped; the Watchman let out a scream of terror. Raffi dived around the mess, out of the door, and ran.

Noise boomed and rang around him, the whole building echoing and throbbing. Left, right, heedless, sobbing and praying, he raced into the dark, down corridors and endless stairways, always down because there was no other way to go. The darkness was thick and airless. Voices rang; once he was sure he heard Carys calling for him and he yelled and screamed her name, banging in the dark against the smooth Maker walls.

And then faintly down at the turn of another black, suffocating corridor, someone said, "Raffi."

"Galen!" He ran, so weak all at once he could hardly keep upright, and the figure waited for him, tall in the darkness. As he came up, he was gabbling in foolish relief. "I'm sorry, I'm so sorry. About everything. This is all my fault. Where's Carys? Where is everyone?"

The shadow did not answer or move. Raffi stopped. Miles back, in the pounding darkness, someone was screaming. He licked his lips. "You're not Galen," he whispered.

A faint mustiness stirred in the darkness. "No." The voice was dry and crackling. "I'm not Galen," it said.

The Crucible of Fire

19

Who can speak of the beauty of Earth?
Not Flain, not Theriss.
Who could bear to remember its loss?
Not one of the Makers.

Litany of the Makers

THE FIRST THING HE KNEW—long before he woke—was that he was warm. Furs were piled on him, and under them were silken sheets, and he was comfortable, so comfortable that his whole body was as relaxed as ever he could remember. Then fear came back and ruined it. He sat up abruptly.

It was dark. Across the room a brazier glowed red with hot coals. He looked around, listening intently, but there was no sound. He swung his feet quickly out of the bed. On the stool next to it were some new clothes, folded and sweet-smelling, and water in a crystal bowl and some soap. He ignored it, heading straight for the door, his legs weak.

It was locked. He shook the handle quietly, then turned his back on it and looked around. It was the room he had seen in the vision on Sarres, so long ago now. The room where the Margrave had been writing. There was the desk, a high, peculiar structure, and behind it the dim outlines of spheres, and shelves of piled books, statues, relics. The room was crammed with objects.

He couldn't remember how he had gotten here. He had seen the Margrave in the corridor, and after that there was darkness, a blur of fever. He had been ill, he knew. The long torment had been too much for him; even now his limbs ached, though his head was clear. Perhaps it had been days. Someone had given him drinks. Wiped his face. Someone. Something.

Panic gripped him. How long had he been here? He tried a sense-line, and instantly felt sick and dizzy. All around him things were distorted and strange. And he must be miles belowground; all its weight lay on his mind. He stank too. He was still wearing his old clothes. Slowly he crossed to the water and looked at it, and then washed, reluctant at first and then enjoy-

ing the freshness and sweet smell of the soap, scrub-
bing his tangled hair clean. When he had finished, it
was almost a shame to pull his ragged shirt back on,
but he did. Then he put a hand out and fingered the
new clothes.

"I had them brought especially for you." The Margrave
stood in the doorway. When Raffi didn't answer, it came
in, closing the door behind it, a deft, small movement. All
the old fear came with it, swallowing him. It came like a
wave and stole his breath, his heart thudding in his chest.
He backed away. The Margrave stood still.

"So we really meet at last, Raffi. And you see me. I'm
not, am I, as terrible as they say?"

Raffi swallowed. Then he surprised himself and managed one syllable. "No."

The creature was taller than a man, but slender. The
face, in this eternal dimness, had jewel-bright eyes with
heavy lids that blinked quickly, and a snout almost like
a jackal's, but it was still a face. Its skin was reptilian, an iridescent shimmer of tiny regular scales, faintly
gold in this light. It smiled. "Good. I am not so beautiful that I keep a looking glass, but the tales the Order

tells of men that die when they see me are unjustified. And insulting. But then, I am evil, am I not? And evil must be ugly."

Raffi swallowed. "Please," he whispered, "let me go."

The Margrave's smile widened, though it had no lips. As it walked its stiff robe rustled. "Now, Raffi, you've only just come. Do something for me. Wear those new clothes."

"No," he said.

"Yours are filthy!"

"I don't want anything from you."

"That's foolish. I suppose you won't eat, either?" The Margrave drew aside, and a servant came in, carrying a tray. Raffi gasped. The servant was a Sekoi. Or had been. Its face had no intelligence, no expression. The short fur was black, its clothes dark velvet, as rich as the Margrave's. With its seven fingers it unloaded dishes of meat and rice and honeyed cakes and a flask of wine. Then it went out, never saying a word.

Raffi stared after it. "What have you done to it!"

The Margrave came and sat near the brazier, the lurid glow lighting its face. "Nothing. There are two of them left—the remnants of one of Kest's programs on longevity. It was never a success and they lost their intelligence through it. They have no speech, and can do only menial tasks. They are hardly companions." It reached over and took a piece of meat, dipping it into the sauce and eating with a flicker of a long tongue. "You see. Not poisoned."

Raffi came and looked at the food. The smell of it made his empty stomach groan. He reached out and took some meat, and ate it.

"Excellent." The Margrave leaned back. "As Carys would say, starving is no use."

He swallowed, hard. "You know about Carys."

"About all of you. Remember, I traveled with you. Or rather, Solon did."

The name jerked Raffi back to himself. He dropped the food and turned away. The Margrave clicked its long tongue irritably. "Ah. Now, that was a mistake. I should have known you would resent all that."

"Resent it!" Raffi turned in fury. "You destroyed him! An old man . . ." He stopped. "Look, what do you want with me? Is it information? Is it to know where Sarres is, where the Coronet is? If so, you'd better call your

Watch thugs and start the interrogation all over again, because I'll never tell you anything." He was shaking, but the Margrave poured wine calmly. Its hands were scaled, with short, ridged nails.

"I never expected you to."

"Then why bring me here!"

"I brought you here to save your life. You have been ill, Raffi, and I have cared for you. For many days." It drank, watching him over the rim. Then it lowered the cup and said, "Your master Galen and his army of thieves attacked Maar."

"WHAT!" Raffi sank into a cushioned chair.

The Margrave's strange eyes blinked. "I warn you, Raffi, this will not be pleasant news for you. But I feel you are strong enough now to know the worst. Prepare yourself." It looked away. "Galen used his Maker-power to open the door of Maar. It was quite extraordinary. No one else in a hundred years has ever managed it. He and your other friends—including Carys, by the way—stormed the building. Or tried to. But Maar was the Makers' first work on the planet and they built it to last. And to defend itself. Laser weapons were triggered, crisscrossing the plain with light, and all the internal force-fields reactivated. As well as a few modifications of my own, of course. With a garrison of four thousand men against them, your friends had no chance."

"I didn't see four thousand men," Raffi said coldly. "It seemed empty to me."

"Did it?"

"I don't believe they even exist."

The Margrave nodded. "Or the weapons."

Raffi was silent.

"Exactly. The Watch is immense, Raffi. You heard the explosions. Don't fool yourself. You know it would be carnage in such a battle."

"Galen," he said stubbornly, forcing the words out, "is more powerful than you."

The Margrave watched him. "Galen, I'm afraid, is dead."

"*No!*" He jumped up, storming off, blundering into the desk, gripping it tight. "I don't believe you!"

"I did not expect you to. Nonetheless, it is true. Galen and your friend the Sekoi prince were killed in the first attack. The warlord Alberic may have escaped. His body has not yet been identified, but many were burned beyond recognition, as you'd expect."

"And Carys?" He whispered it after a second, hating himself.

The Margrave sat back, looking into the hot coals sadly. "I'm sorry, Raffi," it said.

The room was so silent. Nothing sounded down here but the faint silvery tick of some relic in a corner. He didn't believe any of it. He wouldn't. They were all alive, up there in the sunlight. Galen was alive, and they would be searching for him. "I will never believe it," he whispered.

The Margrave shrugged. "I admire your loyalty, but it really makes no difference. You are here now. These are the Pits of Maar. And you will never leave them again." It stood over him. "I want no information from you, Raffi. There will be no torture. I care nothing for Sarres—the planet is dying quickly and Sarres will die with it. But I cannot face eternity without a companion, and I have chosen you."

Appalled, Raffi watched it as it went to the door and turned back.

The Crucible of Fire

"You will find the life easy, and pleasant. No work. No privations. Take some rest now. And welcome to Maar, Raffi."

The door slid shut in the dark. Raffi picked up the new clothes and fingered their richness. Then he flung them, coldly, furiously, onto the fire.

.

TERROR WAS ALL AROUND HIM. He lay curled up on the luxurious bed, waiting, listening to his heartbeat in the silence. Down here in this eternal darkness there was no day; he had no idea what the time was. He felt completely, miserably alone. He longed for Carys to talk to, to plan with; for the Sekoi's elegant stories, even for Galen's intense silences. For Galen most of all. But it hurt even to think of them.

He swore feverishly, over and over, that he would never, never believe they were dead. He had to have faith, in them and in the Makers. And it had been like this for Flain once, lost in the Underworld, and he had found his way out, and all the planet had risen into spring. Flain had been in this hell before him. The words of the Litany came to him and he murmured them aloud to the shadows:

I have been dead. I have been alive. There is nowhere that I have not been.

They had said it on the hill at Sarres. How long ago that seemed.

"I DON'T GIVE UP EASILY." The Margrave picked at its breakfast with a ridged hand. Its voice was full of clicks and rolls and small crackles. "You must wear my clothes, Raffi. It means nothing . . ."

"It does to me."

"You feel that because of your training. The Order puts too much significance into such things. I just want you to be comfortable now you are a little better."

"I am," he said, between gritted teeth. The brazier had gone out in the night and the Margrave had given no orders for it to be relit. He couldn't stop shivering.

The Margrave smiled. "I could have the Sekoi put the clothes on you forcibly."

"That wouldn't mean anything to you, though. No victory."

The Crucible of Fire

It looked at him with bright eyes. "Quite right. Raffi,
I can't tell you what a joy it is to talk to someone like
you!"

Raffi picked at the fruit. He had to find things out.
Much as he hated it. "How long have you been alone?
Don't you speak to the Watch?"

"I give my orders to the Watchlords through relics.
Later, you'll see them. And the Sekoi are dumb."

"You said . . ." Raffi shivered, squirming back in the
seat. "That you'd spoken to Kest."

"Of course." The Margrave blinked in surprise. "Raffi,
Kest created me. Or rather, bred me. I'm the result—the
only successful result—of his most ambitious program, to
synthesize a form of life with the intelligence of a rational
being and the physical strengths of certain animals. Earth
fauna, mostly."

"Earth?" Raffi whispered.

"Ah, yes. A word not to be spoken. One of the Order's
most holy words." The creature made a strangled rustling
creak in its throat; Raffi realized it was laughing. "What
is Earth, Raffi?"

"Earth is the paradise of the Makers." He gave the

311

response reluctantly. It sounded like a betrayal in this place. "After death, we will go there through a door of air."

"Will we now?" The Margrave nodded, amused. "And have you seen images of this place?"

"Once. In the House of Trees." He was caught for a second by the memory of those pictures, the blue sky, the trees, the millions of brilliant and varied creatures.

The Margrave was watching him closely. Its smile faded; it sat back, almost sadly. "It is hard to have to break such wonder as yours. Such innocence. But Kest told me about Earth. And I have images here . . ." It stopped, and then went on gently, "Images of famine, of deserts, of people living in such conditions that you would not—"

"Liar!" Raffi couldn't bear this. "Why are you doing this to me!"

"It's the truth. They destroyed their paradise. They were always seeking to make it again."

"NO."

"Yes, Raffi. Not all at once, but gradually. They could never stop, you see, modifying, interbreeding, experimenting, even on themselves."

The Crucible of Fire

Raffi stood up, pacing quickly among the cluttered furniture. It hurt to breathe. "I know what you're doing. Trying to make me hate them. To sympathize with you."

"I'm telling you the truth." The Margrave sounded mild, matter-of-fact. "Kest explained many things to me. And I spoke to Flain too, when he would deign to come and stare at me. And that bully Tamar." From the corner of its eye it watched Raffi's horror. Then it stood and picked up the new dark velvet jacket it had brought and propped it around Raffi's shoulders. For a second, in his utter disbelief, he didn't even notice, tugging the jacket tight.

"How can you speak about them like that!"

"They were men, Raffi."

"I know, but . . ."

"They were men. Just like Galen. As full of faults."

He stared at it, then noticed the coat and flung it down. But he could not stop shivering.

20

It is the small things that are of most account.

Poems of Anjar Kar

"WHERE ARE WE GOING?"

Ahead, the Margrave walked the dim corridor, the tiny blue lights at floor level casting bizarre shadows under its eyes and snout. "I promised I would show you my communications room. It's not far." It was carrying the second bundle of clothes, even richer than the first, under one arm. Raffi came behind, shivering and uneasy. It was the first time he had been out of the cluttered room; that place almost seemed a refuge now. His fear had ebbed; he realized that he could not hold on to such terror, not for day after day. It was already shrinking, becoming a small cold numbness at the heart of him. He would forget how afraid he should be. He would start to make mistakes.

The corridor was Maker-smooth, and straight. The Margrave came to a doorway, pressed a button. The door slid back, and the creature waved him inside.

He should be concentrating. Carys would already have started counting the doors, remembering the turns right and left. He needed to do that. Without sense-lines, he needed to think like the Watch.

The only things in the room were a gigantic screen, silver-gray, and a chair. The Margrave looked up at the screen. "I've made a few arrangements," it said. Its eyes were bright, but it almost seemed uneasy, putting the pile of clothing down and running a thumbnail along the scales of its ridged face. "I'm sorry about this, Raffi, but you leave me little choice. Operate."

The screen lit. To Raffi's astonishment a man's face filled it; a man he recognized as one of the overseers at Cato's Cleft. The man seemed nervous.

"We can see them." The Margrave's whisper was dry. "But they cannot see us. I prefer it that way." Raising its voice, it said, "Bring the prisoner." The Watchman moved out of sight. For a second there was only the familiar bedlam of the work sledges; then another man was hauled down in front of the screen, filthy and bewildered. Raffi's heart leaped. It was Silas. He looked terrible. His shoulders were a mass of bruises, his face disfigured by a long welt down one cheek. He looked around wildly.

"What have they done to him?" Raffi whispered.

The Margrave smiled its lipless smile. "Why don't you ask him?"

Raffi licked his lips. Then he said, "Silas?"

The man's eyes widened. He looked around incredulously. "Who's that?"

"It's me. Raffi. Silas, listen . . ."

"Raffi! Where are you? Are you dead?"

"No. I'm speaking to you through this relic. I can see you."

Silas made a fumbling sign of Protection. The Margrave gave its creaky laugh and sat in the chair, observing. Raffi tried to ignore its jewel-cold eyes.

"I'm sorry, lad." Silas was almost hoarse. "About telling them . . . should never have. Scared . . . too scared. Should have kept my mouth shut . . ."

"It doesn't matter. What have they done to you?"

"Beaten. To tell them more, but all I know is what you said in your sleep. Mixed-up things—but Raffi, how can you be talking to me?"

"I can't explain." Raffi glanced at the Margrave. His heart was thudding. Silas raised his hand to scratch his filthy hair; his arms were manacled tight. "Raffi," he whispered. "I'm finished. Surely this time I'm finished. Tomorrow . . ." He stopped, staring in horror at something out of the picture.

"Tomorrow, what?" Raffi stepped forward.

"I'm for the gallows." The man was terrified; it came from the screen like an evil smell. "Can you do anything, Raffi? How was it you got free? Can you help me, you and your Order? For God's sake, can you help me?" He seemed to choke into grief and terror.

Raffi faced the Margrave. He was beginning to understand. The pile of clothes lay by the Margrave's chair. The creature looked down at them calmly. "A small price to pay for a man's life," it whispered.

"I detest you." Raffi's voice was icy.

The Margrave scratched its scales. "I feared," it said

sadly, "that this would set our friendship back a little."

Hands shaking, Raffi undid his old jacket. He threw it down, and it was torn and infested, but he seemed to throw his old life down with it, and the lump in his throat and chest hurt him as he drew breath. The shirt next, and the trousers, as the Margrave watched gravely and Silas rubbed his face and whispered, "Raffi? Are you still there?"

"I'm still here," he said grimly, hot with humiliation. The clothes were darkest velvet and silk, a Watch uniform, but more costly than any he'd ever seen, with the finest threads of silver embroidery. They felt stiff and strange as he shrugged into them, and warm too, their fastenings new, their smell sweet, the touch of them on his skin hateful.

"Can you help me?" Silas was desperate.

He kicked his old boots off and pulled the new ones on, silent, raw with the bitterness of betrayal. Then he stared at the Margrave. "Yes. I can help you."

The creature was smiling. "So much better! Now you really look like my apprentice."

"I've promised him . . ."

"And I will honor your promise. Whatever you have

here, he will have. Warm clothes, good food, if you want them for him, you have to take them from me. If you rebel, he will be beaten. If you try to escape, he will be punished. Not you." It settled back and pointed a clawed finger. "This is what power is. Raffi. You have it now. You must use it."

Raffi was so angry, he could barely speak, but as he turned back the Margrave said quietly, "Operate screen," and Silas's eyes widened in his bruised face.

"Raffi! Dear God! I can see you!"

"It'll be all right," Raffi said heavily. "They'll treat you well."

But Silas's joy had already become suspicion. "Look at you! You look like a prince! What have you done! What have you sold them?"

"Myself." Raffi's face was bleak; the man on the screen backed away.

"You've joined them. My God, boy, I never thought . . ."

"It's not like that . . ."

"You sicken me!" Silas's face was harder than he'd ever seen it. "Keep your pity. I don't take favors from the Watch."

The Crucible of Fire

It was useless to say anything. Except, "Listen! What happened at Maar? To the Crow? Was there some sort of battle?"

"Don't pretend you don't know." Silas turned away in disgust.

"I don't! Please!" His voice broke; Silas turned.

"What's going on, Raffi? It wasn't a battle, it was a war! Do you mean you haven't—" The screen went black.

Raffi gave a howl of rage and swung around. The Margrave held up its hands in apology. "I'm sorry. But why be distressed? And you see the ingratitude of the traitor who feels betrayed."

"He helped me."

"And now you are helping him."

"He hates me. You saw. And what about the others! If you've taken Galen prisoner, if he's down here somewhere too . . ."

"He's dead, Raffi. Believe me, I wish it otherwise. I would have liked to talk to Galen." It went to the door, opened it, and looked back. "I could have told him so much about the Makers." Without waiting for him, it went out. Heartsick, Raffi followed. From the door he turned and saw his old clothes lying crumpled on the floor. Like a body the life had ebbed out of.

HE WAS FORGETTING THE LITANY. It had to be nerves, or fear, or weariness, but he was mistaking some of the words, and it didn't help not knowing the right times for prayer, not ever knowing if it was night or day. Or maybe it was the darkness, the terrible darkness seeping into him like a mist, blotting out the edges of his memory. Maybe it was closing in, hour by hour and he didn't know, until it would overwhelm him . . . The Litany, and some parts of the Book. He should have learned them better. Galen would never have forgotten.

There were other books here. The Margrave had stocked the room with amusements for him: statues, books, games, globes, a microscope, and even a cage of jermice that played and rolled and cuddled and slept in a furry pile until the Margrave went too close and they squeaked and hid. At first Raffi had ignored all of it, sullen and despairing; then he had realized the mice would die if he didn't look after them. It was the same as Silas. The Margrave made sure he had no choice. The books were about Earth. He would not even touch them.

The creature was so clever, it terrified him. It would talk for hours about the Makers, about the early days, the way they had worked on the planet, forming it, creating its life. Sitting in the cozy glow of the brazier, its eyes caught the tawny light, and despite himself Raffi was fascinated, lulled by its crackling husky voice and long, jointed fingers.

The musky smell no longer bothered him; maybe he had stopped noticing it. He tried to keep his sense of the creature as horrific, reminded himself that it was a monster, that it had created the Watch, that it was evil, but he knew, helplessly, hour by lost hour his hatred of it was being diluted as it smiled and talked and told him how delighted it was he was there. And how could he pray to hold on to hatred? Was that right? Was hatred—even of evil—ever right?

He tried fasting, but the Margrave knew. It came and stood at his door and said, "Remember Silas, Raffi. He's a little hungry today," and he used that, made himself angry and bitter and somehow felt better. That was the night he tried the sense-lines.

He lay on the bed and carefully opened his third eye. It hurt him, and he knew the aftereffects of the Journey lingered like a soreness in his mind. Gently, he let the sense-line move, into the dark. He touched things. Living things.

They were animals, or lower forms of life. None of them had the intelligence and memory of the trees. None of them could answer him; their minds moved blindly, rubbing and nuzzling against his. He tried to identify species, but they were all wrong, distorted, and there was pain, and things so alien, they made him shudder. And beyond them, once he had pushed through, was nothing but darkness, miles of darkness pressing down, suffocating him.

He jerked back and opened his eyes, gasping for air. He had never liked enclosed spaces; now for a second he had to fight off the desire to run to the door and bang wildly against it and yell.

Slowly he relaxed, unclenching his fingers, breathing deeply. When his heart had stopped hammering he decided on his plan. The sense-lines were his only way out. He would have to climb with them, use them as a rope. Each night, whenever he was alone, he would climb higher, feeling through rock and stone, forcing his mind up. It might take months, but he would do it. Once he reached the level of the deepest roots, it would be easy.

Carys would have approved. *Would* approve.

"I JUST THINK YOU SHOULD see a little more of our kingdom." The Margrave stood by the open door and smiled. "Something tells me you're feeling a little trapped in here." Today it was wearing purple, a deep long robe of it, and under the quilted hems, a dark suit. Raffi followed, silent.

The uniform made him feel like a stranger, grave and tall; his hair was so clean now that it shone, and he was eating far too well. The food was a constant temptation; he tried to be moderate, but the flavors and sweetnesses were so new, and he seemed to crave them, his hand always reaching out for more.

He had never eaten so much. Now he walked alongside the creature. "You didn't make this place."

"They did. Kest added a great deal later. This was the heart of their operations."

"Not Tasceron?"

"Oh, Tasceron was built later," the Margrave said airily. "This was the hub of the planet making. What you call the awen-field. Look."

It stopped at a huge door and opened it. Raffi saw a chamber so immense that the ends of it were shrouded in darkness. Small blue lights winked at him. The vast, dim shapes of huge machines, taller than Watchtowers, hummed quietly.

The Margrave waved a hand. "These control the geophysical nature of Anara. They are accessed by various . . . relics. All lost, I'm afraid, except for the precious Coronet, which is why I was so anxious to get hold of it. When the moon Agramon was moved, these machines were recharged, just for a moment. You should have heard the roar, Raffi. Now they are running down again." It laughed throatily. "Such an irony, that if Solon had gained the Coronet, I would have had control of the

The Crucible of Fire

Unfinished Lands. What an opportunity lost. You and your friends might have saved the world. But you might also have condemned it to death."

Raffi shook his head, aghast. "You wanted it to save the Finished Lands?"

"Why else?"

"To use as a weapon. We thought—"

"I know what you thought." It closed the door and moved on, its voice bitter. "I have lived down here for centuries because of what the Order teaches. And the terrible, unforgiving Sekoi."

"But . . . could those machines and the Coronet really save the Unfinished Lands? And what about this wall?"

The Margrave laughed. "The Wall! It amused me to see them scrambling over it like ants. Who can wall out chaos, Raffi? It will creep in, spore and bacterium. No, these machines only will save us, but their power is fluctuating. But we two will live, whatever happens up there."

Raffi stopped. He couldn't bear this. "We have to use them! To save—"

"Who? The Watch? You hate the Watch."

"Everyone! Galen! Carys!"

"Ah, still holding on. What if I don't know how to use them?"

"We have to find out! All those people!" He had hold of its sleeve. It smiled at him and he stepped back instantly.

The Margrave watched, an outline in the dimness. "My scholar has a great deal to learn," it hissed. "I am not Galen. I am not concerned with the dregs of a planet. My task, Raffi, is far more interesting."

It opened a new door and walked in. As Raffi came after it his mind reeled with the sudden stench. "Look," the Margrave said fondly. "The laboratories of Kest. Of my father, Kest."

21

The supreme tactical triumph of the
Watch came at Mathravale, where the
final remnant of the sorcerous Order
was rooted out, and vast numbers of
keepers cut down. Shrines were burned,
supporters relocated. On this day the
Order died. Brave men and women
were caught in the crossfire. The Watch
has cared for their descendants, as they
would have wished.

Textbook; Glorious History of the Watch

"HOW IS HE?"

The surgeon turned in surprise. "As well as you'd ex-pect, with those burns. It could go either way."

Carys nodded unhappily. She pushed the relic-buttons and the door slid open, Maker-silent. Like all the rooms in the Tower of Maar, this one was dim. Alberic's extravagant bed had been set up in the center; it was surrounded with ranks of candles on stands, and Milo was sitting on a small stool, silent and pale.

The Sekoi turned. "Come in, Carys. He's awake."

"Of course I'm blasted well awake. And cut the hushed

tones, Graycat. I'm not dead yet." Alberic's face looked small on the huge pillows. "Oh. It's you."

Carys came over and sat. "Still as mouthy."

"Too right." His voice was a rasp of pain. "I knew as soon as you turned up we'd hit trouble. You were always trouble. Milo!"

"Yes, Uncle?" The boy scrambled up quickly.

"Wine. A big cup."

"But . . . the surgeon says . . ."

"Hang the surgeon from his own sutures. Chop the toe rag into shark meat. Get it."

Milo looked at Carys, and went out.

"You shouldn't do this," the Sekoi said. It looked around at Godric and Sikka. "You must tell him."

"The chief does what he wants," Godric said acidly. He came over and helped the dwarf to sit up, plumping the pillow behind him.

"And if I fall off the perch, Godric"—Alberic coughed, his face white as paper—"for Flain's sake, take over. That kid has the brains of an addled gnat."

"All right, Chief. Take it easy. We were all young once."

The Crucible of Fire

Alberic glared. "Not me. Now, where's this carnival the keeper's called."

"He'll be along." Godric took the wine cup from Milo and held it gently to Alberic's lips. "A sip! Not too much."

Alberic took no notice. He grabbed the cup, downed half its contents, and sighed. Then he mopped a red drop from his chin with a starched white handkerchief. "Get off me," he croaked.

Carys grinned at the Sekoi. The creature shook its head sadly. Its right arm was heavily bandaged, and she knew that Godric had caught some of the fire too; he limped when he thought no one was looking. She'd been lucky.

The door snicked open; Galen stalked in, and behind him Quist and Scala, with two of Alberic's heavies. They stared at the bed in amazement. The keeper came over and looked down. "You look terrible," he said quietly.

Alberic smiled, a grimace of pain. "Don't get your hopes up. I'm not going to your ragtag Makers."

"I doubt they'd have you. If you want to unburden yourself of your evil doings . . ."

"Get lost, keeper. It would take weeks. You'll have to wait for my autobiography."

Galen nodded. His black hair was tied back; his eyes were dark as he looked down at the tiny figure. "You have great courage, Alberic, for a man of such little faith. We may have come farther than we think."

"Yes. Indeed." The dwarf drank waspishly. "God, the worst thing I ever did was go looking for you. Life was simple. Eat, cheat, steal. Now look at me. For Flain's sake, get on!"

Galen turned. Among the massed candles, his shadows flickered huge on the walls. "First, casualties. Sikka?"

The fair girl was sitting on the bed. She said, "Eighty-six injured, thirteen seriously. Deaths have gone up to forty—Kalesha went this morning."

Grim, Galen nodded. After a moment he turned to Carys. "The search?"

"Finished." She stood up, as if reporting to some spymaster. "The entire building is empty, as far as we can find out. There are twenty-eight levels belowground, mostly unlit, and we've had parties going over every inch. There are relics everywhere, Galen, and I don't know what any of them do, except the descending rooms—there are four of those." She hesitated, not wanting to remind him, but it had to be said. "No one was here except the dead man at the gate and whoever was in that interrogation chamber."

They had found the room early yesterday; one of Godric's men had come staggering back out of it, yelling in stark terror, beating imaginary worms off his clothes. When she and Galen had pushed past him, they had seen nothing but a spilled table and chairs and on the floor a terrifying, ugly mass of worms, hideous threads of red. She had recognized them at once. So had Galen.

She looked at him now. "There were two people in there at least." The undigested fragments had told them that; teeth, fingernails, the metal clasp of a belt, though no one had dared to go and look too closely. The room was locked, with an uneasy guard outside.

"Yes," Galen said. "And Raffi had been there. But I tell you, Carys, he is not dead."

She looked at the Sekoi, who cleared its throat gently. "Galen, we have to consider the possibility . . ."

"He's not dead." The keeper sat on a chair and looked up, eyes dark. "I know that."

"But there's no way out." Carys came over. "Where could he have gone?"

"He's with the Margrave. There must be miles of corridors below us, maybe sealed now, leading right down into the pits. He's there, Carys, I know it."

"Oh, let him believe it if it keeps him happy." To her surprise, the peevish voice was Alberic's. The dwarf waved his wine cup at Scala. "Can't we pull a few fingernails off her and find out?"

Scala twisted her red lips into a smile. "Don't waste your time, little man. Maar's a mystery to me. All I know is that we've lost a great deal of money."

Alberic grinned. "Speak for yourself, sweetie. Your ransom won't be small."

"You won't live to collect it. Half the Watch will be camped outside here in hours."

There was silence. They all knew that was true. The Battle for Maar had been short and deadly, but it wasn't over yet. Carys had dreamed again last night of the terrible searing lights that had scorched from the cube, of the strange energy fields that Alberic's front rank had crashed into and died in, before Galen had summoned all the power he had to make the black arch that let them through. And then the nervous, shadowy progress through the echoing building, ambushed at each room and corner by sparks that leaped and killed, and shafts that opened without warning. Even now, who knew what traps were still lurking undiscovered?

The Sekoi shifted uncomfortably. "The castellan is right, Galen. We must plan quickly. If we are to withdraw . . ."

"Withdraw!" Galen looked up sharply. "We're not withdrawing. I, for one, am going into the Unfinished Lands. I'm going down into Maar, and the pits are the quickest way."

They were silent. Carys had known it would come to this. "Count me in," she said quietly.

"Carys . . ."

"Don't, Galen. I want to find Raffi too. And I've some unfinished business of my own."

Quist was looking at her. He said, "You'll die there. No one can live there."

She looked at him sourly. "No one asked you. Your part in this is over."

Galen stood; Quist rose to face him. They eyed each other.

"I can't believe," Galen said bitterly, "that any keeper . . ."

"I wasn't a keeper; I was a scholar. I ran away. Like yours did. Maybe like yours, I couldn't go through with it."

"To the Watch! In God's name . . ."

"I soon came to hate the Watch. But it had the only thing I wanted." Quist looked sidelong at Scala; she made a small pout and said, "You stayed because I blackmailed you, lover."

"No, I stayed because of you."

Scala looked at Galen. "He's so weak, you see? A complete romantic fool. That's what your Order makes of people."

Galen's eyes were black with fury. "And you're not weak. You simply murder the unarmed and the defenseless."

"That's right." Her gaze was steely; then she looked at Quist with quiet amusement. "But I know him. He's always trying to impress me. Any second now, he'll be telling you he's coming down with you into Maar."

The candles flickered; all the shadows jumped. "Are you?" Galen said quietly.

The Crucible of Fire

Quist said, "Yes. Think about it; you'll need me. I have sense-lines. I can be of some use."

"To find Raffi? You don't even know him."

"To find the truth. To find out who gives the orders. Don't you think the Watch have a right to know it too?"

After a second, Galen limped away; then abruptly he turned. "All right. I haven't got time to argue. But if you betray us down there . . ."

Quist raised his hands.

"And she stays here."

"She certainly does." Alberic wheezed from his bed. "She's four thousand marks on the hoof and she stays with me." He raised his cup to Scala, who looked disgusted.

"So the three of us will go." Galen's voice was somber; there was a split second of silence before the Sekoi languidly said the words Carys had been praying for.

"Four of us."

They all looked at it. It shrugged graciously. "I miss the small keeper."

Galen was watching, intent. The Crow power moved around him, strange shadows and drafts that agitated all the flames. "Ever since Tasceron," he said, his voice a whisper, "you've stayed with us, when you could have gone. To Sarres, to the Great Hoard. Now even to Maar. Why should a Sekoi care so much for Starmen?"

The creature's yellow eyes widened. It seemed a little overcome. "Because we are friends, Galen. We have become friends."

The keeper came up to it and nodded. "I'm very glad of it," he said. "But what do you seek in Maar?"

The Sekoi did not answer.

"All very touching." Alberic coughed painfully on the pillows. "And I suppose now you expect my boys and girls to gallantly hold off tens of thousands while you nobly sacrifice yourselves to martyrdom."

Galen turned. "That's the idea."

"Well, I'll admit the place is good for it. It's worth ten of Halen's castle, and if we can get those hot weapons on the roof to work, I'll fry a few Watchpatrols to a crisp. But get this, Galen. We're not staying around. We're taking anything not nailed down and clearing, as soon as I can scrape myself from this bed. But then, it won't worry you. You won't be coming back."

The Crucible of Fire

"Oh, I'll be back." The Relic Master came over and looked down at him. "You don't get rid of me that easily, thief-lord."

"Get rid of you!" Alberic growled. "I seem to have been trying for years."

CARYS EMPTIED THE PACK. Then she put in water, the food supplies, her lodestone, a spare crossbow, a warm coat. It felt heavy and bulky. She packed the pockets with crossbow bolts. When she'd finished, she took off the Watch uniform and dressed in her old clothes, lacing the green jerkin up. Finally she pulled the insignia—her own—from her neck and dangled the tiny silver discs over the pile of clothes. Then she dropped them.

"So what is this business of your own?" Galen was leaning in the doorway, looking at her. He had his dark coat and his stick, and wore both sets of awen-beads, intertwined, she noticed. She didn't want to tell him. Then abruptly changing her mind, she said, "Mathravale."

He knew the name. His look was sharp. "What does that horror have to do with you?"

"My parents were there. Probably." She didn't tell him Quist had been there too; this was not the time for the black fury that would bring. "I found out that the children from Mathravale had been taken to Marn Mountain. So that solves a few mysteries, doesn't it?"

Galen came into the room. "I'm sorry, Carys," he said. "It must have been a shock."

"Not really." She laced the pack quickly. "I never knew them—not that I remember."

"Still . . ."

"Leave it, Galen." She turned. "Don't tell me they were martyrs for the Makers and that it was good, or that I should take time to grieve over them. I never knew them. It's myself I'm grieving for."

"They *were* martyrs. And it is good." He folded his arms, unmoving, then glanced over at the crumpled uniform. She followed his gaze and swung the pack up. "Yes. I've finished with the Watch. Forever. No more spying, no more lies. It's over." When he wouldn't move out of her way, she laughed drily. "I thought you'd be pleased."

"Raffi would. When he found out we had both planned your capture he was so angry, Carys. I have never seen him so moved. It made me ashamed." He was silent a moment, his face dark with pain. Then he said, "But the Watch is more than a uniform. It's not so easy to put off. Carys, if you are coming with us for revenge . . ."

"I should leave it to you?" She came up to him. "After all, what is your oath for if not revenge, Galen?"

He nodded, gaunt-faced. "Maybe. But I've sworn it now."

As he turned away she said, "Will you do it? Will you kill that creature?"

His back was to her. She heard him breathe, then he said, "Yes." The answer was so quiet, she was hardly sure it was there.

THE GATE TO THE UNFINISHED LANDS was half buried, as if the land outside had bubbled and heaved up against it. The four of them stood there, with Godric and some of his men, and Scala, who had insisted on coming.

"Well, keeper. Graycat." The big man slapped their arms affectionately. "I don't suppose wishing you luck is any use. Flain keep you."

Galen gave him a blessing gravely. "And you, guard the warlord. He's not ready for the Makers. I have a great deal of work to do on him yet."

Godric roared with laughter. "You're a brave man, Galen. I hope you find the lad. I always had a soft spot for Raffi, since I first saw him scared stiff at that cromlech." He nodded at the men; they seized the blackened shell of the door and began to heave it open.

Scala moved up to Quist. "You don't have to do this. We can both be ransomed; I have a few contacts that owe me favors. We'll come out of it well. "

He looked down at her. "When I come back . . ."

"Fool. You won't come back." She looked piqued. "You're a fool, Captain."

Quist ignored her. "When I come back, I'll find you. I promise."

She stepped back. "It makes no difference to me, lover."

"Doesn't it?" he breathed.

The door creaked uneasily apart between them, the metal buckling and corroded. Through the gap a cold wind whistled, heavy with a foul yellow sleet. The Sekoi gave a mew of disgust. Galen gripped his stick and walked

The Crucible of Fire

straight through; Quist followed, with one last look at Scala, and Carys pulled up her hood and marched after them. Godric took out a gold coin and put it in the Sekoi's hand. "Your winnings. From last night's game."

Regretfully the Sekoi spun the coin, "I'm afraid," it said sadly, "there will be very little to spend it on." Tugging a scarf over its face, it followed the others.

The yellow sleet stank of sulfur. Godric watched it swirl in clouds beyond the door. "Get that thing closed," he said grimly.

22

I had thought this the darkest place of the soul, that there could be no worse, but I was wrong. For I had made evil into a shape and spoken to it, and it mocked me. It was my own face in a mirror; when I looked up it was always there.

Sorrows of Kest

"WHAT IN GOD'S NAME ARE THESE?" Raffi wandered down the rows of cages, appalled. Here were all the creatures of a world's nightmares: strange amalgams of species, things with spines and twisted limbs, extra organs, unimaginable diseases. The misery and horror of their minds hung around him in the darkness; he could barely breathe in it.

The beasts fled at his approach, dug themselves into straw. In one cage an apelike thing with pale, hairless skin hugged itself; in another, small snakes shed their skins rapidly, over and over.

"That's a little something for myself." The Margrave

gripped the mesh and looked at the snakes peevishly. "Skin-shedding I detest. I have to undergo it at regular intervals. Kest might have made my skin more durable than yours, but at a price, and I have long worked on the problem. Not with any degree of success."

"It will kill them," Raffi said miserably.

"Probably. It usually does."

He stared at it. Its jewel-bright eyes looked back. "I knew this would disturb you. My policy is to show you everything, Raffi. To hold nothing back. This way." It led him through workshop after workshop, dim gleaming palaces stuffy with heat, their Maker-surfaces reflecting the scuttling shapes of unknowable beasts, of vast machines and racks of glass vials and diagrams that flickered on lit screens. Underfoot, in the shadows, tiny things ran and squeaked.

"A few get out," the Margrave said idly. "Over the centuries they will no doubt have produced some interesting subspecies."

Raffi felt sick, and shaky. Down at the end of the room a dark Sekoi was cleaning out cages. "Why?" he whispered. "Why are you doing it? What is it all for?"

The Crucible of Fire

"Why am I doing it?" The Margrave looked astonished. "But Raffi, this is not my work. It's the Makers'."

He shook his head. "Kest's, you mean. You called him your father."

"So he was, genetically. Does that make me one of the Makers too?" It seemed amused with the idea, rustling into its breathy laugh. Then, seeing his stricken shock, it put a scaly hand on Raffi's shoulder. "Forgive me. This must be hard for you. Come down here."

It walked on quickly, a rustling slender shadow between the high cages. "You see, in your stories Kest had become the one who tampered, the one who created evil, and in a way that is true, but the harsh fact is, Raffi, that all the Makers manipulated genetic material. Some species they brought from Earth could not survive on Anara without modifications. That was the start of it. They introduced new strains of crops, more hardy breeds. But these species affected others. Populations rose or were made extinct; habitats began to be altered and the Makers found they had started something they could not control. Anara is a vibrant, teeming world. Vast colonies of insects spread diseases they had not even known of; interbreeding and mutation were rife; forests were destroyed, deserts appeared almost overnight. The very planet began to warp. They found they were not gods after all."

Raffi listened to it with dread. Its voice mocked him with pleasantry. Coming to a circular staircase, it led him down, muffled and echoing. "'Keep to the program,' Tamar kept saying. 'It will work out.' It never did."

The steps rang under his feet; the air was hot and sulfurous and they seemed to be deep in caves now, cut out of bedrock. Through his misery, Raffi saw that the floor was carved with great channels, and through them lava flowed, curling and crisping to cinders on top, always swept away. The heat was intense. Small bridges spanned the flows; in places huge holes gaped where steam hissed out.

The air was thick with strange gases; he almost choked, his eyes running with water, both hands over his nose and mouth.

The Margrave waved a proud hand. "The very depths of the Pits of Maar. The heart of Anara. There are tunnels down here I have not trodden in centuries. All under the planet's crust they run, who knows where. Once I spent months deep under the Tower of Song; another time I walked for hours through the drains and sewers up into the eternal darkness of Tasceron and explored its alleys, a muffled figure in the dark. So much is unknown, Raffi! So much we might never know."

Raffi whispered, "When they come back, we will."

The Margrave eyed him sadly through the jets of steam and the lurid fiery glow. "You already know, don't you," it said quietly, "that they are never coming back."

He wanted to answer, to scream defiance, to run, to get out, but the airlessness made him weak. He leaned wearily against the wall. "I can't breathe."

"I know. But I wanted to show you this place, because this is where I was born. In here."

It was a chamber in the center of the cave, a sphere of some crystalline glass. It rose out of the steamy chamber like a vast pearl. The Margrave reached out and smoothed its surface. "Kest called it the womb of the world," it said, its voice hoarse. "Flain said it was a crucible of fire."

Raffi stared through the shimmering air, stepping forward. For a second then, through the drift of gases, he had thought he had seen something inside, like a curled body, a mass of wires suspended in fluid. The air choked him. Chest heaving, he tried a sense-line, and knew at once.

"There's something alive in there."

The Margrave looked up at him, its eyes swiveling to his face. "Long ago, Raffi, I knew I could not live alone. Endlessly I have tried to repeat Kest's work." It turned and put both hands on the glass, leaning its face against the steamy heat. "But I cannot make another like myself," it whispered. *"Until I find one of the Sekoi's children."*

For a moment Raffi stood rigid; then he turned and stumbled up the stairs, gasping, tripping, clutching at the smooth hot rail, and when he had hauled himself to the top he doubled over, coughing and retching, his whole body cold with sweat. He crouched, desolate. He felt so alone, as if there were no world out there at all, no sky, no Sarres, that he was alone in this darkness, this terrible nightmare. "Galen." He said the name like a prayer. "Galen."

Behind him he heard the creature's rustle as it climbed up, but he couldn't face it yet, couldn't bear to see it. He stumbled numbly back to the cluttered room.

The Crucible of Fire

LATER, IT CAME IN AND SAT BESIDE HIM, near the brazier. For a while it was silent; then it touched the tray. "You haven't eaten."

"No." He stared listlessly into the flames. It was always cruelty he had feared; the savagery of the Watch. Not this. He hadn't been prepared for this. For kindness. For the creature's way of telling him its secrets. He should hate it—he did hate it, for what it had done, for the destruction of the Order. But if this was hatred, it was strange, it was like pity. Nothing was clear anymore. Nothing was clear.

The Margrave ate quietly, watching him, its long tongue flicking out after fragments.

Finally Raffi spoke. "You're trying to turn me against the Makers. It won't work."

"I'm telling you the truth."

"The Order knows the truth."

"The Order had legends and broken relics. Out of them it has created a dream. A beautiful, remarkable dream."

Raffi rubbed his head in both hands. He felt desperate. "They came from God. They were not evil."

"No, they were not evil. But they created evil. And as for God . . ." The Margrave gave a shrug. "Of that being, I have no knowledge." It smiled its lipless smile, the scales of its skin glistening. "When I was in Solon, and saw the body of Kest, Raffi, what a shock that gave me. To see him again, after so long. In all my long life he has been my only companion. He taught me everything, though he was a quiet, dry man, sparing with words. He had fallen out with Tamar and Flain and Soren, so he stayed here and worked with me. For years no one else even knew I existed. When they found out, they wanted to kill me. But in the end, they couldn't." It shrugged. "And it was too late. For Kest. For the planet."

"What were they like?" he whispered. "Really like?"

"Flain was tall indeed, a man with great authority but frayed with care. Tamar, frankly, I detested, and he me. His expertise was fauna development—perhaps he thought he should have created me himself. Soren, I rarely saw. The others, Theriss and Halen only once, when they came here at the end. Both had been made bitter by their ordeal."

Quite suddenly, the whole room shook. Far below, the machines made a great rumble. The Margrave stood anxiously, but the sound settled and it sat again, slowly. "They will fail soon," it muttered.

"Can I ask you something?" Raffi said absently.

"Of course."

"It's just that . . . in the Book it speaks of the seven Makers, but there are only ever six. Kest, Flain, Tamar, Halen, Soren, Theriss. The other one is never mentioned. There are no stories of him, no images. I asked Galen about it once, but he said it was the deepest secret of the Order and may well have been lost, but I'm sure he knew more than that." He bit his lip nervously. "Was it you they meant?"

The Margrave raised a scaly eyebrow. "I don't know. I know of only six. Though I was kept in here, and never went outside." It frowned. "I have only seen your precious sunlight dimly, Raffi, through Solon's eyes. Kest in his wisdom made a bad mistake with the optical nerves. I cannot bear the light."

Raffi was silent. Then he said, "Maybe he did it deliberately."

The Margrave's frown cleared. It seemed amazed. "Do you think so?" It shook its head. "In all the years, I have never thought of that! It is so good, Raffi—"

"To have me here. I know." His voice was grim.

The Margrave looked piqued. "Come now, my scholar. You will settle. After all, it's better than your other life. Do I insist you starve yourself, make you fast, make you sleep out in all weathers? Are you hunted here?"

"No."

"Do I make you learn huge chunks of unprofitable books?"

"NO."

The Margrave laughed. "And do you have to endure my terrible moods? My black rages? I am a temperate creature, Raffi, compared to your last master."

Raffi's chest ached. "Don't abuse Galen," he snarled, the intensity of it surprising even him.

"I will not, although he deserves it. Your loyalty to him is remarkable. I cannot see how you stayed with him so long." With its taloned fingers, it selected a fruit and bit into it. Raffi stood, restless. "So you miss him," it said quietly.

The Crucible of Fire

"Yes, I miss him! And I miss the sun and the trees and the weather! I can't live cooped up down here! I can't live like this!"

"Then we must do something about it. Perhaps you would be better off without the abilities of the Order— the only things they have that I really envy."

He went cold. "What do you mean, without them?"

The Margrave just waved its hand. "I can take them away. If you want."

Dread stirred in him. "No. Never."

"So be it," it said quietly.

Raffi came and stood behind it near the brazier, red light edging his face. "And what if I killed you," he breathed. "And escaped."

The Margrave almost choked on the fruit stone. "Oh, Raffi," it said, when it had got its breath back. "I am so, so happy to have you here."

THAT NIGHT, IF IT WAS NIGHT, Raffi pushed the sense-lines farther, desperate with worry. It was exhausting, forcing his bruised mind against miles of rock, through tiny fissures, slithering up the cracks in tilted strata. Claustrophobia made him gasp and wheeze; once he had to stop and sit up, shaking. There was nothing but rock, nothing alive, not the merest thread of a root. After hours he had to let himself fall asleep, worn out by the effort.

He dreamed of Sarres. The sunlight was so bright it made him cry out, and the grass was green and freshly cut, the smell of it warm on the breeze. The old house looked quiet, and somewhere Artelan's Well was bubbling its crystal music, but on the lawn among the grazing geese was a silver staircase, and Flain was walking down it, wearing the Coronet, a glimmer in his black hair. Raffi ran toward him, but when he got there he stopped in amazement, because it wasn't Flain at all, but Galen, who said to him irritably, "What's all this nonsense you've been listening to, boy?"

"I haven't. At least . . ."

"Don't lie to me, Raffi. You can't hide it from me. I've been there before you, remember?" And behind him there they all were, Tallis in a dress of leaves, and the Sekoi standing where Tamar stands in the images, and to

The Crucible of Fire

Raffi's delight it carried what must surely be a Sekoi cub, a black furry thing that wriggled and squalled. Behind it was a tall man in dark Watch clothes, and looking at him crossly, Carys, in a coat made of blue sea foam, her red hair grown long. "About time, Raffi," she snapped. "What have you been doing? You keep your mind on us and don't forget it."

She stood back. Behind her he saw Felnia, a little taller now, dressed in heavy crusted gold, sitting on a great throne, far too big for her. She frowned when she saw him, her high voice petulant. "Where have you been? You're always supposed to be bringing me a present—I never get to see it." On her lap was the scruffy toy cub. She waved its paw at him. "Say hello to Cub. And hurry up, Raffi. We're all waiting for you."

"Yes, but who's Kest?" He looked around anxiously. "Is it me? Am I the one?" He was asking the toy.

It winked at him, its eyes jewel bright. "You'll see," it whispered.

23

"Our children break our hearts. We do not speak of them."

Words of a Sekoi Karamax,
recorded by Kallebran

IT SHOULD HAVE TAKEN TWO DAYS to walk to the Pits of Maar—if there had been a road, or if there had been daylight. At first the sulfurous sleet blinded them. Galen made a line of power, a blue crackling thing between himself and Quist, and it wrapped itself around Carys's wrist, tight, and around the Sekoi's waist, and held them as they stumbled. How long the sleet stung them Carys had no idea, but they walked out of it at last onto a desert of green translucent glass, a slippery surface embedded with tiny bubbles.

She pulled the scarf off her face and gasped in air. They

were all filthy; the sleet had left a crust of yellow scum; the Sekoi rubbed its fur in silent disgust.

Galen leaned on his stick and looked around. "That way," he said finally.

She put the useless lodestone away. "How do you know?"

He glared at her. "I know. Now hurry." He would not let them rest. The ground was treacherous, smooth so that they slipped and had to climb the rounded slopes on hands and knees, sliding back as much as they progressed, but also with hidden chasms and ravines of jagged up-right shards of glass. If she fell against them, they would cut her to pieces. The sky was purple, lowering with an eerie storm that flickered, silent among the clouds. As it got darker, the glass flickered too, phosphorescent under their feet. At first she thought they were reflections, then she knew that the sparks leaped deep in the vitreous mass.

"Galen," she gasped finally. "Slow down!"

He gave her a black look, then crouched, breathless.

The Sekoi sank to its knees gratefully.

"We'll have to take more time." Carys took out the water, drank, and passed it around.

The Crucible of Fire

"There is no time." In the storm flicker Galen's face was white. He glanced at her. "This whole area is unstable. I can feel it, Carys, burning and molten and shuddering under us. While it's quiet we have to—" He stopped, staring at Quist.

"What?" she said. "*What!*"

Quist hauled her up, his face ashen. "Run. For God's sake, run!" The ground shook. As she scrambled up, the whole world tilted. The floor was a cliff face now and she was sliding down it, the pack and water flask rattling and rolling in front of her, and as she slid Galen yelled far above her and she screamed, the slivers of glass cracking out below.

RAFFI SAT AT THE DESK, turning the pages of the books. Earth stared back at him, its peoples, industries, armies, machines, vast cities of glass, mud shanties. Over his shoulder the Margrave said, "There was a flood. The sea rose, I understand. I have never seen the sea, myself."

"I have. The Narrow Sea."

"You must tell me about it, Raffi. Really, I would love to hear." It sat in the shadows expectantly, its strange eyes bright. "Tell me what the sea smells like," it said.

CARYS'S FALL ENDED IN a scream of agony. The sense-line around her wrist jerked her up; she hung from it flailing and spinning, clawing with the toes of her boots and her free hand against the impossible wall of glass. A sliver cut straight across her fingers; blood welled out and ran like a tiny red waterfall. "Keep still!" Quist yelled. "Galen! I can't hold her!"

She couldn't see Galen or the Sekoi. Maybe the smashed world had swallowed them. The blue line around her wrist was a searing pain; she felt sick, completely dizzy, and below her there was nothing, a howling emptiness down which shattered fragments clattered. "Pull me up!" she snarled.

"I can't." Quist's face was a blur. "I can't . . ."

The sense-line weakened. It thinned, spun out, became a thread, went to nothing. She yelled in fury and as if in answer, some strange energy surged along it and it strengthened her; she heard Galen's voice say, "It's all right. You're coming up."

Jerking, like a toy on a string, she was hauled out, the Sekoi leaning right down over the terrible slivers of glass. As soon as her feet were over, Galen dragged her upright. "Run," he said. "For God's sake, hurry."

They fled through chaos. The landscape was smashed as if some great fist had pulverized it; now rain came and lashed against it, and out of the cracks tiny crabs came scuttling, many-legged, their shells gleaming like steel. One caught hold of the Sekoi; the creature dragged it off, a pincherful of fur with it. "I thought nothing lived here," it snarled.

The desert became a forest with bewildering speed, a darkness where trees were smothered with vines that sprouted and coiled. Galen led them remorselessly on, between trunks livid with algae and some soft, crumbling fungus that released spores in vast clouds.

"Don't breathe them," Quist warned.

Carys tugged the scarf back over her face.

"Thanks for holding on," she gasped.

"Had no choice."

"If Galen hadn't strengthened the line, though . . ."

"Galen didn't strengthen it." He ducked under a mossy bough. "Neither did I."

"But . . ."

He looked back. "You should try the Order, Carys. It seems you have possibilities."

Amazed, she grinned, slipping under the mutated leaves, trying to ignore the sickening stench. Darkness was thickening; at first she thought it was nightfall, and then she knew it came from something ahead, a great cloud that hung in the air and vibrated. Had that power really come from her? She felt no different. But that pulse of energy—the memory of it warmed her. I'll show you, Raffi, she thought in delight.

They came out of the trees. Ahead was a dry cinderfield littered with odd globe-like yellow growths. Above it, like a swarming cloud, hung the wasps. Thousands of them.

"WHY DID YOU SAY the Sekoi was a prince?"

The Margrave seemed distracted. "What?"

"The Sekoi. You said . . ."

The Crucible of Fire

"Ah, yes. Well, they are a highly secretive race, but I have managed to learn a little about them, down the years. The tribemarks, for instance. Your friend has a mark that shows him to be of high blood—prince is probably the wrong word for it. Has he ever told you his name?"

Raffi shook his head. Catching his reflection in the glass cabinet he tugged the collar of his uniform up. It made him look older. "How did you find out about them," he muttered, not wanting to know. "Have you experimented on them?"

"Yes." The Margrave looked surprised. "Of course. One who seeks knowledge, Raffi, seeks it everywhere. Kest always said there were no limits."

He closed his eyes, then said, "Why do you want one of their children?"

The Margrave smoothed its scales with a ridged hand. "That is not for you to know. The owls guard them."

"The owls?"

"In some secret place. I have never found out where."

"So you have never seen one."

It stood and Raffi thought it was disturbed. "I didn't

say that. But forgive me, Raffi. Something is happening outside." It crossed the room and went out.

Raffi put his head in his hands. For a moment he was lost in the pain of it all, then a draft touched his face. He looked up quickly, went to the door and pulled it. It opened.

CARYS SAID, "IT HAD TO BE WASPS. I hate wasps. Always have."

"And these are agitated." The Sekoi lowered the seeing tube and passed it to her. Reluctantly, she took it. At first they were hard to distinguish, just a swarm, a mass of jagged movement. Then the relic adjusted to her focus and she drew in a hiss of breath. The wasps were orange and black, and small. There were thousands in the swarm. Their buzz made her hands shake.

"They know we're here," Quist said drily. He and Galen had been talking, sitting on the ground. To her shock, as she turned, she saw Quist was putting on the purple and blue crystals. "Those are Raffi's!"

He shrugged. "They have a reservoir of power we need

to use. Don't worry, Carys. Your friend, if we find him, can have them back. If he wants them."

"Too right he will," she muttered grimly, giving Galen a sharp glance. The keeper looked away. She took the spare crossbow off her back and jammed a bolt in angrily.

"What good will that do?" Quist said.

"It'll make me feel better."

Galen took a breath and stood, the dark power in him almost visible. "Now," he said, "we must keep together. I can protect us a little, but anyone who falls behind will be lost. Are you ready?"

She nodded, tight-lipped.

They moved in a close group, and as soon as they were out of the trees, the wasps were on them. Carys hissed, knuckles white on the bow. The air was a turmoil of wings, the swarm flying down, across, hovering, darting, a roar of anger. But keeping them away was a clear space, like a weather-warding she had once seen Raffi make to clear fog; it surrounded them like a crystal sphere and the wasps that barged into it snapped into sparks of flame. The cinderfield was deep in dust. It stretched far to the eastern horizon beyond the swarm, into darkness. Before them the Unfinished Lands shimmered in turmoil.

They tried to stay together. Wasps dived at them; Carys found her shoulders so tense, they ached.

"What are these?" the Sekoi murmured.

They were passing one of the globes; carefully, without touching it, Galen took a sideways look. "Plants."

"Pods." Quist pointed. "Our movements might have triggered it."

The pod trembled. Abruptly Galen stepped back. He whispered something, but the word was lost as the thing gave a great crack and instantly exploded, seed blasting out like pellets, deadly as shot. He took the full force. He went down hard; the Sekoi, half blinded, crashed into him. The Maker-power went out like a light.

Carys raised the bow, but it was useless. "Quist," she screamed. "Do something!"

HIS MIND TOUCHED WATER. It was so tiny; a thread of moisture the sense-lines barely registered, but it was there. He stopped still in the dark corridor. Then he began to move his mind up along it, higher and higher, along the minute gritty channel it had made.

The rock shuddered. Someone screamed. Raffi opened his eyes wide in shock. "Carys?" he whispered.

THE WATCHMAN GRABBED GALEN and hauled him up. Carys caught the Sekoi's arm, beating wasps off her face and clothes, screaming in utter fury and terror. The things stung her arms and hands, crawled into her clothes. She squirmed sideways, lost her footing and slipped, pulling the creature down a low bank, splashing into water.

Water! Instantly she plunged in, the Sekoi and the men close behind. Quist held Galen's face above the surface, but already the keeper was flailing for himself, his black eyes open.

It was a river, and it stank. Foam swamped its surface, and the undercurrent was strong; they were bumped and whirled along in it, with dead animals and logs of wood and terrible slicks of foul rainbow oil. She tried not to get it in her mouth, but that was useless; it stung her eyes and made her retch, and when suddenly the Sekoi's long arm wrenched her out onto a shelving spit of shingle she was violently sick, head down, on hands and knees. The filthy water ran from her clothes.

Behind, the creature's fingers held her tight till the spasm was over. "Better than wasps," it muttered. It almost sounded as though it was laughing.

RAFFI RAN DOWN THE CORRIDOR. He had already met one Sekoi; it had simply stood aside and let him pass. He couldn't get used to their silence. It chilled him. But this was the room. The door slid open. He was lucky. It was empty. He went straight to the screen; it was blank, so he said, "Operate!" but nothing happened. So he opened his third eye and went into the relic at once, drawing its power into himself. After a few seconds it crackled into life.

He saw the tower of Maar. All around the dark cube were camped the forces of the Watch, rank on rank of them, silent as if waiting some signal. From the Watchtower a light suddenly hissed out, a blue searing bolt that struck the ground and made a patrol of horses rear and panic.

Then behind him a voice said, "Enough." The screen blanked; the Margrave came and put its hand on his shoulder.

He pulled away, turning instantly. "Someone is holding the tower. It's Galen, isn't it?"

"Galen is not in the tower."

"Liar!" He felt oddly betrayed. "They're alive! Carys is alive. I know that!"

The Margrave watched him for a moment, then gave a small shrug. "Very well," it said quietly. "She is alive." It looked up at the screen. "As you can see."

GALEN DABBED THE OINTMENT on her face. "Keep still."

"It stings. For God's sake, Galen." She pulled away. "I'll do it myself."

He sat back, letting her take the small pot. They were both soaked and shivering.

"I detest this darkness," she blurted out desperately. "It's like that hell-hole Tasceron."

Galen almost smiled, pushing his dark hair back. As the Sekoi drank and washed its swollen bites, Galen said, "Tasceron was beautiful once. Imagine the great processions there on Flainsnight, and Tamarsday, the people carrying the images, the music, the women throwing armfuls of red spindleflowers in all the streets. Imagine the joy of it."

She nodded wryly. "Only you could think of that now."

"We've lost so much," he said, as if he hadn't heard her. "And I have borne all of that. I've endured it. But to lose Raffi . . ." He glanced up at her, his face gaunt, edged with something dark that made her afraid. "That would break my heart, Carys."

She swallowed, and looked at the others. Quist was somber. The Sekoi looked away.

RAFFI TURNED IN FURY, HIS EYES WET. "You told me they were dead!"

"Yes." The creature's eyes were bright. "So I did. But

380

what a touching moment to witness, Raffi. You must be so happy."

He tried to ignore its mockery. "They're coming here!"

"Indeed. But they will not get through." It looked up at the empty screen. "You would think, to hear him, that he had forgotten his words to you. When he told you you were no use to him. Will he ever realize how much that hurt you? I doubt it."

"I told you not to talk about Galen." He backed away, his throat hoarse. "I see what it is now. You're jealous of him."

"Jealous!" the Margrave hissed; its misshapen face turned quickly. For a second there was a look on its face that shocked him; then its eyes blinked, the long tongue flickered.

He felt the two Sekoi grab his arms.

"I have no reason to be jealous," the Margrave said quietly. "I have what he wants."

THEY WALKED ALL NIGHT. Through chasms and a rocky world, through marsh that gave way under their feet. Weary to the bone, Carys almost ceased to care or notice how the land changed, how the weather churned, remembering only the orchard, the fragment of cherry orchard, all its trees in miraculous flower, askew in the middle of chaos, tilted like a beached fragment of some lost beauty in the light of the moons. Slowly she came to see that Agramon had risen, and all the sisters with her, and that as Galen climbed to an outcrop of rock, he paused there, framed by the coronet of moons. She dragged herself wearily up beside him and stood silently, doubled up and breathless. In front of them, like the wounds of the world, gaped the Pits of Maar.

The Makers

24

There are seven wounds in the world.
They are deep. They lead to dread.
Chaos overwhelms us; we have allowed it.
The world bleeds. Who will save it?

Litany of the Makers

IT WAS A VORTEX, A GREAT SPIRAL.

Looking up now, Carys could still make out the circle of dark sky far above their heads, and for an instant one of the moons, Atterix, among rags of cloud. She turned and clambered down, jumping into the Sekoi's awkward catch.

Once these might have been smooth ramps, a double helix winding down on itself, level below level, but now they were broken, contorted. She felt as if she were crawling down into some vast seashell, or through the complexities and whorls of a gigantic ear into the very body of the sleeping world, of Anara itself. Only it wasn't sleeping.

There had been shocks of white sparks that Galen had managed to stop, but only after a long struggle to gather enough power. Farther down, whole sections of the walkways had suddenly slid and retracted; no one had fallen, but they had had to set up ropes and slide down; the skin on her hands was raw from it. The farther down they went, the darker and more echoing the caverns became. Hour after hour the vast spiral closed over them; near the top, they had barely been able to make out the walkways in the gloom opposite; down here they were close, slithering to the utter blackness of the pit.

Stopping for breath now, she realized how silent it was without their own slips and stumbles and small voices. She turned on her stomach and wriggled to the edge, looking down. For miles below, smaller and smaller, the walkways descended. She could not see the bottom. It made her dizzy.

The Sekoi's long fingers found a fragment of broken rock and held it out over the abyss, then dropped it. The stone fell endlessly; even out of sight they heard the whisper of its bounce and rattle as it rebounded from the leaning rails, deep into silence.

The Makers

"Thanks for warning them," Quist said acidly.

The Sekoi shrugged. "Oh, they know. You, a Watchman, do not think these energy fields are accidents?"

Quist gave a sour laugh. "I never thought one of you would be teaching me about defense."

"The Sekoi are masters of defense," Galen said quietly. He looked so gaunt and weary that Carys was worried.

"We should rest awhile."

"No." He gave her a black look. "That creature knows we're coming. He could kill Raffi, do anything. I'm not stopping, Carys." Scrambling up, he walked on down the metal ramp, a tall shadow lost quickly in the gloom.

She grabbed the Sekoi. "Come on."

It was Quist who muttered, "What he's not telling you, is that someone is watching us."

RAFFI SQUIRMED, but the Sekoi put firm hands on his shoulders; he flung them away. The Margrave turned from the screen in irritation. "This is not good. They should never have got this far!" It paced the floor, its robe rustling, then hissed, "Control!"

A panel rose smoothly out of the floor, the cover rolling back. Small lights winked green on it; a soft whining chatter came and went. The Margrave entered a combination with its scaly fingers.

"Don't hurt them," Raffi begged. "Please."

"If they keep coming, I have no option."

"I'll do anything. Let me speak to them. I'll tell them to go."

The Margrave's voice was a mass of crackles. "And what of Galen's terrible vow? *I swear the Crow will hunt the Margrave down into the deepest pit of hell.* He swore that by the Makers. Do you think anything will turn him back now?"

In despair, Raffi clenched his hands together. "No."

"Nor do I. So I have to stop him. I'm sorry, Raffi." Its fingers pressed one button. The console glowed red.

"GALEN!" AFTER ANOTHER LONG drop down the ropes, it was Carys who saw them first. They came out of nowhere, tiny scorpions, their stings menacing.

"Leave them to me." Quist pushed her on. Out of his

The Makers

belt he took some powder and scattered it over the mesh of the walkway. The scorpions stopped as they touched it, a row of venom.

"Amazing," the Sekoi muttered. "Some potion? A secret concoction?"

"Pepper. An old Watch trick."

"Do you have one that can deal with these?" Galen's voice was grim. Sitting across the walkway, four black shapes waited. They were huge, so dark their features were impossible to see, but in the faint starlight from above, their eyes glinted, alert and watchful.

"What are they?" Carys whispered.

Galen shook his head. "The sense-lines say nothing is there."

"They're not real."

"I think they are. There are things so alien we cannot feel them." He glanced at the Sekoi. "Any ideas?"

The creature's eyes were narrow. It bit one nail nervously. "In stories, such things are. Shadow-beings, made of evil dreams. Half real, half terror." Its whisper echoed down the silent walkways. One of the things raised its head, as if it listened.

"One each," Quist said drily. He looked at Galen. "What can we do?"

Galen was silent. Then he said, "I will go first. You can do nothing against them. Wait and come behind. As soon as you can, pass them. Don't turn your heads. *Don't* come back. Understand?"

"Galen . . ."

"Whatever happens, Carys, get to Raffi."

The Sekoi was as disturbed as she was. "Keeper." Its seven fingers caught his arm. "I fear these beings. More than anything we have seen. Even the Crow may not—"

Galen laughed his harsh laugh. "Maybe. But I'm not planning to die here. Flain will guard me." He stalked forward, down the steep ramp. Before him the four great beasts waited, unmoving.

"IF HE DIES . . ."

The Margrave shot him a sideways look. "There are worse darknesses than death." It gestured to the Sekoi. "Get him out of here. Down to the sphere."

"*No!*"

The Makers

"I'm sorry, Raffi, but there's no reason why you should suffer this." It turned back to the screen. At the door, Raffi wrenched free desperately.

Galen had reached the dark beasts.

HE HELD OUT HIS HANDS. Deep in the silence of the awen-field he spoke to them, and he knew they heard him. "We have met before."

The answer was unheard by anyone but himself. "Many times, keeper. In the Underworld. In the mad-houses. In the cells and prisons. In the silence. You know our names."

Galen was very still. "I know what the Order calls you. You are Hatred, and Untruth, Violence, Despair. But I am the Crow. I command you to let me through."

"We are stronger than you. We have often defeated you."

"No." He fought for control. "Not defeated. All my life I have fought against you."

"And lost."

"And won. The very struggle has made me what I am. Let me through."

"You have failed. The Order has gone. Anara is dying. Your scholar has deserted you."

"That was my fault," he hissed. "I know it."

"You have despaired. You have seethed with anger."

"I have. All my life. But even in the darkest times I have never lost faith." His hands were shaking. All the power of the Crow had drained out of him; he felt weak and the old pain in his leg throbbed. He clutched the stick hard.

"We will overwhelm you." Their eyes glinted in the metallic light; they seemed bigger, towering over him. "You will be lost in us."

"No." He straightened, lifting his hawk face to them. "I am a Relic Master of the Order, and I am the Crow." The words were hard to say; he had to force them out, his whole body icy with sweat. "You will let me through. I command it. In the name of Flain, and Soren and Tamar." The names gave him some strength; he could breathe. "Of Halen, and Theriss. And yes, even in the name of Kest I command you. In the name of his sorrow, and shame, and his bitter repentance. In the name of the planet he betrayed, of its suffering, of all its peoples, all its defiant, beautiful life."

The Makers

At his neck the crystals sparked; their energy flooded him. Behind, all around, darkness gathered, the dark of the Crow, deep and strange. He reached out to it; it streamed into his hands. "I am not ready," he snarled, "to be overwhelmed."

"WHAT'S HE DOING!" Carys caught the Sekoi's arm. The creature grabbed her. "We must do as he said. Quickly."

The thread of light was tiny and growing. It was so brilliant, it hurt their eyes, and it was as fine as a thread of gold, as the light Flain had found in the Underworld. Purest sunlight, it bled from between Galen's fingers, sticky and scorching, dropping onto the ground, spreading to a shining, straight path. The dark beings jerked away from it.

"Now!" the Sekoi hissed. It pushed her ahead and she edged past Galen; as she entered the awen-field the shock of it seemed to go right through her and she gasped, the sunlight a tingle in her fingers and feet and she walked down it, never turning, never looking back, under the very shadows of the vast silent beings. Finally the Sekoi said, "Wait."

She stopped. It was hard not to turn. The vast cavern was silent; her heart hammered.

"Where is he?"

"Carys, don't . . ."

But she had looked, over its shoulder. Galen walked tall and strong down the silver stairway, and it seemed to close up behind him. As he passed the beasts, they turned their heads, their eyes watching him angrily, but he did not even look at them. She had never seen him so calm.

Quist had turned too. And as Galen came up she saw to her astonishment that the creatures were not even there at all, but had been only strange outcrops of oddly shaped rock, the starlight glinting on fragments of quartz embedded in their grotesque heads.

The keeper stopped and looked at them and all power went from him instantly. He staggered, and Quist had to grab him. His face was white and drawn, full of pain. His hands bled.

The Makers

THE MARGRAVE SNAPPED the screen off. "Come here. Now." It pulled out two small boxes and threw them at the Sekoi, who caught them; Raffi recognized them as copies of the blue box Galen had once had.

"Weapons?" he gasped.

"Guard the upper entrance. Don't leave it." The Sekoi fled like shadows. The Margrave caught hold of Raffi and pushed him out. "Down. Quickly."

His heart was racing with a strange joy. "You can't stop him, can you?" he hissed.

It rustled along the dark corridor; behind it, doors snapped shut. "Don't be so sure. I admit he is surprising me."

"Let me go. I might . . ."

"Oh, no." The Margrave pushed him toward the curving stairs. "You're my best weapon, Raffi. My last weapon."

But he could feel it now, far above, exultant, the power of the Crow. It was flooding the pit, storming every tunnel, moving through rock, all the lights flickering on, far behind. Instantly Raffi ran. He raced down the stairs, jumped into the steamy cavern. Leaping the hot lava flows he came up to the crystal sphere. It was empty. The rustle of the Margrave was close behind him. "Raffi!" it hissed.

But Raffi had opened the curved entrance and stepped inside.

"WHERE ARE THEY!" Another blue flash sliced rock next to her face; she jerked back, whipping the crossbow up.

"At the base of the stairway." Quist reloaded quickly. He came around the rock and sent a bolt into the dark. "I can see them."

Galen, weary and haggard, said, "They are not men. But you must deal with this. I need to save as much as I can now."

Quist grinned. "Leave it to the Watch." A searing explosion sent fragments of rock flying.

"It's just like the old days," Carys muttered.

THE MARGRAVE STOOD STILL. "What are you doing?"

Raffi ignored it. He moved his mind deep into the relic;

it was full of power, it charged him with strength. The pain of it racked his chest; spreading his arms out, he touched the inside surface of the sphere with spread fingers, sent sense-lines deep into every filament.

"Raffi, please come out. You'll be hurt."

"Maybe." Even his voice was different, harder, fiercer. "But that's not what you're afraid of. Let them through or I destroy this sphere. I can do that. I can use its own power to do it."

The Margrave stepped back. "I don't doubt it. But you will kill yourself and me as well."

"I know." His hands ached; he held them rigid, controlling the energy. "But maybe that will be best, because then Galen won't have to do it, and I will have shown him what sort of a scholar I can be. What I can do."

The Margrave was silent, its strange profile lurid with the red light. And then, to his utmost astonishment, it laughed its throaty laugh. It came over and leaned on the open door of the sphere, one ridged hand resting on the glass. "But you are my scholar now," it hissed.

"You can't stop me." His voice was a question, a whisper of dismay.

"Oh, but I can, Raffi. I'm afraid there is something else, you see, that I have lied to you about. Something that makes all the difference."

"THIS WAY!" Carys raced down the corridor, Galen a dark shadow in front of her. Doors slid open before him. Quist kept the rear, the crossbow pointing back. Between them the Sekoi was grim and silent. It had not spoken since it had risen from the bodies of the black Sekoi.

"Carys." The keeper had found a staircase. As he grabbed its rail the whole thing lit; it was silver, crackling with power. He raced down it, two steps at a time.

At the bottom she banged into his stillness.

IN THE STEAM-FILLED CHAMBER the Margrave sat elegantly on an impressive throne, raised on two wide steps. At its back, tall and grave, a Watchman stood.

It was only when Galen whispered his name that she realized it was Raffi.

25

I am so changed, you would not know me.

Sorrows of Kest

E LOOKED OLDER. Different, as if he had passed through some great ordeal. It made her realize how long it had been since she had seen him.

"Raffi?" she said.

"Hello, Carys." His voice was quiet; he made no move forward.

Galen turned on the Margrave in wrath. "What have you done to him!"

The creature on the throne smiled. Carys stared at it in uncontrolled curiosity, its bright eyes that took them all in, their dismay, their hesitation. The ripple of its scaly skin fascinated and repelled her, its musky smell in the dimness, and when it spoke, its voice, a whisper of clicks and rustles.

"I have done nothing to him. But your rescue attempt is ill-conceived, Relic Master. He is my scholar now."

The sly way it said *Relic Master* filled Carys with unreasoning anger. She raised the bow and pointed it at the creature. "Come on, Raffi. Now!" To her dismay he came from behind the throne and stood between her and the Margrave; she swerved the bow away with a curse.

"Don't, Carys, please. You don't understand."

"Too right, I don't." She glared at him. "What's happened to you?"

"I haven't betrayed you," he said quietly.

"It looks that way to me."

"We can't kill it." He turned to Galen, his face pale. "If we do, we destroy ourselves."

The keeper's face was dark. "How?"

Raffi looked back; the Margrave shrugged, so he said, with an effort to control his voice, "There are machines here, vast relics; the Makers used them to control the Finished Lands. They can reverse what's happening to the world, if we can link with them. For that we need the

The Makers

Coronet. But only the Margrave knows how to operate them."

"And you believe it?" Galen stepped toward him; then he put his hands out and caught Raffi's arms roughly. "Dear God, boy, after all I've taught you, you believe it?"

Raffi nodded bleakly. "Yes. I do."

Galen was silent. Unexpectedly he said, "Then I must too." He looked hard at Raffi. "You look well. They haven't ill-treated you?"

"The opposite."

"It calls you its scholar."

Raffi shrugged, uneasy. "That's nothing." Then he said abruptly, "I thought you wouldn't . . ."

"No." Galen's sharp sense-lines made him look up. "Don't say that! You must have known we would never desert you. I would never desert you. I'm a reckless, bitter, angry man, Raffi, and I will never forgive myself for the things I said to you. I drive myself and everyone else hard, but you I've driven hardest, always, and I know it."

"It's not that." Raffi's voice was so low, only the keeper heard it. "Not the way we live. It's just . . . I thought you despised me. I let you down."

Galen's eyes were dark. "No, I let you down. And our lack of trust in each other has brought us both to this." He pulled Raffi close.

In the charged silence the Margrave's whisper was cool and amused. "Don't be taken in, Raffi. He will never change."

Carys took a step sideways. "Keep him there, Galen."

Galen flung his hand out at her. "Keep still, Carys."

"Indeed you must. Because my scholar is right." The creature's bright eyes watched them all in the dimness, from Quist to the silent figure of the Sekoi just inside the doorway. "You see, the machines have been mine so many years. I have learned much about them—they are not like other relics. There are code words and combinations even you, Relic Master, could not access for months. I have altered them too, put something of my consciousness in them. If I die, they will die with me." It folded its ridged fingers. "So you need me. And what I want from you is the relic known as the Coronet. Then, perhaps, I will give the boy back to you."

"He is not yours to give."

Galen glanced at the Sekoi. The creature was rigid with

hatred, its fur swollen. It said thickly, "Do not listen to its lies, keeper!"

The Margrave stood. Its tongue flickered as it said, "The Sekoi will never believe me anything but evil."

"I have just come through your handiwork."

Carys had never seen the Sekoi so moved. It was haggard and worn, its long fingers trembling with suppressed wrath on the relic-weapon it had snatched up. "Out there, I have destroyed all your filthy mutations."

The Margrave blinked its heavy eyelids. "I can easily breed more," it hissed.

For a second they both faced each other, an instant when anything might happen, until Galen put Raffi aside and said heavily, "I should kill you anyway, master of evil."

"If you feel you must, go ahead." The Margrave turned calmly and walked to its throne, the long robe slithering behind it. "I have no guards, no Watchmen. I have always been alone here. You may kill me if you wish, but all the world will die with me. Besides . . ." It leaned forward, interested. "Your Order forbids you to kill. And I am an intelligent being, am I not? Or am I an animal, or am I some new thing? Where is the boundary drawn? Do I have a soul? Would your act be murder, or the culling of some dangerous species? I will enjoy discussing these things with my scholar when you've gone."

"All I know is that you're a poison in the heart of this planet." Galen's voice was harsh. "It seeps out from you like . . ."

"Not so!" The Margrave pointed a taloned finger at him. For the first time it trembled with anger. "I have not poisoned the world. Your beloved Makers did that! Those god-like beings you so revere, Flain and Tamar, all of them, they did it! They corrupted a whole ecology and could not stop it. They ruined Anara! Ask the cat creatures. They've always known."

Raffi glanced at the Sekoi. Its yellow eyes caught his, expressionless.

Galen stood dark and tall. "They made mistakes."

"Believe it, Relic Master! They blamed Kest, but none of them were innocent, not Soren with the crops she bred, not Tamar with his cloned beasts. And when it all became too much, when the planet seethed and boiled with disease and alien microbes, they abandoned it when they might have saved it. And you!" It glanced at Raffi. "And me."

In the silence, somewhere above, the vast machines hummed. Carys felt the thrum vibrate inside her. She wanted to scream at it to stop.

It was Quist who said, "You?"

"Yes, Watchman." It smiled a bitter smile. "I too am a victim. Left to survive, half blind, never knowing a friend. Do you wonder I made the Watch for myself as a great toy to amuse me, that I brought my stories to life, brought the planet under my hand, that I hated the Order because it revered the Makers and all the things of the Makers?" Its eyes never left Raffi as it whispered, "They killed Kest. They made him fight the dragon, but there was no dragon that they had not made themselves."

Galen turned away, the agony of his indecision stabbing them all.

Carys couldn't keep quiet any longer. "The Watch is yours. The Watch killed my family and enslaved me. I should kill you just for that."

"Ah, but how you profited." It looked at her shrewdly. "You would just have been some other farm girl, illiterate, overworked, bewildered by superstition. Now you are so much more. The Watch gave you a new life."

She drew her breath in to scream at it, but Galen turned. His face was set. "No, Carys. I'll do this. I have sworn it."

The Margrave sat back on its throne. "What an irony. Your vow will destroy all the world."

Galen raised his hand.

"It's telling the truth," Raffi whispered in horror.

"Get out of the way."

"Galen."

"I have sworn to the Makers, Raffi!"

"IT WILL BE WRONG!"

Desperate, Galen shoved him aside, sparks crackling from his fingers. The Margrave smiled mirthlessly. "Do it, keeper," it hissed. "Do it. I welcome it."

Galen swung around and flung a great bolt of power out of his very soul. The energy scorched; it jerked Raffi back, shot across the dim chamber, searched in a great arc around the Margrave's throne. But it did not touch the creature. And it snapped instantly into nothing.

In the long, drained silence that followed, the Margrave stood. "Well," it said, its voice a dry rasp. "You are true to yourself. I respect that. I will wait for the Coronet. Come, Raffi."

Galen stood, utterly silent. And in that instant the cavern trembled. The noise of the machines changed; rose to a high whine.

"What's happening?" Quist looked around.

"The machines." The Margrave pushed past them, ignoring all weapons; it raced up the stairs. They followed; halfway up Galen found the creature protecting its eyes from the blazing lights. "Put them out," it whispered.

Raffi said, "It's all right." He looked at Galen. The keeper gave a shrug; instantly the lights died.

"My thanks." The Margrave hastened up into blackness. "The power is fluctuating. This happens often now. Soon there will be none left."

THE HUGE CHAMBER with the Maker-machines was open and the noise was deafening. Red lights flickered. The Margrave turned. "These are what I control, keeper."

Galen stared at the relics, appalled, then moved his

mind rapidly through the complex systems. He shook his head. "It's failing."

The noise was unbearable. Raffi grabbed him and pulled him outside. "The Coronet! We can make the link with Tallis from here . . ."

Galen dragged back his hair. "I can't do it alone. Not even the Crow—"

"The Makers can."

Galen looked at him in despair. "The Makers aren't here."

"Yes they are."

They stared at Raffi in shock. The Margrave came up behind, looking suddenly intrigued. Raffi caught hold of it and pulled it toward them, and grabbed Carys with his other hand. He felt wild and reckless with sudden certainty. "The Makers are here," he yelled. "The Makers have never left!"

26

It was then Flain said to the Crow, "Fly to the peoples. Tell them the World is theirs. To heal or to destroy, forever."

"Even to the Sekoi?" the Crow said. "Even to the evil, and the uncaring, and the dead?"

"To those most of all," Flain answered.

Book of the Seven Moons

"RAFFI."

"Listen to me, Galen." His voice was strong and sure. "This is my vision. This is what I bring from my Deep Journey. *Today, we are the Makers.* The power they had is the power we use. This is our world, and they want us to heal it. All of us. You, me, Tallis, the Order, the Sekoi, the trees, even the Watch. 'The world is not dead,' remember? 'The world is alive, and breathes.'" His face was alight with energy; Carys felt it crackle through her wrists.

"Flain told you this?" Galen whispered.

"In a dream. We can stop the decay of the Finished Lands. We can do it here and now."

"The link with Tallis, yes." Galen shook his head. "You and I and Quist, with a great effort, might even reach through the grid as far as Tasceron. But these machines . . ."

Raffi turned to the Margrave. "That's why you must join us."

"Me!" The creature's eyes blinked in astonishment. "You ask me to help you? And you believe the keeper would trust me?"

"I will trust you," Galen said with immense difficulty. "If Raffi says so."

"I do." Raffi's voice was quiet.

Carys felt the Sekoi's disquiet. But neither of them spoke.

The Margrave was silent a moment. Then it hissed, "You make me feel something like shame, Raffi. But why should I care what happens to Anara?"

"We can't do it without you." He took a step closer. "And I will make a vow too. If we succeed, I will stay with you, here, in the darkness. For as long as you want. As your scholar. As your son."

They were all silent, stricken. Only the machines

roared. Small red reflections flickered on the Margrave's scaly skin. "You swear this?" it whispered.

"Yes." Raffi looked at Galen, then Carys. "I swear it by Flain."

THE CAVERN RUMBLED.

Galen laid the last crystal in the hasty circle and stepped inside. Carys and the Sekoi, Raffi and Quist waited where he had put them, outside, four corners of an invisible square. The keeper turned. "Now you," he said.

The Margrave entered the circle warily. Face-to-face, they looked at each other, the darkness between them. "We must touch?" the creature said. It held out its hands, but Galen gripped its arms at the elbows. "I should have killed you," he whispered.

The Margrave smiled its lipless smile. "Have faith, Relic Master."

THE SENSE-LINES CAME, out of nowhere. In the dark, for the first time, Carys could feel them, and she cried out with the pain they made, as her mind rippled, caught up in the sudden surge of power spinning from Raffi and Quist, and even the Sekoi, its lines of story circling her delicately.

And she joined with them, felt herself being drawn deep into the relics, down their dark circuitry, her senses choked with the rank smell of oil, scorched by tiny sparks, made and remade in a million instant connections. Spiraling down with her were all the things she had never known existed: voices of calarna trees, and sheshorn, birch and yew; the slow intelligences of tiny animals; fiery energies of birds and salamanders. All the complex tales the Sekoi tell were there and the stream of sounds and minds became a living thing, unfurling and uncoiling. It infiltrated the Maker-devices, growing into them; it sent out roots and uncurled leaves; it sprouted branches through the minute tunnels of wire and microchip, making a new thing, an organic machine, a great tree rooted in the ground, the seven moons high in its branches.

At the heart of the tree Tallis was waiting. She wore the Coronet of Flain, and all her three ages were in her at once, and over her in the filaments and branches a dark bird came down and perched, and at her feet a lizard slithered, its bright eyes unblinking.

Out from the tree all weathers came, and Carys became them, one by one, the frozen numbness of snow, the slash of rain. She became soil and rock; she ran and splashed and trickled and drowned in the deep hollows of great rivers.

She became all the people of the world, sick and well, young and old, male and female. She became Sekoi and Starman. She breathed air and water. She ached with every worker on the Wall. She became the dead, their lost consciousness all around her, their pain and longing and peace. She became her mother and her father, her small, sickly brother, all the long lineage of her family. She became the Makers, as wise as Flain, as strong as Tamar, as ingenious as Kest. She was the Interrex, and knew herself a queen. She squirmed with Alberic's asperity.

Raffi was there, and she relived the terror of his Journey, and she knew Quist's longing for Scala and the Sekoi's secret name. She became the Crow, crackling with its darkness, the strength and compassion of its power.

And last of all she became the Margrave. Deep in its

blind loneliness she was evil and she was lost; she was ashamed and exultant.

She became them and they were Anara. They had no end and no beginning, only the circular spin of the seasons. They were together and no one was alone. They were the tiniest seed, the greatest forest of quenta. They moved now, out over the planet, deep in its soil, through its oceans and hills and relics. They overran Tasceron, taking the darkness of its wound with them from streets and domed shrines and ruined houses, and sunlight filled the city, and deep in the House of Trees every relic of the Makers' came to life. They crossed the Narrow Sea and spilled their joy over pasturelands, over woods and lanes, over Sekoi tombs and cromlechs, over the Wall, raveling up the land behind them, healing the hurts in atom and molecule, through enzyme and bacterium. They came to Sarres and swept up its power. They ordered themselves and aligned themselves.

They were dead. They were alive. They were in balance.

And they left the planet and turned outward, and sped through the stars. Galaxies flashed by them, novae flared and burned. All through the vast interstellar silences they spread, until far off they saw the point of light, tiny at first, that grew, as they hurtled into it, to a great inferno, the heart of an explosion of life that never stopped, that scorched them as they fell deeper and deeper, burning them, dissolving them, making them new.

"CARYS." THE VOICE WAS DISTANT, a long way off. "Carys!" An arm was around her shoulders. "Drink this," the voice said.

It was water. She gulped it, spilling it, suddenly deep in such a terrible thirst she thought it would kill her. The pain brought her sight back and she stared at Raffi.

"All of it," he said quietly.

She emptied the glass, both hands shaking. "Is it always this bad?" she croaked.

He smiled. "Nearly."

Over his shoulder she saw Quist looking down, and Galen kneeling over the Margrave. The creature seemed as distraught as she was; it was on hands and knees, and the keeper had to support it. "Did we do it?" she whispered.

"We did something." He shook his head, overwhelmed. "Did you feel it, Carys? Did you feel the glory of it?"

"Get me up," she said irritably.

Around them the Maker-machines hummed, a steady, efficient sound. Raffi had to hold her. She had never felt so weak, so utterly useless. "If this is being a keeper," she muttered, holding on to one of the machines, "you can keep it."

He grinned, but the Sekoi's voice, oddly harsh to her raw nerves, interrupted. "I've got something, Galen."

The creature had the control panel up and had found some image on the screen, blurred and grainy. Galen helped the Margrave to a chair and came over quickly. He seemed to have barely enough energy to control the screen, but finally they knew they were looking at the Unfinished Lands.

The silence was intense.

"It's just the same," Carys breathed. She felt devastated.

"Don't be so sure." Galen struggled to get the image closer; Raffi had to help him.

The land was barren, a chalky sand, but as they closed

down on it, they saw rain was falling, a calm, steady drizzle.

"There!" Galen pointed. "Look there." It was nothing much. A tiny green shoot, barely breaking the surface. But they all stared at it in stunned delight.

"Raffi." The Margrave was standing, unsteady. "Did we succeed?"

Carys didn't need sense-lines to feel that abrupt end of Raffi's joy. But he answered calmly. "Yes. I think we have." He turned to Galen, awkward. "I'm sorry," he muttered. "But otherwise it might not have . . ."

"You made your vow, and you at least must keep to it." Galen's eyes were dark; the darkness was in the hollows of his face and his long, glossy hair. He took something from his pocket. "These are for you. I made them ready a long time ago. I knew you would need them." They were a keeper's beads, green and black. Raffi stared, but Galen put them gently around his neck, all seven strands, and stepped back. "You have finished your Deep Journey after all, Relic Master," he said.

For a moment in silence they both stood there as if they could not bear this. Then Raffi said, "I must go."

Behind him, the Sekoi spoke. "Stay where you are, small keeper."

"No!" He turned, sense-lines alert. "No. *NO!*" But the flash of blue light seared past him and past Quist. It flung the Margrave back against the machines, a shocked, crumpled heap, and as it lay there the Sekoi came forward, firing again and again into its chest, coldly accurate, until the air was acrid with a choking smoke and the stunned agony of the snapped sense-lines.

For an instant Raffi was blank; then he found himself kneeling by the Margrave, dragging it up, calling it desperately. Its soul barely flickered; the strange touch of it moved through him, and he lifted it, body and spirit, and it reached for him. "Kest," it breathed, "my scholar." And its life slid into the Maker-machines and was gone, a whisper in the darkness.

Galen's hands were tight on his shoulders. Raffi turned to the Sekoi, his face drawn, searching for words. "I never asked you . . ." he screamed.

"It was not for you, Raffi." The creature was tall and controlled; it dropped the weapon with weary distaste. "It was not for any of you. Or for Solon, or Marco. It was for a Sekoi cub that was lost from us eons ago. The only one we have ever lost."

Raffi choked. He couldn't speak.

Galen said, "It was captured?"

"Brought here. Experimented on. Altered." Its voice was raw, almost unrecognizable, as if it could not bear to say the words, and it turned away quickly.

"The Margrave did it?" Raffi had to know.

The Sekoi did not turn. "It *became* the Margrave," it whispered.

27

*The world is not dead. The world is alive
and breathes. The world is the whim of
God, and her journey is forever.*

Litany of the Makers

THEY SAT TOGETHER in the cluttered room, all but the Sekoi. Raffi had found some food, but no one even looked at it. Galen brooded in a corner, deep in prayer and remorse. It was Quist who looked up and said, "We will need to bury it."

Raffi put a plate down abruptly. The shock of the Margrave's death kept coming over him, like an unending series of waves, each time harder, more real.

Carys looked at him anxiously. "Yes. But we need to get out of here, and it should be soon. We have to find out what's happening outside."

"Alberic!" Galen looked up, remembering. He stood quickly. "Carys . . ."

"He'll be gone, Galen! Long gone!"

"Not if he's in the Watchtower," Raffi said numbly. "I saw it, on the screen. There was an army all around it."

Galen made straight for the door, Carys close behind. Then she came back. "Are you . . . ?"

"I'll stay here." Raffi glared at Quist. "On my own."

THE SCREEN SHOWED CARNAGE. It looked as though there had been several attacks; the ground was churned with horse tracks, the black flowers mangled and bloody. The tower seemed to have held out so far; but the numbers of the Watch army made Carys turn cold.

"Well." Galen looked up. "The thief-lord has done us proud after all."

"He'll never get out alive."

"Of course he will." The keeper gave her his wolfish smile. "When the Watch fall back."

The Makers

"You're mad, Galen. They will never withdraw."

"They will if they're ordered."

She stared at him, suddenly understanding. Quist said, "But who . . ."

"You. Or me. It doesn't matter." Galen adjusted the controls carefully. "They never saw the creature, remember? Raffi says it only spoke to them. They won't know that their master has been replaced."

The screen flickered. They saw a Watch commander with a bandaged face, his uniform torn. Galen glanced at Quist. The captain licked his lips, then said, "Report."

"We have made five separate attacks. The rebels control the tower weapons, and have inflicted heavy losses. Commander Resh five forty-nine has been killed."

"Enough. Listen carefully, this is a priority message." Quist's voice was hoarse. "The attack is to be called off. All troops are to be withdrawn to Cato's Cleft."

The commander's face flickered with astonishment.

"Called off? Lord, we are so close . . ."

"Do you question your orders?"

Surprise vanished. The man's face closed. "No, lord."

"Then carry them out."

The bandaged man nodded, and vanished.

Quist let out his breath.

"There is something to be said," Galen muttered from the controls, "for such blind obedience."

Quist glanced at Carys. "Not from everyone," he said wryly.

She nodded. "And it will destroy them. It's clever, Galen. Sly, in fact."

Galen looked up. "In slyness, here's an expert."

Before the picture came, they heard the singing. Carys winced; Alberic's poet seemed to be arriving at some tuneless crescendo. Then, in a flicker of light they saw him, and the dwarf, in a golden breastplate and greaves, picking moodily over a plate of stale dewberries.

"Hello, Alberic," Galen said softly.

The song stopped in mid-note. The dwarf stood slowly, unsheathing a bright, curved sword. His bodyguards stood around him. Carys could see the back of Milo's head, dirty and uncombed, turning this way and that.

The Makers

"Keeper?"

"Yes, thief-lord."

"Where in hell's name are you?" He circled warily.

"You've got your back to me," Galen said.

Alberic turned. His neck was scarred and raw from the burns; he moved painfully, but he was grinning from ear to ear. "Are you dead, or is that too much to hope for?"

"Far too much. You've cheated death yourself, I see. What's in front of you?"

"A wall. With my idiot nephew against it." But Milo had already scrambled up, and stood by Godric.

"There should be voice controls," Galen said irritably. "But maybe this . . ." Milo gave a yelp.

Alberic said, "We see you. God, you look worse than I do. Did you find your boy?"

Galen came forward and stood looking up. "We found Raffi," he said, his voice quiet.

"And the Margrave?"

"The Margrave is dead."

"Smart move." Alberic sheathed his sword. "We've made a few killings here. Held them off for you, just like I said we would."

Carys snorted. "You liar." She waved at Milo. "No hard feelings."

He shrugged, and stammered, "Well, no, but . . ."

She smiled sweetly. "I couldn't have done it without you."

His face lit. "Thanks," he whispered.

"My gallantry," Alberic said briskly, "brings the price of this shebang up to three million." He turned, as if someone had come in with a hasty message, then swung back, his narrow face transformed. "They're pulling out!"

"We know," Galen said calmly.

"Did you arrange it? God, keeper, that's a trick I'd give a lot to master."

"Listen." Galen was impatient. "We'll make our way back. Get your people ready."

Alberic turned his back. "If you think I'm going anywhere . . ."

"You're escorting the Interrex into Tasceron. An imperial escort, Alberic. Think of the luxury. The food, the wine. The palaces."

The dwarf turned his sly face and spat. "I know your

idea of luxury. A ruined hovel with no roof, that's all you're offering. Besides, Tasceron is a black hole."

"Not anymore."

The dwarf stared. Then he moved closer, his voice shrewd. "Are you telling me the truth? Does this mean the Watch are finished? That it's over?"

"It will take time"—Galen looked at Quist—"but yes. We have infiltrated the Watch. They will be healed, like the planet, from within."

Godric said, "Good news, Chief."

"If it's not all mumbo jumbo and claptrap." Alberic smiled sourly. "Will there be any mercy for thieves under the Order though, eh? I doubt it. Give us ten years and we'll be nostalgic for a few hangings and a firm hand. Maybe I should stick around after all."

"You do that." Galen moved to the controls, but Quist said, "Wait." He looked up. "Is she safe?"

"Safe!" Alberic turned in disgust. "She's driving me crazy."

Scala was lounging on the bed, smiling. "So you're alive, lover. It's more than I thought. This means our reward is gone, then?"

"And any ransom." Quist's voice was low.

"So we ride free?"

He nodded. Then he said urgently, "Scala, you will wait for me?"

She picked a fruit from the bowl and threw it playfully at Alberic. "To be frank, lover, I can't promise. The company here is less than classy."

The screen dimmed. Quist was smiling; when he saw Carys's look, he shrugged. "She's crazy about me," he muttered. And then, to himself, "Or she will be."

RAFFI SAT SILENT in the dark room, his feet up on the seat, his head sideways on his knees. When the door creaked open he did not look up, or around. After a moment, the Sekoi came in and sat by the brazier, in the Margrave's chair, staring deep into the red coals. In the silence the fuel settled, a light tinkle of sifting cinders. When the Sekoi spoke, its voice was gentle. "My actions have threatened our friendship, Raffi."

He didn't answer, so it went on, "You had grown fond of the creature."

The Makers

"No."

"I think so. You came to find something likeable in it. That is nothing to be ashamed of."

Raffi said, "It used to sit there. It told me about the Makers, how it used to talk to them. It told me such things . . . and such lies, and now I'll never know what the truth is." He couldn't bear it; he jerked his head up and hissed, "Why did you do it! I don't understand why! It had helped us."

"I waited until it had done so."

"You betrayed it! All of us! Did you plan this from the start? Have you always despised our ways so much that . . ." His voice broke. He shook his head. "I just don't understand," he whispered.

The Sekoi smiled unhappily. "Do you remember how once, long ago, Galen warned you that the Sekoi could not be trusted? That we have our own beliefs as you have yours, and hold them as dearly? He and I knew there would be a time when those beliefs would conflict. That time has come. Raffi, I cannot explain to you the . . . hatred the Sekoi felt for this creature. And the pity."

"Pity!"

"Yes." It scratched its fur. "It was one of us once. Kest took it and mutated it over the years. He used the genes of animals, and of Starmen. Your stories say it was a man he used, but that was not so, and the Sekoi have always known it—it has been our deepest shame. And each of us is taught that if ever we should even glimpse it, it must die."

Raffi rubbed his face. He felt weary and lost. "It called you terrible and unforgiving."

"So we are." The Sekoi leaned forward. "We are not like you. I knew Galen too well. He could not kill. And Carys is becoming like him. Only I could do this. And with it I have made amends for my betrayal of the Great Hoard. It was harsh, but evil must not be allowed to spread. The innocent must not be corrupted. It would have corrupted you, in the end. If the Makers had only acted long ago . . ."

"It wasn't evil," Raffi hissed. "It did evil things, but . . ."

"What is evil, if not that?" The Sekoi stood. "I will have to go before my people for their judgment. But before I do, I would like to have your forgiveness. If you can give it."

Raffi pushed back his hair and looked up. "Why me? I should thank you. I could never have survived down here."

"Nevertheless, it is you I ask."

He was silent a long time. Then, with an effort he said, "I hate what you did. But I will never hate you."

The Sekoi nodded sadly. "Then I will have to be content with that."

It was halfway through the door when Raffi whispered, "That was the way I felt about the Margrave."

GALEN CARRIED THE MARGRAVE'S body down and laid it in the crystal sphere, its ridged hands clasped. He closed the door and then, to their surprise, spread his arms and chanted the long prayer of Atonement, said only for keepers. Raffi joined in, his voice hoarse. He felt so strange. Through the thick crystal he watched the face of the being that had lived so long, that had spoken with the Makers, that had hunted him through the world, had terrified him. When had he stopped being afraid of it? When had he begun to think of it differently? He couldn't remember. But it had changed him, and now it was dead. Although, in the heart of the machines, somewhere in their hum, in the energies of the awen-field, something of it lingered. For no one dies, the Book says. Not even the worst of us.

HE TOOK SOME OF the Earth books, pushing them into Carys's pack.

"What are these?" she asked.

"I want to take them. Don't tell Galen."

"You're not his scholar anymore, Raffi. Take what you want." Shoving them down in the pack she said, "What will happen if we get to Tasceron?"

"Felnia will be crowned." Galen stood in the doorway, the Sekoi behind him. "And we will call a great meeting of the Order. Everyone left alive will come, keepers and scholars, out of hiding, out of terror." He put an arm around Raffi's shoulders. "We will choose a new Arch-keeper."

The Makers

"It should be you."

"Not me." Galen laughed darkly. "The Crow will have much to do. There is a whole world to be remade; it will not happen quickly."

Tugging the straps on the pack tight, Carys was silent a moment. Then she looked up. "Galen. You've lost your scholar."

"Not lost."

"Yes, but what I mean . . ." The strap would not go through the buckle; she threw it down in exasperation. "What I mean is, are you looking for another? Another scholar?"

He scowled. "Carys, if you mean that nephew of Alberic's, I'm sorry but . . ."

"I mean me."

"*You!*"

"Yes." She couldn't help grinning. She had finally done it. For the first time since she had known him she had utterly astonished him.

He stared at her, wordless.

"Don't you think I can do it?"

"Of course you could," Raffi said.

"I agree," the Sekoi said softly.

Galen took a breath. His voice was quiet. "I am not an easy master, Carys."

"Oh, I know. Neither was the Watch. And I warn you, I'm not going to be the easiest of scholars. Is there some test I have to pass?"

The keeper said, "If there were, you would have already passed it." He put his hand in his pocket, took out the beads that had been Raffi's, and tossed them to her. "Welcome home, Carys," he said quietly.

RAFFI WAS THE LAST to climb over the lip of the pit. The Sekoi helped him up, and he stared in utter joy at the sunlight, the pale moons, at the blue dome of the sky. All around them after the rain, the desert had bloomed, a glorious flood of tiny fragile flowers, red and palest pinks. They stood among it all in silence. And along the sense-lines a voice came to him, and the voice was Flain's.

"I have been here before you, Raffi," it said. "And the Deepest Journey starts here."

Carys looked back at him. Galen said, "They will

The Makers

still come." He looked out at the miles of sunlit land. "Remember those words we heard in the House of Trees. *Wait.* We might have completed their work, but we still need them."

Raffi nodded. "I know," he whispered.

Don't miss
CATHERINE FISHER'S
New York Times bestselling duology:

AND

IT GIVES LIFE.

IT DEALS DEATH.

IT WATCHES ALL.

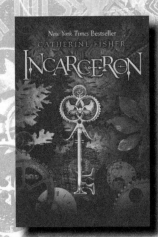

NAMED A BEST BOOK OF THE YEAR BY:

The Washington Post

Horn Book

SLJ

Kirkus

PW

CCBC

YALSA

Praise for INCARCERON

THE ONLY ONE
WHO ESCAPED . . .
AND THE ONE WHO COULD
DESTROY THEM ALL.

An Indie Next List Top Ten

Kirkus Reviews Best Book of the Year

Praise for SAPPHIQUE

—⊲○○○⊳—

★ "A modern masterpiece."

—*Kirkus Reviews,* starred review

★ "Fisher further explores themes of reality, illusion, and freedom without losing her intensely original world-building and authentic characters."

—*Booklist,* starred review

"A dark, interesting foray into vivid imagery, danger, surprising twists, and intriguing revelations."

—*School Library Journal*

"Readers who have pieced together Incarceron's clues will no doubt find satisfaction in its sequel as they unlock its secrets." —*The Bulletin*

"The plot builds to an inexorable climax—a fitting finial on Fisher's grand invention." —*The Horn Book*

About the Author

CATHERINE FISHER, acclaimed poet and novelist, was born in Newport, Wales. She graduated from the University of Wales with a degree in English and a fascination for myth and history. She has worked in education and archaeology, and as a lecturer in creative writing at the University of Glamorgan. She is a Fellow of the Welsh Academy.

Of the Relic Master series, Catherine says, "This quartet of science fiction/fantasy novels are especially important to me; first because of the characters (Galen, Raffi, Carys, and the Sekoi, some of my favorite characters out of all those I've written about), and second because it was the first time I had really let rip and created a whole new world and everything in it."